Three

Times

Over

Printed in the United Kingdom

First Printing, 2020

ISBN UK e-book 978-1-9993113-8-4
ISBN UK printed 978-1-9993113-9-1

Jackiemcmillan2@gmail.com

Print on Demand service
Self-Publishing

Three Times Over

By

Jackie McMillan

Part One

Understanding

Chapter One

Everyone has their own share of loss throughout their lives. For me, I've had more than my fair share. How you deal with those losses is different each time. It depends on how old you are, what the circumstances of the loss are and who you have lost. Regardless of the circumstances, you are never the same as you were before you were told the news.

My first loss was when I was not much more than a baby. I don't remember much about it just flashes. My aunt Abby can tell you more and she will soon. This is my story. I would have kept is secret, but someone thought the world needed to know.

I'll start at the beginning when I was glad to get home from the hospital. All I wanted to do was sit on my couch in my comfy jammies and zone out watching tv.

I knew that I wouldn't be doing that as I had to get food in as I had been away for a few weeks. I didn't even know if there would be spoiled food in the fridge when I opened it. I put my bag down and took the step towards the kitchen to see if I needed to buy a new fridge rather than food. I was surprised when I opened it and found it empty and clean.

Abby must have been over and cleaned it out. I didn't know how I felt about that, but I was glad at this moment as it was the last thing I wanted to do.

I headed back to where I had dropped my bag, lifting it and headed into the bedroom and sat down on the bed feeling tired but knowing I shouldn't be as I have rested enough over the last few weeks. I lay down on the bed just for a few moments only to wake a couple of hours later.

I got up, showered then decided that it was time to find some food. I knew the fridge was bare but there should be something in the cupboards that I could eat. I dressed in my comfy jammies and headed back downstairs.

I had been living in the two-bedroomed house for the last three years and I loved it. It was an ideal size for me, and I knew as soon as I saw it that I had to have it. The spare room was a spare room and not just somewhere to let things pile up until I decided what to do with them.

I had gradually worked my way through the house, doing it up to my tastes. It had an old world feel to it with lots of deep dark colours and large furniture. I remembered searching for every piece I had and knew when I had found the right one.

I had dragged Michael all over town looking for pieces to bring into the house. I stopped where my thinking was going as I wasn't up to thinking about him just yet. It still hurt too much that I couldn't handle that on top of everything else.

I headed into the kitchen to see what was there for eating. I put the kettle on to boil as I opened the cupboards to see what I could find. I really needed to get some groceries. The cupboards were almost as empty as the fridge, but I did find a can of soup that was still in date.

I lifted this out and put it on the worksurface then pulled out a mug for it. I took out a pot and set it on the stove and lit it. Fortunately, the can was one that had a ring pull rather than one that needed a tin opener. I opened it and tipped it into the pot for it to heat up.

As it was warming, I looked out into the small back garden that I had. That was my next task. It was badly overgrown and looked more like a jungle than a garden. I had tried to keep on top of it, but it was a losing battle. I knew what I was going to do with it, but I just needed to get it into a condition that would allow me to work.

I heard the soup starting to bubble and took a spoon out and stirred it. Once it was ready, I poured it into the mug then headed into the living room and sank down into my favourite chair and let my mind wander as my hands held the warm mug.

The last few weeks had been a whirlwind even though I don't really remember much about them. I was still trying to understand it all. I ached all over from the accident and from lying in bed doing nothing for two weeks, but I still wished that he were here with me.

I knew he had my best interests at heart but to hide it from me, hurt me. He knew my history and how much it would have hurt. I couldn't bring myself to contact him just yet. It was too soon. When I had awoken, the nurses had told me that he hadn't left my side since I had been admitted.

I tried to understand but it had been too much for me. Everything was still too raw. I felt the tears forming in my eyes, but I did nothing to stop them from falling. I let all the pain and sorrow that I had suffered out, I cried for the loss that I had suffered over the years. I cried for myself being so alone in the world. I cried for those that tried to help me, but I refused them.

When I finally stopped, I felt lighter as if I had finally let go of something that had been holding me back for years. My soup was now cold, so I took it through to the kitchen and re-heated it in the microwave before drinking it.

I looked about the kitchen looking for my bag when I remembered I had taken it upstairs when I had arrived home earlier. I headed up there drinking my soup as I went. I pulled out the papers that the hospital gave and that I had to hand into my GP. I flicked through them and stopped when I saw another document.

On a couple of sheets of A4 paper was a rough outline of the story of my life. Stapled to the top corner of it was a business card. I went to throw the papers in the bin, but something stopped me. After everything I had been through maybe it was time to let others know that it wasn't the end. There was life that could be found and lived to its full potential.

I knew looking at the plain card that this was a turning point for me and that I was going to make a phone call that would change my future. I didn't know how it was going to change but it couldn't be any worse that what I've already been through.

I stood where I was and began reading the papers. It was amazing how much she had done when she hadn't even spoken with me about it all. It must have been Abby that had given her all the information she had used. For once, I didn't feel betrayed, I felt relieved.

There was the outline of my life but a lot of gaps that only I could fill in. I knew I was to call her. She hadn't pressured me whilst I had been in hospital even though she had gone behind my back to get the information she had.

When I had finished reading, I knew that she had my best interests at heart and the way she had written it down, gave a good understanding of what I had been through and that there are people and organisations out there that can help people in the same situation.

I lifted my mobile and dialled the number from the card. I kept standing as if I knew that I had to stay strong to get through what was to come even though, I had accepted it all. The ringing continued in my ear making me think that no-one was going to answer. I was about to hang up when it was answered.

"Hello?" I found myself unable to talk suddenly. "Hello? Is there anyone there?" Before I lost the courage again, I spoke.

"It's Catriona Mont-Clair." There was a small gap before she answered back.

"How are you feeling? Are you still in hospital?"

"No, I got out earlier today and I feel about as well as anyone could be in my situation." I paused before continuing. "I read what you left for me. It's good, a lot of gaps but good."

"Thank you. It is only an outline of what the full story can be. My editor likes the idea of the story so much that it may become a feature in the paper rather than just a news story. I didn't have a lot to go on only hearsay from Susan as she had been talking to who I presume was your aunt and someone called Michael." I felt my heart leap at the sound of his name knowing that I would never be over him. I just had to find it in myself to forgive him.

"It's okay. It's time I get this out and let others know that nothing is insurmountable. Are you free tomorrow?" I heard a few clicks before she answered.

"Yes. I'm free all day."

"Ok, I'll talk to you, but it is on my terms and on my timescale. I can't tell you much about the early years, so I'll need to get my aunt to fill you on that part. The rest, I can handle."

"No problem, where do you want to meet?"

"My place at two pm. If there is any change, I'll let you know." I gave her my address.

"Ok see you at two tomorrow and thank you for giving me the opportunity to tell your story. You are an inspiration to others in the same and similar circumstances."

"I don't know about that but it's my life and I want you to tell my story. I don't know any better. See you tomorrow." I hung up feeling the nerves kicking in about what I'm about to do. Putting my life story out there for all to see was hard but if I could help even one person to deal with loss, then it would be worth it.

Chapter Two

I awoke the next morning feeling lighter than I had ever been. Making the decisions I had yesterday given me a sense of hope that things were going to be okay. I know they say not to make any life changing decisions after something major has happened in your life, but if I listened to that, I wouldn't be where I am today.

I got up and the first thing I did was grab my phone and make a call. It was one that I was dreading but knew it had to be done. The call was answered immediately throwing my off a little.

"Cat, thank god. I've been worried about you. You need to let me explain. I never meant to hurt you." I cut her off before she could see anything else.

"Abby, stop." I took a breath before continuing. "Can you come over about two this afternoon?"

"Yes, I can come over just now if you want."

"No. this afternoon is fine." There was silence for a few seconds before she spoke again.

"Cat, I am sorry. I wanted to tell you, but Michael wouldn't let me. Time went past, and it was harder to even think about telling you."

"Abby, it's fine. I'll see you this afternoon." I hung up before she could see anything else. Just hearing his name made it hurt even more than I had when I woke in hospital. I knew I needed to speak to him, but I needed to get through today before I could see him. I didn't know how I was going to get through that meeting, but it was something for another day.

I got washed and dressed and did an inventory of my bare cupboards which didn't take long. I needed everything. I grabbed my bag and keys and headed out to my car. I stopped a few feet from it as my heart began to race and I felt the panic race through me at the thought of driving. I knew that it wasn't reasonable as I hadn't been in the car when it happened, but it still freaked me out.

For god sake, I came home in a taxi yesterday and I was fine but then again, I was still a little dazed about everything. I've had a decent nights' sleep and I am more aware of what is going on around me. I told myself I could do this and hit the button to unlock the car. I moved slow and got in the driver's side. I put my bag on the floor and turned the ignition on. I was sweating but my heart had calmed a little. I put my seatbelt on then put the car into gear and reversed down my driveway. My hands were sliding on the wheel with sweat, but I wouldn't let it get to me.

All the way to the supermarket, I could feel the sweat coating my body and sliding over my skin. I probably shouldn't have been driving but I had to do it sometime and now was as good a time as any. I pulled into the parking lot and parked up taking some deep breathes before prying my hands from the steering wheel and getting out.

I gave them a shake a few times to get the circulation back into them as I hadn't even realised that I had been gripping the steering wheel so hard. I got out the car locked it up and heading into the supermarket. I picked up a shopping cart outside and heading inside.

Doing something as mundane as shopping would help me feel normal again and not let me think too much about what I was going to go through this afternoon. I didn't really know much about my early years only a few flashes that came now and again.

I was nervous and scared about what Abby was going to say. Anytime I had tried to get her to talk about it, she shut down and would say nothing. I have imagined horrible things over the years about what happened and now, today, I was going to find out exactly what happened to my parents all those years ago. I put my bag in the top of the cart and started down the first aisle. It was going to be a long day.

A couple of hours later I pulled back into my driveway feeling better at driving but exhausted. I had to gather the strength to get out of the car and the thought of carrying the bags of groceries into the house was too much for me. I staggered through my front door and all but collapsed into the nearest chair.

I told myself a few minutes rest would be enough to recharge me before bringing in the shopping. I knew that I would be tired doing things after being asleep for so long, but I hadn't realised how much it would drain me. Before I could drag myself back up out of the chair, my eyes closed, and I was soon fast asleep. I awoke to someone banging on my front door. It seemed as if they were doing their best to try and break my door down. I pulled myself up out of the chair glancing at the time as I went. What I thought was a short nap turned out to be a few hours' sleep.

"Hold on, I'm coming no need to break the door down." I pulled open the door only to duck as a fist came right at my head. "Hey, watch it." As I stood up again, I saw Abby standing there looking worried.

"You're early."

"I know, I was anxious to talk to you. Are you alright?"

"I'm fine as I can be when someone wakes you from a deep sleep by trying to break my front door down." I stood back and let her enter. "Why didn't you use your key?"

"I didn't know how you would take it if I did. I need to explain why I did what I did. I wanted to tell you but as the year's went by, it got harder and then I thought it would be best to leave it. I know it was wrong, but I didn't want to lose you."

I walked into the kitchen after closing the door behind Abby trying to keep my emotions calm at what she was saying. I knew that she had my best interests at heart and that she would never want to hurt me, but it did. I told myself that it would pass. I had to hear her out if I was going to get by this.

I got a couple of mugs out to make some tea only to realise that I still hadn't brought in the shopping from the car. I turned away as I could feel her watching me from across the room. I grabbed my car keys and saw the look of panic on Abby's face. She moved to block me from leaving.

"Cat, please, let me explain everything and if you still don't want me around, I'll leave. "She reached out to stop me from leaving. I looked at her hand then up at her face. She thought I was walking out on her.

"I'm going to get the groceries from the car. I didn't bring them in when I came home earlier."

"Oh!" I opened the door then turned back to her.

"Do you want to help me?" She dropped her bag and walked past me out to the car and stood waiting on me opening the vehicle.

We worked in silence for the time it took us to empty the car for the bags. By the time we had finished I felt drained again and it must have shown as Abby made me sit down as she finished putting everything by. I watched as she knew exactly where everything went. I glanced at the time and knew that it wouldn't be long before my other visitor would be arriving.

I sat in silence watching as Abby found things to do in the kitchen as she avoided looking at me. I was trying to keep myself together for what was to come as I knew that I was going to hear things that I never knew, and I was hoping that I could handle it.

"Cat," Abby said but stopped when there was a knock at the door. I knew who it was, but she didn't. I stood and crossed to answer it.

"Hi, is this still a good time?" I must not have looked okay for the woman to ask me that, but I replied.

"It's fine. Please come in." I stood back and let Rose Maguire, journalist into my home. She stopped when she saw Abby across the room.

"I can come back later if you are in the middle of something?"

"No, now is perfect. Please have a seat." I gestured to the chairs waiting for her to take a seat before sitting myself. I knew Abby was looking at me wondering who she was and what was going on. Rose sat on the chair that faced the door as the uneasiness increased in the room. It was time to end all this and have the truth out there. I moved to stand beside the sofa before I spoke again.

"I read what you left, and I'm impressed. It's a brief account of what's happened but you need more. I can't give it all to you, but Abby can." I was watching Abby as I spoke seeing the confusion as to what was happening.

"Abby, this is Rose Maguire, a reporter from the Gazette. She's done a brief piece on me but needs more." I turned to Rose. "This is Abby McIntosh, my old babysitter and stand-in parent figure. She will be able to tell you about the first time and up to where I can take over. Between us both, you should have more than enough to get the full story of my life." I let my gaze switch between the two of them. One was eager to get started wondering what else is going to come out. The other, was of relief and the proudness of a parent.

"Now, would you like anything to drink before we start? I have a feeling that it is going to be a long afternoon." Rose shook her head and I moved to sit on the sofa. Abby seemed to come back to the present and moved to sit on the chair beside me.

I was nervous at what was going to be told but I had a right to know as it was my life they were talking about. I don't know why I never asked before, but it had seemed to hurt Abby anytime I had brought it up in the past, so I left it alone. It was time now for me to know exactly what happened to my parents.

"If you want or need to take a break at any time let me know. I don't know how long this will take so I am hoping you are here for the duration."

"I've got nowhere else to be. My editor is looking forward to seeing the full story. I gave her a brief run through of what I've got so far, and she loves it. I know we are only a local paper but this story, your story, has what it takes to make the nationals."

"I don't want it all to be a sob story. Yes, it is sad, but I want people to understand that despite it all, I came out ok. The only person who can stop you moving on or holding back is yourself. You have to be open to that and realising that there are people out there who can provide support if you need it."

I glanced at Abby and saw the pride shining out of her face. If it hadn't been for her, I don't know where I would have ended up.

"Ok, let's get started. If you don't mind, I'm going to record everything then transcribe it later." I nodded and saw Abby do the same. "Right, Abby tell me how you met Catriona and where her story started."

Part Two

History

Chapter Three

25 years ago

Abby stood outside a house that was double to size of the one she grew up in. This was the first time she had been here and was doubting her decision to come. She had answered an ad from a couple that were looking for a babysitter for their eighteen-month-old daughter.

She wiped her hands down her legs then knocked on the door. As she heard footsteps approach, her heart began to race. The door opened and there stood a woman who looked not much older than herself and was dressed in an outfit that she would never be able to afford.

"You must be Abby, I'm Isla Mont-Clair. Please come in." She stepped back and Abby walked past her employer to be and into a home that she could tell was well loved. It was decorated tastefully with lots of warm colour. She began to feel at ease the more she looked around, feeling Mrs Mont-Clair come up behind her.

"You have a lovely home Mrs Mont-Clair."

"Please call me Isla. I feel like my mother when you call me Mrs Mont-Clair." Abby smiled at her.

"Ok, Isla." Before she could say anything else, she heard a wailing from down a hallway to their left. They both turned towards it and Abby saw a tall handsome man walk towards them cradling something gently in his arms.

"I don't know what's wrong with her tonight. She just won't go down." As he came closer, Isla moved forward and lifted her daughter from his arms.

"Stewart, this is Abby." He held out his hand.

"Pleased to meet you Abby. I'm sorry for the behaviour of our daughter. She is usually much more behaved than this."

"That's ok, babies sometimes just feel the need to let it out. She may also be able to tell that you are leaving her. Have you done that before?"

"No, I only recently went back to work, but this is an important night for Stewart, and I can't let him go alone. We have left here during the day, but this will be the first time at night." She was trying to soothe the child but with no success.

"May I?" Abby put her bag down on the nearest chair and waited to see if Isla would hand over her daughter to a stranger. She did and as Abby felt the softness and weight of the child in her arms, she knew she was where she was meant to be.

She moved the child around until she could see the baby's face and she was treated to the greenest pair of eyes she had seen in a long time. Them combined with the dark hair made her stand out and Abby felt herself falling in love with her.

She caught the baby's gaze and she felt a connection and she stopped crying and reached out her hands and hit gently against her face. Abby forgot who else was in the room, only concentrating on the baby.

"Well, I guess you're hired." Stewart said. "We haven't really discussed money, but I'll pay you twenty per hour. I've never known her to quieten or take to someone so quick."

Abby smiled at the little girl. "What's her name?"

"Catriona or Cat for short."

"Ok then Cat, it's you and me tonight. What are you up for doing?" The baby laughed and completely forgot about her parents.

"We won't be too late."

"It's okay, we'll be fine. Tonight, is about us getting to know each other." Abby started walking around the room getting her bearings and pointing things out to the child.

"Well, I think we have made the right choice. I have a feeling that those two are going to be inseparable." Isla tried to stop the tears but couldn't.

"I think you're right. Let's go before we are late." They closed the door knowing that their daughter would be safe and headed out.

The next year and a half went by quickly with Isla and Stewart calling upon Abby whenever they needed her, growing close to the family.

When her mother fell ill, they helped her out by making sure she got to whatever treatment she needed.

Abby could never repay them for all they had done for her. They didn't even mind when a few times she had to bring her younger brother along when her mum couldn't watch him. The first time she brought him along was a wet day. Her mother had to go to hospital for tests and would be away all day. It was the school holidays, so she had no-where to take him to except with her.

She parked the car in the driveway as usual and turned to him.

"Now, I need you to be on your best behaviour. I love this job and don't want to lose it. I know you wanted to stay with mum but she's at the hospital all day and can't watch you." He kept looking out the windows and not at her.

"Michael, do you hear me?

"Yes Abby, I hear you. I'll be on my best behaviour. I promise." He turned to look at her as he finished, and she could only hope that he kept that promise.

They got out of the car and walked up to the front door. She opened it and called out. There was no answer, but she did hear voices coming from down the hallway. She turned and pulled Michael into the house. He kept close to her and stopped at the junction of the hallway.

"Isla? I'm here." She put her bag on the table and headed towards the kitchen where there were noises of someone moving about. She turned to Michael giving him a warning look then left him standing there. She found Isla in the kitchen sorting food out.

"Abby, thank God you're here. She is being a right pain today not doing anything we tell her to. It's as If she is trying to keep us here."

"She's only two and a half and doesn't understand that you need to leave."

"Yeah, well tell that to her. Now, the casserole will be ready in an hour so help yourself." She came away from the stove, taking off the apron that she was wearing. "Let's go and see the monster."

They walked back the way she had come but stopped as they saw Michael.

"Isla, this is my younger brother Michael. Mum is at the hospital all day for tests and I have no-one else to watch him. I hope you don't mind me bringing him."

Isla stepped closer to the boy who looked about eight years old. He was dressed in a faded t-shirt, jeans and sweatshirt that had seen better days but were all clean. The way he was standing made Isla on guard as he looked like he would cause trouble in an empty house. He looked as if he would rather be anywhere than where he was at that moment. Before Isla could say anything, Stewart called out from the hallway.

"Cat don't you run away from me." A small figure shot down the hallway heading straight for the table between them, hitting it and landing on her back. Before anyone could react, the boy was there lifting her up. The tears and wailing that had begun suddenly stopped as she looked up to see who had picked her up.

"Hi, are you okay? I'm Michael." Abby walked over and knelt beside Cat as her parents looked on.

"Cat, this is my brother, Michael." She switched her gaze from the two of them then she pulled herself to her feet and reached out and grabbed his hand and started to pull him down the hallway. The look of fear on Michael's face was priceless but Abby motioned for him to go with her. The three adults stood watching as the toddler led an eight-year-old into a world he couldn't imagine.

"Well, that's something you don't see every day." Stewart said. "Your family has an interesting effect on my daughter Abby."

"I'm sorry Isla, I don't know what happened." She stopped her talking by putting her hand on her arm.

"It's ok. I knew we made the right choice in hiring you, but I never expected the connection you have and now it seems your family has with her not to mention myself and Stewart."

Abby didn't know what to say. "If you're stuck again for Michael, please bring him back. I'm intrigued to see how that relationship will evolve."

Over the next few months, any time Abby went to the Mont-Clair's she found herself with Michael tagging alone. Somehow the connection between the two of them was instant and the change in Michael was substantial. He was behaving more and helping out more at home. It was as if he knew he had to step in and take care of her.

Abby stopped talking and looked to Cat. She could see in her face how this was affecting her, she looked at Rose who was busy writing stuff down even though she was recording it all. She sat closer to Cat and took her hand as she knew that this next part was going to be hard for her hear.

"Keep going." Abby searched her face before she began talking again.

Chapter Four

She was running late. Her mum was doing well today but Michael had been off school the last few days with the flu. When he had found out where she was going, they had gotten into an argument with him trying to persuade her to go with her. He tried to tell her that he was better and would be back at school soon, but Abby was having none of it.

Over the last six months, he had been going with her when she had been watching Cat and the two of them had gotten extremely close. It was getting difficult to separate them when she was leaving. The winter weather had hit them hard in the last 24 hours and it was another reason for Michael to stay inside in the warmth.

He had been shouting at her as she left the house whilst her mum had been sitting watching them. It was as if the roles were reversed and Abby was the mother, and her mum was the child. She was used to it but at times, it weighed on her. She was only nineteen and not much more than a child herself, but she took it as it came at her. She was no stranger to hard work.

She gave a sigh of relief as she pulled into the Mont-Clair's driveway knowing that it must be important if they were going out in this weather. The snow was falling thick and heavy and Abby began to wonder if she would even be able to drive home tonight.

She lifted the brightly coloured package out of the car and made her way carefully to the front door. It was Cat's birthday in a few days, so she had brought over her gift early as she knew that her parents had something special planned for her. They had asked her to go as well but she had an exam at college so she couldn't make it.

She knocked on the door then opened it with the key they had given her. She put the present down in the corner so that it would be hidden until she could move it into Stewart's study where the rest of her presents would be kept.

"Sorry I'm late." She walked in looking about for Isla and Stewart. It was Stewart who appeared first.

"Evening. How's the weather doing?"

"The snow's falling heavier and it's icy on the roads. You'll need to be careful whilst driving. I may need to stay here tonight pending on how the weather is when you get back."

"Not a problem. The spare room is always made up for you just in case. I'll be careful driving as Isla hates driving or even travelling in this weather, but I can't not go tonight. I can't miss my own promotion and awards ceremony."

Abby smiled at him.

"Isla will get over it. She just doesn't like not being in control."

"Don't I know it." He lifted his suit jacket and put it on. "Honey, we're going to be late if we don't leave now."

"I've left a present for Cat by the front door.

"You didn't need to do that."

"I wanted to. I love that little girl and Michael wouldn't let me not get something. He helped pick it out." Stewart's eyes filled up and he looked to the floor then back up at her.

"Thank you. I know she loves you too. Now can you please go and see what is taking my wife so long whilst I put the present away with the rest."

Abby walked down the hallway knowing where she would find Isla. She stood at the door and watched as she played with her daughter. One was dressed in a designer gown, the other in Disney princess pyjamas. As soon as the little one caught sight of her, she was up off the floor and running across the room.

"Well, I can see I've been forgotten now." Abby smiled down as she picked up the toddler who was giggling away. When she looked back up, it was to see a worried face looking at them both.

"Isla, what's wrong?" She moved Cat into a more comfortable position then crossed to where Isla was standing. There were unshed tears in her eyes and Abby felt her heart begin to race and all kinds of things running through her head.

She put Cat down motioning for her to go and play again. She seemed to know something wasn't right and did as she was told. Abby stepped closer to Isla and laid a hand on her arm. Her face was one of hopelessness and loss and Abby couldn't work out why.

"Isla, what's wrong? What's happened? Are you ill?"

"No, I'm not ill and neither is Stewart or Cat. Everything is great."

"No, it's not. You wouldn't be looking like you are if everything were great. What's wrong?" Isla looked at Abby then down at her daughter who was playing quietly and seemingly oblivious to the tension in the room.

"I swear everything is fine. It's just that I have a bad feeling. It has been dogging me for the last few days and I can't seem to shake it."

Abby didn't know what to say. She seemed so upset that there must be something that she wasn't telling her but there was no way to get it out of her. Isla smiled and hugged her tightly before leaving them alone as she went into her room. A few minutes later she came back out with her makeup repaired and her coat and clutch bag.

"Now, we shouldn't be too late but knowing Stewart, he'll talk all evening and it'll be the middle of the night by the time we get back. If so, then we'll see you in the morning."

Abby went to Cat and pulled her up from the floor carrying her through to where her father was waiting on them. He kissed her goodbye telling her to be a good girl and he waited on Isla who was saying her own goodbyes to her daughter. Finally, they were done and were heading out the door as Abby and Cat stood watching them leave unknowing that everything was going to change forever later that night.

A few hours later, Cat was sleeping soundly, and she had been catching up on some revision for her exam in a few days. She was startled when there was a knock at the door, and it was only then that she saw how late it was. As she stood from the table, she went to check on Cat who was sleeping, and she knew that Stewart and Isla weren't back yet as their bedroom was lying open as it was when they were not in.

The knocking became more insistent and louder, so she hurried to the door before whoever it was woke Cat up. She didn't want to deal with a grumpy little girl this late at night. She unlocked the door only to open it to find that her life would never be the same. Standing on the front porch was two police officers. Their look was grim, and Abby knew that something bad had happened.

"Is this the residence of Stewart and Isla Mont-Clair?"

"Yes. How can I help you Officers?"

"May we come in?" Abby hesitated for a few seconds before stepping back and allowing them to enter.

"Please, this way." She took them into the main living room and sat down. Her heart was racing knowing they were going to say something bad but wanting to put it off for as long as possible.

"I'm Officer Gordon and this is Officer Mitchell. What's your name miss?"

"Abby McIntosh. I'm babysitting their daughter. What's happened?"

"Is there anyone else here?"

"No, it's just me and Catriona. Tell me." Abby was shaking as she waited to hear how bad it was.

"The Mont-Clair's were involved in a car accident earlier this evening. I'm sorry to inform you that they didn't make it."

Abby had known it was going to be bad, but she hadn't expected that. She could see the officer talking to her, but she couldn't hear what he was saying. She felt something on her leg, and she looked down at it seeing a hand, so she looked up to its owner. Doing that had brought her out of the daze she had been in.

"Do you need me to identify the bodies?"

"No. They had ID on them."

"What happens now?"

"We will need someone to collect their personal effects and sort out what to do with their daughter. How old is she?"

"Three, well nearly, she'll be three in two days. How am I going to get her to understand that she'll never see her parents again?"

"Kids are resilient. It may take time, but she'll be okay. Child Services will be here in the morning to take custody of her."

"What! You can't do that. This is the only home she has ever known."

"Miss, it's the law. There is no other family, so she'll become a ward of the state until she is either adopted or reaches the age of eighteen."

"No, she'll stay with me. I'll take care of her."

"How old are you?"

"Twenty." The older looking officer smiled sadly at her as if he knew that she was lying about her age. She knew that she didn't look that old.

"Miss you can't take her on. You are barely legal yourself. What about your family? How would they react?"

"They'll be fine. My little brother already knows and adores her, and my mother will also love her."

They stood to leave, and she stood with them.

"We'll see what Child Services say. You may have temporary custody, but I doubt it."

"You can't take her away." Abby didn't know where this stubborn protective streak was coming from, but she was going to fight. She didn't want that little girl thrown into a strange house with strangers or worse, a group home. She'd heard too many horror stories about kids that ended up there. The officers moved closer to the door and the older one spoke.

"I'll be back in the morning with Child Services." Abby saw the look on Officer Mitchell's face but before she could reply, a cry could be heard through the baby monitors.

"We'll go and let you deal with her. I'm sorry for your loss." They closed the door behind them leaving Abby standing staring at it. She moved when the cries became louder and hurried into Cat's room.

"Hey, what are you doing awake?" she asked as she crossed to the bed.

"Bunny." Abby looked around and saw he favourite stuffed toy lying at the bottom of the bed. She picked it up then sat on the bed as she gave the toy back. Abby didn't know how she was going to tell her that her parents were never coming again.

She sat with her until she fell asleep again then left the room quietly. She made it outside before the tears came. She found herself sliding down the wall outside her room as the tears flowed out of her.

She cried for the loss of two people that were like family to her. She cried for the little girl who would never know her parents. She cried for all the things that they would never get to share with their daughter. She had to get it out of her system tonight as for tomorrow, she was going to have to tell her and she would need to be strong to get through it.

Chapter Five

When Abby work the next morning, she found herself lying in front of Cat's bedroom door. She must have fallen asleep after breaking down. Her eyes felt heavy and her face was probably red with all the emotions running through her along with her crying episode.

She dragged herself up the wall and stood, opening the door slightly to make sure that Cat was still asleep. She moved stiffly down the hallway to her room and cleaned herself up. As she came out, she heard her mobile ringing and she rushed to answer it so that it wouldn't wake Cat.

"Hello."

"Abby, when are you going to be home? I have to go out this morning and I don't want to leave Michael alone in the house."

"I'm not sure. Something has happened." She looked down the hallway to Cat's room feeling the tears begin to build again.

"What's happened? Is Cat ok?"

"Cat's fine. It's Isla and Stewart." Abby took a deep breath before beginning to speak again. She didn't want to tell her mum over the phone that they had died. "They were in an accident on the way home from the party last night. They skidded on the ice trying to avoid a car that had run a red light." She stopped talking trying to keep herself together knowing that her mother would know how she felt.

"How is Cat? Which hospital are they in?"

"She doesn't know yet. I'm going to tell her this morning when she is awake which should be anytime now."

"Well, once you have, bring her home with you and we will look after her. She needs people around her."

"I'll try but I'm not sure if it will be possible. The police will be back this morning with someone from Child Services to take her into foster care." Abby had moved around the room as she had been talking to her mother. She stopped at the window staring out at the back garden where they had spent a lot of time this summer. There was a sound from behind her and she turned to see Cat standing bleary eyed looking for her mother. "I need to go mum, Cat's awake. I'll be home at some point today."

She hung up the phone and slipped it into the back pocket of her jeans then crossed to where the little girl stood. She crouched down.

"Hey sleepy head. How are you this morning?"

"Mum." Abby knew this was going to be the hardest thing she had ever done. She lifted the little girl and headed back into her room where she would be the most comfortable. She didn't know where to start or how she was going to cope but she would get through it. She had to for Cat and for Isla and Stewart. They would have wanted her to take care of their daughter.

She put Cat back down on her bed and pulled the covers back up over her. The little girl had a strong grip on Bunny as if it would protect her from what is to come. There was sadness on her face as if she knew something had happened but looked at her as if she wasn't about to shatter her world.

"Cat, I've got something to tell you. You know that I'm here because mummy and daddy were out last night?" The little girl nodded bring Bunny closer to her little body. "Well something has happened."

Abby could feel the tears welling in her eyes as she tried to form the words that she needed to say. She was only three years old. How was she supposed to make her understand that she would never see her parents again? She was the only one who could tell her. She couldn't leave it to the authorities, she owed Isla and Stewart more than that.

Cat was a bright child and Abby knew that she would understand that her life was going to change. She was going to have a long road ahead of her but she would get over it. With her being so young, she would recover and her life will be what she will make it. She would make sure that she made it regardless of what the authorities did. She would watch over the little girl and ensure that she had a happy life ahead of her.

"There was an accident on their way home last night. They won't be home again." She kept her eyes on the little girl as she spoke. She could tell that she was listening, but she wasn't sure if she was taking in what she was saying. "They are now angels, watching over you."

Cat pushed the covers back and crawled into Abby's lap. She pulled Bunny along with her and Abby felt a single tear fall as the little girl wrapped her arms around her neck. More tears fell now and Abby was chiding herself at being weak when she was trying to tell the most devastating news.

Cat pulled back and lifted her hand to her face, touching the tears that were falling from Abby's eyes. "Mummy, daddy?"

"Yes, mummy and daddy." Abby wrapped her arms around the little girl and held her close. She could feel vibrations from her and knew that she was now also crying. It hurt so bad as she held the little girl, but she was here for her always.

She knew she was holding on tightly, so she loosened her arms and the little girl climbed off her lap and headed to the chest of drawers on the other side of the room. She struggled to pull the lowest drawer open, but she managed. She pulled out the clothes that were in it until she lifted something else out.

Abby was about to tell her to stop but she stopped herself as she stood from the bed. The little girl had turned back to her holding a sweatshirt that was too big for her. As she came back to the bed, Abby sat again and the little crawled into her lap again and pulled the sweatshirt close along with Bunny.

It was then that Abby recognised it. It was Isla's. She had seen her wearing it about the house and knew that she had lost it last week. Now she knew where it had disappeared to. Abby's heart shattered as she held on the little body as the tremors flowed through the paid, of them.

She didn't know how long they had been like that but sometime later, Abby pulled back and glanced at the time. Child Services would be here soon, so she needed to get Cat ready to go.

"Ok, time to get dressed. We have a lot to do today." She lifted the little girl and stood her up. Her face was read and blotchy, but she loved her and would fight for her. "What do you want to wear today?" Cat held up the sweatshirt.

"No, that's too big for you just now. Let's find something else for you wear." She crossed to where Cat had pulled the clothes out and searched through them. She picked up a top and turned back. "How about this?" Abby watched the little face brighten slightly as she had hoped it would. The top was one which Isla loved on Cat. Abby moved to the wardrobe and pulled out a pair of jeans to go with the top and a sweatshirt to go over it all.

"Ok, bathroom now to wash that face clean." She laid the clothes on the bed and took her hand as they headed into the bathroom. Once they had both washed and brushed their teeth, they headed back to get dressed. Abby left Cat in her bedroom as she went down the hall to get changed herself.

She called out to her as she made her way into the kitchen.

"How about pancakes for breakfast?" Cat stood at her bedroom door as Abby stopped at the other end of the hallway. "With loads of blueberries." The small smile that crossed Cat's face made Abby feel as if she were doing something right. It may not be much, but it was something.

Cat came down the hallway as Abby held out an apron for her to put on. She put one on as well and began pulling the ingredients for the pancakes from the cupboards and fridge. Cat climbed up on the bar stool at the other side of the breakfast bar and Abby handed the eggs to the little girl.

"Ok, get going on smashing the eggs." Abby had out three small bowls in front of the little girl and let her get on with it. She may only be three, but she could crack an egg like a pro. Abby got started on measuring out the flour and milk before lifting one of the bowls and mixing the egg into the flour and milk mixture.

Abby turned to the stove and put the pan on to heat up. She lifted the blueberries and handed the bowl to Cat allowing her to add how many blueberries she wanted in her pancakes. Once completed, she poured the mixture into the pan watching for any splashes that may occur.

Once Abby had a few pancakes, she tipped them onto a plate for them both and put the syrup in front of them. Cat began eating the pancake then stopped and lifted the syrup and poured some over the pancake then began eating again.

Abby stood watching as she ate knowing that she didn't know where they would both be come the end of the day. She ate hers then began clearing up the dishes. She turned back and saw Cat staring at her.

"It'll be ok. Everything will be ok." Abby didn't know if she was trying to convince Cat or herself. "Go on and play for a little while. I'll finish cleaning up in here." She watched as she got down from the stool and came around to where she was standing. She looked up at her then threw her arms around her legs and held on tight. Abby held back the tears as Cat let go and headed back to her room.

It was going to be a tough day for them both and she didn't know where they were going to end up. She hoped it would be together, but she couldn't count on it. She would fight to keep hold of her, but she didn't know if she would win.

Abby looked in on Cat after she had finished cleaning and saw that she was playing quietly in her playroom. She turned away and headed to her bedroom and started pulling clothes out for her. She piled them on the bed then went into her cupboard and pulled out the small suitcase that they had bought for her a few months previous.

She began folding the clothes into it leaving her mother's sweatshirt to the end so that she would see it when it was opened. She also put in her other favourite toy, a stuffed tiger that she'd also had since she was born.

Abby was starting to feel numb as she packed the case. Everything was becoming unreal even though she knew that it was real. When she had finished, she left the suitcase by the door and was headed back to her when something caught her attention on the bedside table. It was a picture that she had taken of the three of them last summer in the back yard.

They had been playing in the paddling pool when Isla and Stewart decided to join Cat in the small pool. They were splashing each other, and Abby had grabbed her phone to take a picture just as the pool burst and the water had flooded into the garden. She remembered getting soaked with it but the sheer joy on their faces made her take the picture.

It had been sitting at Cat's bedside since she had gotten it printed. She lifted the picture frame and slid it into the front pocket of the case just as there was a knock at the door. Abby felt her heart skip a beat knowing that was the authorities come to take her away.

Chapter Six

Abby wiped her hands down the side of her jeans as she got closer to the front door. Whoever was there knocked again seeming impatient at not answering quick enough. Before they could knock a third time, she pulled open the door to see one of the officers from the night before and a woman the looked to be in her early thirties.

"Morning Abby."

"Morning Officer. I didn't think you had been serious last night about coming back this morning."

"I told you I would. I don't go back on my promises." Abby swung her gaze to the woman standing beside him. "This is Susannah Croft from Child Services." Abby watched as she held out her hand to greet the newcomer. She didn't want to like her but she did.

"Please, come in." Abby stood back and allowed the two of them to enter the house. She gestured to the living room and they walked on through with her following. She knew this was it but now she was nervous.

"Miss Croft is here to take Catriona into foster care."

"Can't she stay here? This is her home."

"Not anymore. She will become a ward of the state as there are no other family members."

"I can look after her. I can move in here so that she doesn't need to leave. It'll be easier for her."

"Abby, isn't it? You are no more than a child yourself. You can't take on the care of a three-year-old. You don't understand the amount of work involved."

"I do understand. I have been looking after my younger brother for the last few years and ensuring my mother gets to hospital appointments. I can handle a three-year-old." Susannah smiled at her.

"You have just proven my point. You have enough on your plate without taking on the care for a small child. You are what, eighteen? You don't know how much work a young child is. How old is your brother?"

"He's nine, nearly ten."

"A ten-year-old can be a hand full. I'll bet that it hasn't all been plain sailing with him?" Abby couldn't respond as she right. It had only been in the last year that Michael had started behaving better than he had ever been.

"You say you take your mother to hospital appointments. It must be serious if she has a lot, on top of an eight-year-old. Have you finished school yet?"

"I graduate this summer."

"Well there you go. You have final exams coming up something else for you to think about. A young child is not what you need at this moment."

"I'll manage. I'll get a job now and I'll be able to take care of them all. Please give me a chance."

"I would love to but rules are rules. You are not family and we cannot leave a young child in the care of someone who is not related to them. We need to make the hard decisions in the interest of the child." Abby had been watching her as she spoke. She seemed genuine but she couldn't let her take Cat out of the only home she has ever known.

"Now, where is Catriona?" Abby stood silently then pointed to the room at the end of the hallway. She watched as she walked down towards where her heart had been left.

Abby turned away and saw that the police officer was standing against the wall near the door.

"Why are you letting them take her?"

"I can't stop them. They are in the right to take her away until permanent arrangements have been made for her. I know that you want to stay with her but it may not be possible. It will be a hard road to travel if you wish to go that way."

"If I wish…. Of course, I wish to go that way. I want to be able to look after Cat and watch her grow up in a loving home not some group home waiting for someone to take pity on her and take her away."

She heard Miss Croft talking but there was no response. Abby turned away and headed down the hallway to see Miss Croft kneeling on the floor across from where Cat was playing. Abby crossed the room and sat down beside her.

"Cat, come here and meet Miss Croft." Cat eyed the stranger warily before crossing to Abby and leaning against her. She hid her face into her body not wanting to look at the new lady. Abby pulled her away from her leg and turned her towards where Susannah was sitting.

"Hello Catriona, it's very nice to meet you. My name is Susannah or Suzie if you prefer."

Abby watched as the little girl eyed the stranger trying to work out if she was friend or foe.

"Cat. My name is Cat."

"Oh, I'm sorry. Well it's nice to meet you Cat. Who do you have there?" Abby kept an eye on Cat as she looked down to Bunny.

"Bunny."

"Well it's nice to meet you as well Bunny." She took the stuffed paw and gave it a shake leaving her hand where it was. Cat lifted her small hand and put it in hers. "Who else do we have here?" Cat moved away from her leg and Abby watched as she went to Susannah. She turned and left the room and back to where the police officer was still standing.

"Officer Gordon, isn't it?" He nodded. "What happens next?"

"Well Catriona will be put into the foster care system until a family is found to put her with. If no-one comes forward, then she will go into the system until she is either adopted or becomes an adult."

Abby felt her breathe catch as he spoke. She knew that there was the danger of her not being adopted so she didn't think about it. She would have her back with her before long she hoped.

"What about the house?"

"That will be in the hands of the lawyers. I'm sure they would have something in place in the event of anything happening to them. As Catriona is so young, any outcome will be held in trust until she is of age most likely then she would be able to gain access to it."

"How long will it take?"

"It's lawyers, they always take their time but I would suspect that it would be quite quick as it is clear there are not other relatives. They won't want to drag it on as it will be a fixed fee due to the circumstances." Abby nodded as he spoke trying to take it all in and what her next step was going be.

"I would suggest that if there is anything here that you would want to keep for Catriona, then I would put it aside otherwise everything will be sold. Anything that was in either of their names will be sold and the proceeds held in trust until she comes of age."

"How long do I have with her?"

"Not long. Most likely Miss Croft will want to take her with her today so that she is getting the proper care immediately. They left her here last night as a courtesy but that's it."

Abby heard voices behind her and wiped her face of the tears that had fallen. She turned to see Cat coming down the hallway with a smile on her face holding Susannah's hand. She smiled at her as Cat stopped and looked at her.

"Ice-cream." Abby looked at the others then back at Cat. "Chocolate ice-cream."

"I've told her we're going for some ice-cream. Do you have her bag?" Abby felt rage inside her at the lie. She opened her mouth to say something but stopped when she saw the look on her face. She wouldn't win this just now.

"I'll get it." She walked past them and back to Cat's room to pick up the suitcase. She knew that Cat would recognise it and know that she was going away. She kept it hidden behind her until Officer Gordon took it from her hand. She watched as she held out her hand the Cat took it. She took a few steps before stopping and turning back to her.

"Abby?" she said. Abby knew what she was asking.

"I can't come with you just now. I need to sort out some things for your parents." She seemed to think on this then tried to pull her hand from Susannah's. She couldn't as she held on firm.

Cat began pulling with all her strength but couldn't get free. Abby wanted to go to her but knew she had to let them leave. Susannah lifted Cat up and headed to the door all the while Cat was screaming and kicking trying to get down. Abby wanted to turn away but didn't she wanted to keep her eyes on Cat even though her heart was shattering into a thousand pieces.

Officer Gordon opened the front door and allowed them to walk past. He followed them out carrying the small suitcase. As the door closed, Abby turned away and let out a scream. She wanted to throw something but knew she couldn't so she let it out in a way that wouldn't hurt anyone, by screaming.

Chapter Seven

Abby pulled herself together a few minutes later knowing that the police and that woman would have heard her. She felt someone behind her before she lifted her head again. She turned to see who it was and saw Officer Gordon standing looking down at her.

He bent down and lifted her up to standing then guided her over to the sofa and sat her down. Abby watched in disbelief at what he was doing. She didn't know why he had come back or even what he was doing there.

She watched him as he disappeared into the kitchen and she heard cupboards opening and closing and guessed that he was making tea. She stood on shaky legs and crossed to the entryway holding on to the wall to keep her upright. He had his back turned to her, but he knew she was there.

"Why don't you go and clean up a bit. The tea will be ready by the time you are back." Abby knew that he was being kind to her, but she didn't know if she could take it anymore. "Go on now. Get cleaned up."

She moved towards the bathroom in the hall and as she closed the door, she caught sight of herself in the mirror. She looked a mess. Her eyes were red and swollen, she had tear streaks down her face and as she lifted her hands to her face, she noticed them shaking. She held both hands together for a few seconds then began to run the water.

It would help a little, but it would take time for her to look like herself again. She had it easy. Cat had the hard task as she had to understand why she wouldn't see her parents again. She wanted to be there for her as she would help to ease her into her new life without her parents. She would fight for her. She would need to find a lawyer that could help, how she was going to pay for it, she didn't know but she would find a way somehow.

The funerals. She had to find out what was happening with the funeral arrangements. She didn't know whether it would be the county that would organise it or if this was something that she could do. She would ask Office Gordon and see if he could help her out.

She ran the cold water and splashed some water on her face a few times, jumping at the coldness of it. It would help to reduce the redness on the outside, but the inside will take a lot more to heal.

When she felt steadier, she headed back into the living room and found Officer Gordon standing at the window looking out over the gardens. She saw the teapot and cups sitting on the table, so she crossed to this and began pouring.

"Milk? Sugar?" the Officer turned around.

"Yes please, just one sugar. My wife keeps getting me to stop it altogether, but I can't let go of that last one. I used to take three sugars." He crossed to the chair and sat down allowing Abby to sort the cups and hand one over to him.

"Why are you helping me?" Abby watched him as he hesitated before beginning to speak.

"You remind me of my daughter. My granddaughter is about the same age as Cat and I would hope that there would be someone there for her just like you are for Cat if, God forbid, anything like this happened to my Sammy."

Abby didn't know what to say. "But she would still have you and your wife. She wouldn't be totally alone."

"No, she wouldn't but having someone there with her at that moment, is something that can never be forgotten. Being there for someone when they have lost a loved one, is the best thing that anyone can do. You wish you could take away the pain from them knowing that you can't and that everyone goes through that at some point in their lives."

Abby couldn't respond. She didn't know how she would cope if, and when, she lost her mother or Michael. She was older and understood that loss was a part of life, but Cat. She was too young to understand, and she just wanted to be there with her and help her through the coming months. Abby lifted the cup and took a drink. She felt the heat doing down into her body and warming her. It removed the chill that she hadn't realised had been there.

"What is happening about the funerals?"

"Once everything has been completed at the morgue, the County will arrange for them to be buried if they don't already have something in place." Abby looked puzzled at him. "Some people put plans into place regardless of how old they are. They want to make sure those left behind don't have to deal with sorting out the arrangements along with dealing with their grief. Their lawyer will be able to confirm if they have anything like that."

"Please site down Officer. You are making me nervous standing hovering over me."

"Martin. My name is Martin."

"Well Martin, please could you sit down." He hesitated for a second or so then sat down at the other side of the table. Abby took another drink of the tea before speaking again. "What about the house? What happens to this?"

"Again, it will depend on what has been put in place. Most likely it will be sold, and the proceeds will be put into trust for Cat until she becomes of age."

"How soon?"

"Again, it will depend on what has been agreed, but I would assume that it would be soon. After today, no-on will be allowed back inside this house until it is ready to be sold. I would recommend that if there is anything here that you want Cat to have, then I would pack it up today otherwise, she won't have anything left of her parents." Abby put down her cup. "There will be officers here later to lock up the house until that time. I told them I would be here this morning, so they won't be here until later, but it doesn't give us much time."

Abby stood and looked around the room trying to work out what to pack for Cat. Her mind was going in different directions at the thought that it was up to her to make sure that Cat didn't forget her parents.

"Take a deep breath. That's it and again." Abby felt hands on her shoulders, and she looked up to see Martin standing in front of her breathing deep that she felt herself do the same.

"I…I…I… don't know where to start."

"That's ok. We'll get through it together. Now, do you know if there are any packing boxes around?"

"There may be some in the garage."

"Ok. I'll go look and you start thinking about what Cat would like to keep of her parents." Abby nodded her head as she felt herself calm down and watched as the Officer, Martin headed into the garage for the boxes. What would Cat like? Abby felt herself moving down the hallway into Isla and Stewart's bedroom.

She stood at the door and looked around seeing the way the room had been left the previous night. She felt the tears begin again but gave herself a mental shake to say that she had to get on with the task at hand.

She walked in and looked around. She headed to the closet and opened it to find rows of clothes that she would never be able to afford. She told herself she needed to detach from this so that she could decide if she was keeping anything from here.

She pulled all the clothes to the side not seeing anything that would be worth keeping until she saw a box on the top shelf. She pulled it down and opened it to find all baby things that they had kept.

There were scan pictures, receipts for furniture, small baby grows, photos. This was something that needed to be kept.

"What's first to be packed?" Abby looked up then back down at the box she had in front of her.

"This is first. I'll keep looking here."

"Ok. How about you go through things and leave them out and I'll come behind and box then up for you. That way, we will get done quicker."

"Ok, sounds like a plan." Abby began putting the items back into the box and pushed it towards Martin. She turned back to the closet and looked again on the shelf. There were more things there from when Cat was a baby.

She pulled the boxes and stuff down and laid them on the bed. She moved to the dressing table and began looking at the jewellery to see what she would keep.

She pulled out the jewellery box and glanced through it. Most of this was costume stuff but she knew that Isla kept her good stuff in the bottom drawer. She knelt and went through the drawer until she found the few velvet boxes. She opened them to ensure the items were still inside, then closed them over before putting them on the dressing table.

They worked together until there were about six or seven boxes piled up at the front door. Abby had somehow switched off as she was going through everything but knew that what she had picked would be things that Cat would treasure when she was older.

"Is there anything else?"

"No, this is the last box. Are you sure this will all fit in your car?" Abby looked at everything piled up.

"I hope so. It needs to as I'm not leaving any of it."

"Ok. Let's get started filling your car." Abby pulled her keys from her bag, lifted a box and headed out to start packing her car. It didn't take them long to get everything in and she could just about fit herself in the driver's seat. She began doubting herself at where she was going to put everything once she got home. But she would find somewhere.

Abby went back inside for a last look around then lift her bag and headed out to where Martin was waiting on her. She locked the door for the final time and walked down to where he was standing at her car.

"These are yours now." She handed him the keys and turned to look back again. She hadn't been coming there long, but it had felt like home. Now she had to go home and tell Michael what had happened.

Chapter Eight

Abby looked over at Rose before she turned her gaze to Cat. She could feel the emotion coming off her and she wouldn't look her in the eye.

"That must have been a difficult time for you being not much more than a child yourself." Rose said.

"It was but I did what I had to do until I couldn't do anymore at that time. All my thoughts were about Cat and how to get her through this." Abby felt drained as this was the first time, she had really spoke about what had happened. It was also cathartic feeling making her feel lighter than she could ever remember. She swung her gaze back to Cat who had now turned to look at her.

"I never knew what you did for me. What you had been left to deal with."

"I didn't know what else to do and I wanted you to have some things that belonged to your parents." Rose cleared her throat and looked between the pair of them.

"I think this is going to take longer than we have today. We don't we call it a day and meet again tomorrow. I can work with what I have just now."

I nodded knowing that I couldn't keep track of everything that had been said. I never knew how tough it must have been on Abby as she was only a teenager, but she stepped up to the mark to get things done.

I thought back over how I had treated her over the years and felt ashamed. I should have been more grateful for her rather than acting like a spoiled child. I vowed to try and make it up to her at some point I didn't know how, but I would.

Rose stood, gathering her bag and recording device before heading to the door. I know words were exchanged but I couldn't tell you what as my mind was whirling over everything else. At the door, Rose turned and put her hand on my arm bringing my attention to her.

"Thank you for allowing me to hear and tell your story. I can't even imagine what you must have gone through in your life, but you will be an inspiration to others." I nodded again but still couldn't bring myself to speak.

"Is ten o'clock tomorrow okay for you?"

"Yes, that's fine. We'll be ready to go again." Abby had answered but I could hear the strain in her voice. If I was feeling like this, then I couldn't imagine what she must be feeling as she lived through it. I have a few flashes here and there but not much else.

Abby opened the door and said goodbye before closing it and turning to me. I felt frozen in time, but someone was guiding me away from the door and back to the sofa. I sat down going over everything again.

I had known that Abby had dealt with things for my parents, funerals but I hadn't realised how much she had dealt with. I knew that her mother hadn't been keeping well at that time, so she had been looking after her little brother in between going to school and looking after me when required.

I really wished I had been better to her in my teenage years. Growing up in foster care was not the worst thing that could have happened and when I had finally been adopted, I felt loved again. I hadn't known that there had been someone out there who did love me and had tried her best for me.

She had never told me that she had wanted to keep me. This was the first I was hearing about this and I felt my heart crack over finding that out. There wasn't anyone else in my life that fought for me as much as Abby had and for that I can never repay her.

It was frightening to know that someone loved me that much to do what they could to protect me and make sure that I was safe. My mind immediately drifted to Michael, but I pulled it back I had too much going on to bring him into it yet. I had to deal with what was in front of me first and I had a feeling, there was a long way to go before I could allow myself to think of him without the hurt.

I glanced at the time and was surprised to see that it was only mid-evening. It felt a lot later as so much as had been told already, I felt as if it should be the middle of the night.

"Why don't you go for a lie down, you look done in." I looked across at Abby who was standing a few feet away from me.

"I think I will. Give me half an hour then I'll make dinner."

"Don't you worry about dinner. I'll sort something out for when you get up. You need rest. You are still recovering, and you need to build your strength for what is to come."

I nodded feeling like one of the nodding dogs you get but headed into the bedroom. I sat down first thinking that I'll never be able to sleep but I turned and lay down anyway. I could hear Abby moving about and sorting stuff out. I closed my eyes and soon found myself drifting off.

When I opened my eyes again, I found that I hadn't moved on my bed from where I had laid down, I turned my head to see what time and it was shocked to find that I had been sleeping for two hours. My stomach made a noise as I pulled myself out of bed and headed to the bathroom.

When I came out, I headed down to see if Abby was still there. I knew she was as I could hear her voice.

"I'm not going to force her to talk to you. Give her time. She's been through enough and the next few days is going to take its toll on her." I stood hidden by the wall listening. "I know you love her Michael, but you need to give her time."

My breath caught at his name, but I made myself step out so that she could see me.

"I've got to go. I'll speak to you tomorrow." She hung up the phone and put it on the table where I could see her laptop open and papers surrounding it. She was working.

"Sorry I slept so long."

"Don't worry about it. You must have needed it. Now, sit down and I'll make you something to eat. You must be hungry."

I moved and sat at the table glancing over the papers sitting there. A name caught my attention, and I pulled the papers towards me. It was McArthur account that I had been working on before all this had happened. I was close to finalising the details before everything went to hell. I Quickly read through the papers knowing what I was looking for and found everything to be in the right place. Nothing had been changed.

"We needed to close on the account, so I picked it up and finished it off. You had done a great job with it. Even caught the small details that others would have missed."

"I like to make sure everything is covered and that the best deal has been struck for both parties." I turned to the final page where the signatures would be and stopped. It was my name that showing as the person who closed it.

"If you sign, it'll be a done deal and you'll get the commission for it. It's the biggest account you have closed on in all the time you have been working with me. I am impressed that you got the best deal for both sides."

I looked up and saw Abby holding out a pen for me to sign my name. I took it and signed my name that gave the me the biggest commission of my career. I felt heat wondering where it was coming from, but I looked down and saw a bowl of soup in front of me. How did that get there? Before I could say anything, my stomach let out a growl but before I began eating, I spoke.

"I didn't know if you'd still be here."

"I'm not going anywhere. Now eat up whilst I clear these papers away." She began to gather the papers and folders, putting them in her bag before closing the laptop then just sat as I ate the soup.

"I've re-arranged my schedule tomorrow so that I can be here when Rose comes back. I've got a courier coming by early to pick up the contract and take it in. I'm not leaving you alone."

"I'm not a child Aunt Abby. I can take care of myself."

"I know you can but I'm here more for support and I've still to finish off my story to Rose."

"It's not finished?" Abby shook her head.

"No. There's still more to come."

I didn't know what to say. Of course, she would have more as I couldn't pick up from where she had left, I still don't remember much from then. I'm now I'm wondering what else she has to say. I wouldn't get anything out of her tonight so it will need to wait until morning. I had a feeling this is just as hard on her as it is on me.

It was making me realise how much she had done for me without me even knowing about it. I knew she wouldn't expect any repayment as if that could ever be done, but I felt I wanted to do something for her, but I didn't know what.

As I finished my soup, I looked across at Abby and I could see her getting older, but she still had the energy of a twenty-year-old. I didn't know where she got it from as I know I would struggle to do what she did every day.

"All finished?" I nodded and before I could stand, the bowl was lifted away from me and in the sink for washing. "You go through and sit down. Find something to watch and I'll be there as soon as I've finished this and changed."

I stood and did as I was told as I didn't have the strength to argue but it also felt comforting knowing that someone was looking out for me even if I didn't want it. I sat on the sofa, curling my legs up underneath me and flicked through the channels to find something to watch.

My mind was wandering as I pressed the button to change channels. I thought back over what I had been told earlier today about Abby describing the night my parents died.

I was glad I didn't remember it, but I was also sad. She had to go through that alone and it wasn't fair on her. I recalled the many times when I had been horrible to her, but she still stood by me. Not many would have. I owe her so much that I knew I could never repay it all.

"Oh, I haven't seen that in years. I remember it used to be your favourite." I pulled myself out of my own mind and looked at the tv. I smiled when I saw what was on it. I had stopped on a film that I hadn't watched in years but did remember the countless nights that I had sat and watched it. It was an old film but still one I loved.

"Do you want anything?"

"No, I'm fine, sit down so that I can select and start it." I waited until Abby had made herself comfortable at the opposite end of the sofa then hit play. I felt myself sinking back into the sofa when I felt I felt something on my leg.

I looked down and saw a blanket being spread over both of us and I felt myself transported back to the first time she had done this. I moved from where I sat to be closer to her, leaning against her and hiding the tears that had begun to form in my eyes.

I settled in and watched the film know that tomorrow would come soon enough and that I would deal with it then. I felt my eyes getting heavy not long into the film and before I knew it, I was fast asleep feeling safe with one of the people that had always had my back.

Chapter Nine

When I awoke, I knew that I had fallen asleep on the sofa as I felt stiff all over. Usually it wasn't bad when I slept on this but after what I had been through, my body was telling me to stop it.

I swung my legs over the edge the blanket that had been covering me, fell to the floor. I stood lifting the blanket and pulling it around my shoulders as it was cold. It was late and I needed more sleep. I was awake but I felt as if I was still sleeping.

I headed up the stairs and peeked into the spare room to see Abby asleep but not peacefully. She was tossing and turning, and I backed out of the room as I didn't want to wake her. If I were finding it hard to hear what had happened, I couldn't imagine what it must be like for her to relive it all again.

I was going to find out the truth about my early years. I had tried to get Abby to talk about it before, but she always fobbed me off. Now she was facing the hard times that I had known nothing about. It had been draining today and I had a feeling that it was going to be the same until she had finished.

I crossed to my bedroom to sleep the rest of the night. It had been a draining few days and I knew I was going to need my strength and awareness to get through what was to come. I laid down on my and sorted the blanked over me. I was too tired to even get changed. Soon after my head hit the pillow, I was asleep again.

When I awoke again, it was light, and I could hear voices in the kitchen. I rubbed my eyes to make them open better and looked at the time. It was late and I didn't have much time before Rose would be back.

I opened the blinds and blinked my eyes closed as the brightness seemed too much for me. Gradually my eyes got used to it and I could see that it was a nice day. Everything seemed normal looking out there, but I knew different. Things had changed for me and I had accepted that, and I was going to accept what was to come today. I could only deal with a day at a time.

I closed the blinds again before turning away and went into the bathroom switching on the shower. When I looked in the mirror, the bruises had faded but my body still felt stiff. I knew that would pass but I felt as if I would break into a million pieces if someone hit me.

When the shower was warm enough, I stripped and got in. As the hot water fell over my body, I let out a sigh feeling the heat going into my body. I stood for a few minutes before I washed my hair and body.

When I came out, the bathroom was full of steam and it felt good. After I had brushed my teeth, I headed back into the bedroom and got dressed. Comfy clothes were asked for, so another pair or jogging bottoms and sweatshirt were called for.

After I was dressed, I headed downstairs hearing the voices become louder as I got closer to the bottom. I froze just above the last step as I recognised one of the voices. My heart skipped a beat at hearing it again. It was Michael. I knew it was wrong to listen in, but I couldn't help myself.

"I need to speak to her. I need to explain why I didn't tell her that you were my sister."

"Not just now, she is going through enough that she doesn't need that added."

"But I need to talk her."

"I know you do Michael, but it's best if you keep away just now. She is going through a lot and she needs to process this first before you come in and tell your side."

"Can't I see her? I'm lost without her. I need her."

"I know you are, but this is the best way for now. Maybe in a couple of days, you can come around and see if she will see you."

As I stood listening, it was taking all my strength to remain where I was. Michael sounded so sad that it was breaking my heart. I wanted to take that last step down and around the corner so that I could see him. I knew that if I did that, I would be in his arms shortly afterwards and I wouldn't let him go.

Even though I was still hurting over what he had kept secret from me, and I had begun to forgive him for doing so. I wasn't there completely yet, but I knew it wouldn't be long. I needed to hear the rest from Abby before I could face him again. I knew that I wouldn't part from him again once I was back with him.

I must have made a sound, as Abby told him to go. I heard the back door open then close again. I gathered myself together then, stepped down the last step and headed into the kitchen.

"Who was that?" I asked.

"Who?"

"I heard the back-door closing."

"Oh, that was the courier here to pick up the contract to take in." I had to give it to her, she was smooth with her response. "I've been able to clear things up so I can stay as long as you need me. Now, did you sleep ok? I didn't have the heart to wake you last night when you fell asleep watching the movie."

"I slept fine. My body doesn't agree with me as that sofa is not really designed for sleeping."

"No, it's not. You should get one that is comfier so that if you did fall asleep you wouldn't wake feeling as if you'd been in the ring with Mike Tyson."

"Maybe I will but I like that sofa, lumps and all." I smiled at her and I felt as if things were going to be ok. I didn't know why but I just knew that things were going to be okay.

"Now, what do you want to eat? I had some things brought over. I have eggs, bacon, sausages, pancakes mix as I didn't see any of that in your cupboards yesterday."

"I think coffee first then maybe just some toast. I don't feel up to anything more than that just now." I moved towards the coffee machine to find that it was already set up for me. I turned back to her.

"I know what you are like if you don't get your coffee in the morning, so I set it up for you." I turned back and switched the machine on, pulling a mug down as it heated up.

"Do you want one?"

"Yes please." We stood in silence as the coffee machine made gurgling noises as it made the strong coffee. When complete, I emptied out the used capsule and put in another one and pressed the button to start.

I took a sip from it and felt better as the caffeine went down. I knew I drank too much of it and that it was strong coffee, but I couldn't do without it. I leaned over and pulled the bread out and popped it into the toaster.

I leaned against the countertop watching Abby over the rim of the coffee mug. She was acting sketchy and I knew it was because Michael had been here. She was hiding that from me, but I was giving her a pass on it as she had given me a lot to think about from yesterday. She jumped when the toast popped up.

"You okay?" I asked her as I held out her coffee mug.

"I'm fine." She took it from me then turned away from me and began looking at the papers that were on the table that I hadn't even noticed. I put my mug down and pulled the butter from the fridge and began to spread the toast.

"You sure?"

"Yes, I'm okay. I'm preparing myself for what I've got to say today." I lifted a piece of the toast and began eating. It tasted like cardboard and I was trying to work out what else Abby had to say today. How much more had she been keeping from me?

As I finished my toast and as I went to get a second cup of coffee what she said stopped me in my tracks.

"Michael was here." I froze where I was as I hadn't expected her to tell me that. "It wasn't a courier you heard leaving it was Michael." I looked at her, but she wasn't looking at me. I crossed to her and as I got close, she looked up at me. There were tears in her eyes and I could see the anguish on her face.

"He came over to see you, but I wouldn't let him. None of this was his fault, it was all mine. Even though it started out as his, it became mine. I thought it was best to keep our relationship from you, but I know that was wrong. I should have come clean with you a while ago, but I just couldn't bring myself to do so. "

"Michael's a grown man, he could have told me himself."

"Yes, he could have, and he was torn about it. He wanted to tell you as he didn't want to keep any secrets from you, but he was being loyal to me. I feel terrible about the position I put him in and if I could change it, I would."

If I had partially forgiven him before now, then I had just completely forgiven him now. I watched as Abby collapsed into the chair and the tears fell from her eyes quicker than she could wipe them away. I grabbed some kitchen roll and handed it to her. I pulled up a chair next to her and wrapped my arms around her.

I had to keep telling myself that even though this was my life, there were others that had been hurt through it. I needed to be there for them as they were there for me. We held each other and I felt the pain easing inside me. Telling my story to Rose was being cathartic not only for me but also for Abby who had lived it.

I leaned back a bit and watched as Abby pulled herself together. It was humbling seeing her in such a state compared to the image that she puts across. People think she is hard, cruel and unforgiving but she's not. She's driven and if they could see her now, they would be astonished at the change in her.

"I need to get through this with Rose first before I can speak with Michael. If you can pass on a message for me."

"Anything." She said nodding.

"Tell him that I understand what he did but I need to sort it out in my own mind before I see him again. I'll contact him when I'm ready. He's a part of my story so I need to tell him what I'm doing. Unless he already knows?"

"He knows something but not the full story. It wasn't my place to tell him. He knows we are talking to a reporter but that's all. I wanted to tell him, but I held back."

"Thank you for that. You can tell him the full story as he's going to find out soon enough anyway."

"Ok. I'll tell him later." We hugged each other and I felt as if the bond between us was being strengthen. Before we could say anything else, there was a knock at the door. "

"That will be Rose." I pulled away and stood. "Go and clean up a bit and I'll let her in." I headed to the door to allow the one person who was telling my story to the world in.

"Morning. It's a beautiful morning isn't it?" I stepped back and allowed Rose to come in being a little surprised at how cheery she was. In fact, I would even go so far to say that she looked more wired than cheery.

"Would you like a coffee?"

"No thanks. I think I drunk enough last night to keep me going for days. I couldn't sleep so I began working on your story. I know we only had one day but I think it will be better if I can write a little of it after each sitting with you." Rose was moving about the living room unable to sit still.

"You want any tea then, something to calm you down a bit?"

"No, I'm fine, I need to keep going." She was still pacing when Abby came in. She took one look at Rose then looked at me. I smiled.

"Rose has been up most of the night writing and drinking lots of coffee." Abby smiled as well as she knew how it was when you pulled an all-nighter. "Rose, why don't you have a seat and we can get started." She sat on the chair she used before and pulled out her notepad and recording device.

"Are you both ready?" We nodded and sat down in the same seats as the previous day. Rose leaned forward and pressed record. "Abby what happened after you handed the keys to the police officer?"

Chapter Ten

Officer Gordon brought me out of the daze I was in.

"Sorry?" He gave a small smile as he repeated what he had said.

"How far away do you live?"

"About five miles, why?"

"Well, considering the size of your car and the number of boxes that are packed into it, I don't think it's safe for you to drive that far." I turned from the house and looked at the car. He was right. I would just be able to get into the driver's seat. I would struggle to see out the side mirrors and forget about seeing out the back window.

"I suppose you're right. I'll take it slow and I'll be ok. The roads will be quiet so it shouldn't take long."

"No, let's put some into my car so that it is a bit safer for you to drive." Abby started at the officer unable to believe that he was helping her this way. Yes, he said that she reminded him of his daughter, but this was over and above his duty.

"Are you sure?"

"Yes. I wouldn't be able to forgive myself if anything happened to you on your way home." Abby nodded and opened the car to take out some of the boxes and transferred them into Officer Gordon's car. When they had finished, they stood staring at each other.

"I'll follow you." Abby nodded and got into the car. She felt numb over everything that had happened, but she kept going. She had to. She started the car and pulled out of the driveway knowing that she would never be back there again. It hurt so bad and, in a way, she was glad that Cat was just too young to fully understand what had happened.

Abby pulled out into the road and started driving home with Officer Gordon behind her. The roads were quiet, due to the weather and the time of day. Most people wouldn't want to be out in weather like this if they didn't need to be.

She kept to the main roads as she knew these would have been treated but it still took time to get home. A journey that would normally take about fifteen minutes took double that. As she pulled into her driveway, Abby had to pry her hands from the steering wheel as she had been holding on so tight. She let out a sigh of relief at being back home again safe. She looked in the mirror and saw Officer Gordon get out his car and come up to her.

"You okay?" He asked as she got out the car.

"Just glad to be back home safe. The roads are treacherous. I don't blame people not wanting to be out on them." As she spoke, she rubbed her hands to get the circulation back into them.

"It is dangerous out there but you're home safe now. I would advise you to stay inside until this weather clears. We don't need you to have an accident." Abby shivered at the thought then nodded at Martin. "Why don't you go and open up and I'll start bringing the boxes in for you." Abby nodded and headed carefully up the pathway to the front door. She pulled her keys out and opened the door. She put her bag on the hall table then turned back outside to help with the boxes.

Martin was halfway up the path to the door, so she waited for him to reach her before standing to the side and motioned for him to set the boxes down just inside the door. She didn't know where she was going to put them, but she would work that out later. She followed him back out pulling the door over behind them and brought the rest of the boxes inside.

Abby turned to Martin rubbing her hands together again.

"Thank you for all your help. I know you didn't need to do this, but I really appreciate it."

"As I said before, you remind me of my daughter, and I would hope that someone would help her if she was in the same situation."

"Well, thank you again." Abby didn't know what else to say so she reached out and gave him a hug to say thanks. She knew it probably wasn't the correct thing to do, but at that moment, she needed to feel someone else. As she pulled back, he held out something to her.

"What's this?"

"The number of a lawyer friend of mine. He knows what happened and he wants to help. I spoke with him last night and he is waiting for your call."

She didn't know what to say as she looked down at the name on the card, Jonathan McCartney. She recognised the name as one of the big law firms in the city. They were expensive.

"I can't afford them." She went to hand the card back, but Martin closed her hand around it.

"Don't worry about it. He won't charge you. And before you say anything, he does this regularly looking at cases for people who wouldn't normally be able to afford him."

"I can't ask him to do that. Even if he has done this before. I don't want to be beholden to anyone."

"You won't be. He doesn't know if he can help but he is willing to see what he can do for you. Just give him a call and see what he has to say."

"Ok. I'll call him." Abby put the card in her pocket and stood awkwardly. She didn't know what to say now. She felt the tears gather in her eyes and at that, Martin stepped forward and Abby gave him a hug again but this time, she felt him hug her back. He pulled back before he spoke.

"Well, I'd better go. My shift starts in an hour. Good luck." He turned away and she watched him as he got into his car and drove away. She had a lot to do but now, she didn't want to do anything. She turned and went inside locking the door. She had just locked the door when someone spoke.

"Who was that?" Abby looked up to see Michael standing in the hallway. She now had to tell him about Cat, and she had no idea how he was going to take it.

"Come into the living room for a minute. Is mum still sleeping?"

"Yeah, I checked on her a few minutes ago." He walked towards her still in his pyjamas looking like the kid that he was. Abby glanced around the room trying to work out how she could fit another child into their small house. She would make it work somehow but she was getting ahead of herself. She still had no idea if she would be allowed to bring Cat home or not. She wanted to believe she would, but she had a feeling deep down that she wouldn't be. She would fight though to try.

"Abby?" She sat down on the sofa next to Michael and looked at him. Even though he was only eight, he was growing up fast and would be a man before she knew it.

"Michael, something has happened to Cat."

"Is she ok? Where is she?"

"She's fine, she's with Child Services." She could tell that he didn't understand. "Her parents died in a car crash last night and they have taken her into foster care."

"Why? She could have come here. We'd look after her." Abby smiled.

"They won't let her come here as we are not family."

"Why not? We love her as if she were part of our family. We'd take care of her and look after her and make her safe. I'll protect her like a big brother would."

Abby felt the emotions inside her warring as the sadness of not being able to give him what he wanted but also feeling proud at him standing up and wanting to help despite his young age.

"I know we do but the law doesn't work that way. I have the name of someone who may be able to help but we'll need to wait and see." He seemed to think on this before speaking.

"Ok. When are you meeting with him?"

"I don't know. I haven't called him yet. I'm going to once the offices are open." He nodded at that then leaned towards her an gave her a hug.

"If you need any help, I'm here for you. I know I'm just a kid but I here for you." The tears fell now as her little brother was acting more like a man than some she knew. It's wouldn't be long before he wouldn't need her at all.

"Thank you. Now go on back to bed. It's still early. I'll see to mum." He nodded and headed back to his room. She was so proud of him that she felt as if she were going to burst. She pulled herself together a little before heading to look in on her mother. She headed down the hallway and pushed open her door slowly just in case she was still sleeping.

"Come in Abby." She pushed the door fully opened and closed it behind her. She crossed to the bed as her mum sat up in bed and switched on her bedside light. She knew that she didn't have long before her mum would know everything. As soon as she came into the light, her mother knew.

"What's happened? Who died?" Abby sat down on the bed and pulled herself together. Telling Michael had helped but her mother was different. The roles would be reversed.

"It's Cat's parents." Her mum just opened her arms and Abby collapsed into them as she told her mother everything that had happened since she left last night. As she finished, she sat up and tried to dry her eyes with her t-shirt. Her mother looked strong sitting there, but she knew the illness had taken its toll on her.

"She'll come to us."

"I don't know if she can."

"Well, we'll see about that. We need to get a lawyer first."

"I've got a name and number already."

"Well then, let's call them and see what they have to say." Abby glanced at the time and decided to chance it. She pulled the card and her mobile from her pocket and made the call. She was expecting to get an answer machine, but she was wrong. Jonathan answered after a few rings. She told him who she was then she didn't say much after that.

As she hung up a few minutes later, she felt in shock at how quickly everything seemed to be moving. It seemed too fast and too good to be true but she couldn't stop herself from getting her hopes up.

"Well, what did he say?"

"We have an appointment at three pm at their offices in town."

"Good. We have time to prepare. Let me get up and we'll start planning how we can approach this and what we'll say when we meet them."

Abby had to move from the bed as her mum was getting up and moving around the room. She was moving with a determination that she hadn't seen in a long time. She watched as she pulled out a dress that she had bought on a whim before she had gotten sick. It was navy blue and white and smart looking. She hung it up in front of the wardrobe then began looking for her shoes. She found then and set them out.

"What are you doing standing there? Go pull out your dress that you are going to wear at your graduation. It's smart enough for a meeting with the lawyers. Now who can I get to watch Michael whilst we're out?

"No-one." They turn to the voice. "I'm coming with you. I have my suit that I can wear. I just need help with the shirt and tie." Abby wanted to tell him no, but she felt as if she needed all the support she could get if she was going to get through this.

"Ok. Go lay it out on your bed and I'll help you later." She turned to her mother and saw the same look on her face that she must have had when he had offered his help earlier.

"We better get up and dressed as we have a lot to sort out before this afternoon."

Chapter Eleven

Abby couldn't believe that things were moving so quickly. She had never expected someone to help her out. She spent the morning sorting out where she was going to store the boxes and her normal chores. Michael was being uncharacteristically helpful. It was as if a switch had been flicked and he had gone into adult mode.

After they had lunch, she got showered and changed into something a little more appropriate for meeting with a lawyer. She came out her room and saw her mum and Michael waiting on her. Both had dressed in their best clothes, with Michael wearing his Sunday best and Abby knew he didn't like wearing it. She felt the tears gather but held them back.

She parked as close as she could to the address but even that was a little distance away. The multi-storey parking garage was one that she didn't really like using but knew it was closer than the one she normally uses. They walked the few blocks to the office building and her stomach was doing somersaults at the thought of what could happen.

She tried to sort her thoughts out as they walked but knew that it wasn't going to happen. She had too much going through her mind. She pulled open the door and allowed her mum and Michael to enter before her. They walked up to the reception desk waiting until the woman on the desk looked up before speaking.

"I have an appointment with Jonathan McCartney." The receptionist checked her computer.

"Ok. If you take the elevator to the seventh floor, the receptionist will meet you there."

Abby nodded and they headed to the bank of elevators to their right. The elevator opened immediately, and the ride up was smooth and quick. Too quick for Abby. They got out when the car stopped looking around for the reception desk only to see it directly in front of her. They walked forward but before she could say anything the receptionist stood up.

"If you take a seat over there, Mr McCartney will be with you shortly. Can I get you anything, coffee, water?" Abby stood still before speaking.

"No, we're fine thank you." The receptionist motioned to the left of the desk and Abby saw the waiting area. As they sat down, she began to fidget. Her mum reached over and put her hand over hers and stopped her. Abby looked at her and the smile she was given was one that always made her feel better when she had been younger. Michael sat across from them and despite him being so young, Abby could see the man he would become.

"I'm sorry to keep you waiting." They stood and turned to the voice seeing for the first time, the person who wanted to help them. He looked to be in his thirties dressed in a suit that looked expensive. He held out his hand to Abby.

"Jonathan McCartney."

"Abigail McIntosh. Abby."

"Pleased to meet you Abby. Is it ok to call you Abby?" She nodded. He turned to her mother.

"This is my mother Elizabeth." He reached out to shake her hand as well.

"Please call me Beth." He turned to Michael who had been hanging back slightly.

"This is my younger brother Michael."

"Ah, the man of the house." He reached out and shook his hand as well. Abby watched as Michael seemed to straighten and grow in front of her. "If you all follow me, we'll get started."

He motioned for them to head down the corridor and he followed them then overtook them. He stopped in front of an office and motioned for them to enter. He came in behind them closing the door. Abby looked about the office. It was all dark wood but the window behind the desk was enough to lighten the full office.

"Please have a seat." They sat on the sofa that he gestured to as he sat down in a chair that he had turned around from his desk.

"Can I get you anything, tea, coffee, water?"

"No thank you. We're fine." Abby began to fidget again, and she could see that he had noticed as well. She was struggling to get the words out and what she wanted to say. Jonathan took that from her when he spoke first.

"Abby, I'm sorry for your loss and what you are going through. Martin gave me a brief outline of the situation, but I want to hear it from you. How did you meet the Mont-Clairs?"

Abby felt relief that he had started, and it gave her the courage to tell him how she came to meet them. He took notes and asked questions to all of them. When she had finished, she felt lighter but still tense. Both her mum and Michael had answered Jonathan's questions honestly and she felt comfortable with him. She had to quash her hopes down as they were starting to rise.

"Well, I will be honest with you, the situation isn't unusual but there will be problems to overcome. First your age. You are barely old enough to be an adult. Second, your mother's health. Third you are taking care of both her and your brother whilst trying to finish school. It doesn't look good, but we can put forward a strong case for you as a family to gain custody. It will not be easy or smooth going so I need you to be prepared for what is about to come."

"I'm ready. We're ready." Abby kept his gaze as she spoke. "What's the next step?"

"Now, I contact the courts to put in application for you to become Catriona's legal guardians."

"How long will that take?"

"A week or so. I'll submit it in the morning and see where we go from there. I do need to say that it is going to be hard. It all depends on the presiding officer and how they interpret the law." Jonathan stood making Abby and the others stand as well.

"I'll be in contact as soon as I have any updates." Abby nodded and held out her hand to shake his. She crossed to the door with the others following.

"Thank you for trying to help. I know you didn't need to and that you aren't taking payment from us."

"I like to take on cases that are interesting and with people whom I can help. This is one of them."

"Thank you again."

"I'll be in touch soon."

Abby nodded then headed back down to the corridor to the elevators. The receptionist wasn't there, and she caught the time. They had been in there for a couple of hours. As they exited the building, her mum spoke.

"How about we go to Franco's for dinner? Michael, do you want to go there?"

"Uh-huh." He looked as drained as she felt. They headed back to where the car was parked and headed to their favourite restaurant. They had taken Cat there a few months ago and she had loved it.

It was a strange feeling walking into the restaurant. Even though it had only been the once, it had felt right. As it was early enough, before the dinner rush, they were seated quickly and ordered some drinks. She saw Franco heading over to the were they were seated carrying the colouring stuff that Cat had loved. She shook her head at him slightly and he stopped with a frown but put the books down realising that something was wrong then came over.

All Abby wanted to do was lay down and cry, but she wouldn't make a fool of herself like that.

"We don't usually see you through the week, fancied a change?"

"Not really, couldn't be bothered cooking so thought we would come to the place with the best home cooked food." Beth replied.

"Well, just for that, I'll make you something special. Are you up for trying something different Michael?"

"Ok." Franco's expression changed to one of worry but wouldn't say anything until they did.

"Be right back with some appetisers." Abby excused herself a few minutes later to go to the ladies. She found Franco at the kitchen door.

"Franco, I'm sorry about that it's been a hard couple days. Cat's parents were killed in an accident and I'm trying to gain legal guardianship of her. We've just come from the lawyers and I really don't know how it's going to go." The tears started to fall, and Franco put his arms around her and held on as she let the emotions out. Once she had gathered herself back together, she left him and headed to the ladies to try and sort her face out. He hadn't said a word, but she knew that he was feeling it as well.

As she got back to the table, the appetisers were there and not long after the main course arrived. They made small talk as they ate not really knowing what to say. When they were finished, Franco came back with boxes of food. They tried to decline but he was having none of it. There was enough there for the next few days possibly longer.

By the time they got home Michael was near enough sleep walking. It wasn't that late, but it had been a trying day. She put the food away and her mum put Michael to bed. When she looked at her mum when she came out of Michael's room, she could see that she was doing all she could just to stand upright. She went over to her and put an arm around her and helped her into her room.

"When are the funerals?"

"I don't know. I would assume soon but I don't know. I'll call Officer Gordon to see if he can help me find out."

"Ok. Once that's over with, everybody can start to heal. Now, go to bed. You've been strong enough for one day. Go and have a good cry to yourself. You'll feel better for it." Abby nodded and left her mum's room and locked up the house before heading to her room. As she sat on her bed the tears began slowly before they came faster and harder. She fell side wards on the bed and just lay there and let it all out.

Chapter Twelve

As Abby looked from Rose to Cat her heart was breaking all over again at the look on her face.

"I never knew you tried to keep me."

"I know you didn't. I didn't want you to feel as if I had failed you. I just let you believe that I had walked away. It was easier that way."

"After the way I treated you, you still stood by me."

"I didn't want to let you go but I was out of options."

"What happened?" Abby told her.

A week after the meeting with Jonathan, the funerals were held for Isla and Stewart. There were some people from their workplaces there but not many others. Cat was there with the social worker. Abby had fought them on that as she hadn't wanted her to attend as she wouldn't understand what was happening. She got told that she had no business telling them that she couldn't go as she was not her guardian. She had to say goodbye to them, to get closure despite her young age.

When Cat saw her, she had tried to get away from the social worker and run to her, but they wouldn't let her. Abby's heart had completely gone now. It was too hard to stay away from her, so she walked around the gravesite to where the social worker was holding on to her.

Abby bent down and picked the little girl up and just held her close. Her arms were choking her, but she let them as she didn't know if this would be the last time, she would hold her.

"Where have you been Abby? I've missed you."

"I'm sorry Cat. I've tried to come and see you, but some people are keeping us apart. I am trying to fix that just now." The little girl put her head into her shoulder and Abby could feel the tremors through the little body. She put her back on her feet and took her hand giving the social worker a look that said don't even try it.

Abby stood holding the little hand in hers as the service was completed and her parents were put into the ground forever. Soon enough it was over, and it was time to go. Abby saw the social worker taking Cat's other hand even though she tried to fight it she let them go. She stood there long after everyone was away, and she began to feel the cold seeping into her body. She knew she must already be cold, but it was only then that she had begun to feel it.

Once she was home, she called Jonathan for an update. He hadn't called and she was getting anxious to know what was going on but there was no news. He was still waiting on a response for the courts.

She called Susannah Croft, but was told that she was on annual leave and would be back the following week. That explained why is had been a different social worker at the funeral and not her. She left a message to ask for her to all her back on her return.

Abby got a call late Sunday night from Susannah who gave her an update.

"Abby, it's Susannah Croft."

"Hi, thanks for calling me back. I wasn't expecting to hear from you until next week."

"Well, I thought I would call you today and give you an update as I assume that was why you called in the first place."

"Yes, you're right." There was silence on the other end of the phone as Abby waited to hear what was going to happen.

"Cat's going into a permanent foster home tomorrow. I know you are trying to gain guardianship of her, but I don't think that is going to work. We need to keep the welfare of Cat at the top of the list and getting her into a more stable, permanent family surroundings is the best thing for her." Abby didn't know what to say.

"I'm waiting to hear from my lawyer about that and he is hopeful that it will work out in my favour."

"Abby, can I be frank with you."

"Yes."

"I don't think that is going to work out. I've heard that the judge is going to throw out your claim and that Cat is going into the adoption system. Foster care is a steppingstone to that, and they wouldn't be doing that if they were going to award you custody. I think you need to prepare yourself for the loss."

"No, it's not over yet. Until I hear it from my lawyer, I am keeping it on the table." Even as she spoke, Abby knew that she was being told the truth. It had been longer than Jonathan had said it would take and that was never good news.

"Can I still see her?"

"I don't know. You shouldn't really and if it was up to me, I would let you as I know how much you love her. It will be up to the foster parents' if they will allow you. I'll speak with them tomorrow and see what they say. I'll call you and let you know."

"Thank you. I'll speak with you tomorrow." Abby hung up the phone and took a deep breath. Even though things were moving quickly, they felt as if they were going too slow for her. She knew there was nothing she could do until she called back, so she went to bed hoping for a miracle to happen.

Abby was on her way home from school when Jonathan called her. It wasn't good news.

"Abby, they are denying your petition to be Cat's legal guardian. They are putting her in the foster care system to wait for adoption. I'm sorry I couldn't help you anymore. I tried everything I could, but they wouldn't allow it."

"It's ok. I think I knew deep down that this was what was going to happen, but I had to try. Thank you for your help and if I ever need any legal help again, I'll know where to go, but no offence, I hope I don't need that kind of help again." Jonathan laughed.

"I hope in the absolute best way that we don't see each other again as well. Good luck with the future. I'm sure you will be a force to be reckoned with in the workplace." They hung up and Abby just sat waiting for something to happen. She didn't know what it would be, but she was expecting something. She jumped when the phone rang again and when she looked at the number she answered quickly. It was Susannah.

"Can I see her?" Abby dispensed with any greetings as she wanted to know if she could see Cat.

"Under certain conditions. They want to meet you first and speak with you before they allow you to meet Cat. They asked if they could meet with you next Tuesday at one pm. They want to allow her to settle in first before the decide if they will allow her to see you."

"I'll be there. What's their address?" Susannah gave it to her, and she was glad that it wasn't that far away. It meant that if things went well, she could still be in Cat's life. She went inside and found her mum helping Michael with his homework.

"How was school today?"

"I'm glad I've not got long to go. I'm ready to get to college and start working on our futures. What's the homework?"

"Math." Abby put her bag down and sat the other side of Michael and they both helped him with the math problem.

Abby looked across at Rose who was listening intently and writing something down. She glanced at the voice recorder on the table that was taking in everything that she was saying. She was afraid to look at Cat as she didn't want to know what she thought about what she had just said but in the end, she couldn't avoid it and looked up at her.

She was staring at her with surprise as this would be the first time, she had heard how hard she had fought for her.

"I'm sorry Cat, I tried to keep a hold of you, but it was out-with my control. The system wouldn't allow me to. I hate that it put you through all that but the only thing that was in the back of my mind was that you were so young, I hoped that you didn't really remember much about it."

"You're right. I don't really remember much from them and after listening to you, I'm glad. I don't know how I could have gotten through it otherwise."

"You would have. We all do somehow even though at the time we feel as if we can't go on."

Rose spoke up.

"What happened at the meeting with the foster parents? Abby took a deep breath and took herself back to that time and continued her story.

Abby pulled into a driveway that was in front of a very nice house that gave off a happy vibe. The front garden was big enough and surrounded by a fence that made it safe for youngsters to run about without getting run over. She got out of the car, smoothing her skirt down as she straightened then she leaned in and lifted her purse then locked the car.

She walked slowly to the top of the drive and opened the little gate there and entered the garden. She walked the pathway and knocked on the door when she came to it. She turned around and looked at the surrounding houses. They were similar family homes, and she knew that it would be best for Cat to live here rather then, in the small 3 bedroomed flat that she, her mother and Michael currently lived in. She would have fresh air here and plenty of friends.

"I remember that place. The Watsons'. I stayed with them for about a couple of years until Mrs Watson became ill a lot. I didn't know at the time, but it was a high risk pregnancy. They couldn't keep me as she was ill a lot with the pregnancy." Abby was surprised that she could remember that as she was only three. "I remember feeling safe there and I remember you coming to around as well. Why didn't I remember that before? I don't have many memories, but some are coming back to me after listening to you."

I couldn't believe it. The early part of my life was a black hole and I had always felt frustrated at not having any memories from when I was young. I know that you don't retain memories from an early age, but even after that there was nothing. My first real memory I have was when I was about six years old. Nothing before that. When I found out about my parents, I assumed that it was the trauma of losing them made me block that time out until I was feeling safe again.

Listening to Abby, was making all these memories come back to me and I was struggling to hold back the emotions on them. I remember spending time with Abby and the Watsons' being happy and moving on. Finding out that Abby hadn't forgotten about me was making my heart break and mend at the same time. I had been horrible to her over the years and I had always blamed her for walking away from me. I never realised that she hadn't walked away of her own volition but was forced to walk away by a system that was so outdated it was nearly stone age.

I could see how much it was taking out of Abby as she was talking but it was like a weight had been lifted from her shoulders. I had to remember that she had been living with all this for the last twenty-five years. I can't imagine the burden this must have been on her and I wish I had been more understanding when I had been younger. But then again, we all wish we were something different in hindsight.

"As I stood waiting for the door to open, I had never felt as nervous. I could feel my body shaking and I was sweating even though it was cold outside. I don't think I've ever been as nervous as that time until recently. I knew that this was my last chance to keep in touch with you."

I knew then that the death of my parents had increased the determination in Aunt Abby's life. She had fought for me even though I didn't know it. She fought the way she had for anything else that she wanted in her life. She took a chance when she wasn't much more than a child herself and it had backfired on her but she was determine not to let it get it to her so she shook it off and did what she could to make sure that I was safe and happy.

I stood from the chair I had curled up on and crossed to her and gave her a hug. She stood and we held each other letting all that had gone before now flow away. This was going to be a new beginning for us even though we were only at the start of the story. I pulled back and sat down beside her.

"Aunt Abby, what happened next?"

Chapter Thirteen

As Abby stood waiting for someone to answer the door, her stomach felt as if a flock of butterflies had taken up residence. She turned around when she heard the door opening.

"Mrs Watson, I'm Abigail McIntosh." Abby stood holding her hand out. The woman who answered seemed surprised, but she took the hand and shook it before stepping back and letting her in the house.

"I'm Susan Watson, please come in." Abby walked past her and into the main living space and moved her eyes around the room taking everything in. It was homely and lived in.

"Please have a seat. Can I get you anything to drink?"

"No thank you." Abby sat in the first chair and Mrs Watson sat in the chair opposite. There was an awkward silence as they both waited for the other to speak. Abby got in there first.

"I want to thank you for allowing me to visit you. I know this must be hard, but I want you to know that all I want is for Cat to be happy and if that is with you then it is fine with me. You know that I tried to gain guardianship of Cat but failed but I am not bitter about it. I am disappointed but the result is whatever is going to be best for Cat and from what I can see so far, this is the place. All I want is for Cat to be loved."

Abby stopped and took in the expression on Mrs Watson's face. The shock was big and unexpected as she was assuming that Abby had gone there to make trouble and try and take Cat from them. Mrs Watson stood before speaking.

"I think I'll make some tea." She said in a shaky voice before leaving Abby sitting in the living to go into the kitchen which seemed to be through an archway at the other side of the room. Abby kept herself under control even though she wanted to let her body go and the shakes to take over her. To take her mind off them, she glanced around the room again and saw some photos on the wall next to the kitchen entrance. There must have been about thirty or forty pictures and as Abby stopped in front of them, she could see that there was a happy smiling child in each of them. Some of them she could tell that Mrs Watson was in them as well along with another man whom she assumed was her husband.

She was so focused on the pictures that she didn't hear Mrs Watson come back into the room and it was only when she felt someone beside her that she looked round.

"This is what we call our wall of fame. These are all the kids that we have fostered over the years in emergency situations. Some were with us for a few months, others a few years, but we loved each one of them regardless of their circumstances. We were never blessed with children of our own, so we did the next best thing and that was helping those that needed it."

Abby felt herself becoming emotional and tried to hide it but failed. She felt a hand on her back supporting her and she leaned a little into it. She knew then that this was the best place and that Cat was going to be loved. Even though she had said those words earlier, seeing these pictures, she knew that it was going to be true.

"Let's sit and chat. You can tell me all about yourself." She let herself be guided back to the chair she had been sitting on before and watched as a cup of tea was poured and handed to her.

"Mrs Watson,"

"Susan, please call me Susan. I think we are more than strangers now."

Abby could feel Cat staring at her as she stopped talking.

"I don't remember you coming around when I was there."

"I didn't. Even though I wanted to spend time with you, I could see you were happy and settled and I didn't want to change that. I knew that me coming back to see you would hurt more and I didn't want that. I came to an agreement with Susan that I could watch you from afar but not to let you see me. I was there for every part of your two years with them.

"I started college that year and the first year was tough so I didn't get there all that often but anytime you were doing something special like when you started taking dancing lessons and were in your first show, I was there. Christmas pantomimes, summer plays I was there. I understood after that first year that I would probably have dropped out of college as it would have been too much taking care of you along with Michael and mum."

Abby knew the tears were gathering again and she felt as if that was all she was doing the last day or so. Bringing up the memories of the past hurt more than she thought it would. She could only imagine how Cat was feeling and she forced herself to look at her. She was sitting next to her and holding her hand.

"How about I make some tea?" Rose said then stood and walked into the kitchen to find what she needed. She was giving them space. A short time later, Rose came back with a tray of tea things.

"Thanks Rose. Did you find everything ok?" I asked

"Yes. It's almost the same layout as my own so it was a shoo in. The only thing, I couldn't find was something to nibble on."

"Sorry, I must have forgot to get something when I was shopping the other day."

"No worries, how about we have this then take a break as it's almost lunchtime and I know a great place that delivers."

"That's fine with me Aunt Abby, you ok with that?" I watched as she nodded. I never knew that Abby had felt so strongly about me until the last few days. I knew she loved me, but I hadn't realised how much she had gone through to ensure that I was safe and loved.

I was still feeling the aftereffects of the accident, but I was also feeling strangely energised and drained at the same time. It was a weird kind of feeling. I felt as if the weight had been lifted off my shoulders that I hadn't really known was there. I liked the feeling and wanted to hold on to it for as long as I could as I had the feeling that it would be back before the end of my story was told.

My mind drifted to the one person I was trying to stay away from, Michael. I knew that I had hurt him badly by turning him away after the accident, but I needed to get my head on straight after what I had found out. I knew I was going to forgive him, but I needed to get through my history first before I could speak with him. He had known things about me that I didn't and that is taking time to settle in me. I realise now that what he done was not out of malice, but out of love. It was still lying, and he could have told me at any time, but he didn't.

I drank the tea and watched as Rose place a lunch order for us even though I don't feel very hungry now, I knew I would need to eat something. My life history seemed to be falling into place in a way that I hadn't known and I was beginning to feel part of something rather than being apart from everyone.

"Abby, please continue where you left off. We have about an hour before the lunch will be delivered." Rose stated.

Abby and Susan must have been talking for a couple of hours when they heard the front door open. Susan stood and headed to the doorway whereas Abby stayed where she was. She could hear a man's voice over a child's crying.

"There, there, it's okay, you're okay." Abby stood as she waited for the new arrivals to enter the living room. She could hear the whispered voices but couldn't make out what they were saying over the crying. She put her purse on her shoulder and was prepared to leave.

Susan turned back to her and a man came to stand beside her. His expression said it all that he didn't want her here. Abby's gaze went from the man to Cat in an instant and she felt her heart pull at the heart wrenching sobs from the little girl. Nothing that was being said to her was making the crying stop.

Susan motioned for Abby to come forward and speak to Cat. The closer she got she finally found her voice.

"Cat, what's wrong?" there was a pause in the crying and the head lifted from the shoulder and turned to her direction. When her eyes cleared enough to see, she started kicking to get down and the man put her down and the instant her feet touched the floor, she was running to Abby.

Abby went to her knees and caught her as she ran at her. She held on tight and looked up at the couple watching them. She tried to convey an apology in her face but in a way she wasn't sorry. She pulled back from her and pulled a hanky out and wiped up the tears that had been falling.

"What's with all the crying?" Abby waited for her to stop crying enough to talk. At first it was muffled but then she made out what she was saying, and her heart skipped a beat.

"It's okay, you're okay. Don't pay attention to what the other kids say. You are not different or weird. Yes, you are an orphan, but there are people who love you. Me, Grandma Beth, Michael, The Watsons."

Abby stood lifting her as she went and sat back down in the chair she had vacated recently. She just held her and rocked her to sleep. When she was out, she looked up and didn't see Susan anywhere, but she could hear her in the kitchen. She could tell by the voices that it wasn't a pleasant conversation, but she wanted to get Cat in her bed to sleep off the upset. She stepped through into the kitchen and stopped them mid conversation.

"Where's her room?"

"This way." Susan said and moved past her, and Abby followed to a perfect little girl's room fit for a princess. She laid Cat out on the bed, taking off her shoes and jacket and pulled the covers up over her. She moaned a little when she let go but Abby leaned back down.

"I'm here Cat. You're safe. It's okay." She settled and Abby left the room and headed back to face the music with the couple that were her temporary parents. She stopped in the doorway and waited for Susan to see her. She motioned for her to come in and she stood beside the dining table.

"I'm sorry about this. I'll leave you two alone to talk."

"Don't be silly, stay. Please sit." Abby didn't know what to do. She wanted to stay but she wanted to leave as the man was anything but happy about her being there. Susan noticed the glare he was giving her and nudged him a little.

"I'm sorry, I haven't introduced you two yet. Abby, this is my husband Raymond." The glare didn't vanish.

"Please to meet you Raymond. I know you are not happy that I am here, but I only have Cat's best interesting at heart. I know I can't take her away from you, but I just want to be in her life. I can tell her about her parents if she asks. I know about her history."

Abby waited to see if he would speak and he only did once Susan gave him another nudge, this time bigger.

"I'm sorry, we really like having Cat here and we don't want to lose her. I know we are only her foster parents, but we can help her through this difficult time."

"I know. That's why I want to do this as well. She is a three-year-old who has been ripped from the only home that she's known and lost everyone that cares about her. I just want her to be okay and come out on the other side of this with as little mental scarring as possible. All I want to do is help."

As she waited for a response, Abby felt as if a change was on the horizon and that he held the key to it.

"Ok. This is the first time this has happened, and we have been used to dealing with the kids on their own without someone from their previous life. I can see that Cat loves you and you were able to calm her down quicker than we could have. I'm sorry for how I acted, and I would like it if you kept in touch. But remember, we are her parents not you."

"Thank you, Mr Watson. I only want to be in her life. We can work out when you allow me to see her and I'll stick by it. What about Miss Croft?"

"She doesn't need to know. We can keep this between us." Abby smiled and couldn't believe her luck. She was still going to be able to see Cat grow up. She couldn't wait to tell her mum and Michael. She wasn't going to push her luck and ask if they could see her as well, she would ease into that.

Chapter Fourteen

The next few years were hard going for Abby with college work, a part-time job, looking after Michael and trying to see Cat as much as she could which turned out to not be as often as she had wished.

The rug was pulled out from under her again just a few weeks before her twenty-first birthday. Her mother took ill and was admitted to hospital from which she never left. She found herself at a loss only to have more added to it when she found out that there was a family that wanted to adopt Cat.

She was having dinner with them one Sunday night when the other bombshell was dropped on her.

"Abby, we've got something to tell you." Abby waited to see what it was. She knew that Susan was pregnant and that with her being older the risks were higher. She was hoping that there was nothing wrong with the baby. She watched as Susan and Raymond looked at one another before back at her. It was Raymond who spoke.

"Cat is being adopted." Abby felt a smile cross her face.

"That's great news. What made you decide to adopt rather than just foster her?" There was silence and Abby felt he smile disappearing from her face.

"We are not adopting her but another family, the Smythe's, are adopting her."

"When?"

"Next week. We have known for a while that they had been interested but we didn't want to say anything until it was official. It's a good thing as we were trying to work out how to tell you as we couldn't go on caring for her. As Susan's pregnancy advances, there is a higher risk of complications and we need to focus on that and not leave Cat out." Susan got up and came around the table.

"We were going to tell you last week but with your mum's funeral it didn't seem right. We waited as long as we could, but it was now or never." Susan put her arm around her shoulders to comfort.

"When does she leave?"

"Sometime next week, we don't know the exact day, but we will be packing her stuff up over the next couple of days. I'll try to let you know but they can come at any time."

"Thank you for telling me. I think I'll go home now." Abby stood and walked away in a daze. She must have said her goodbyes, but she can't remember doing so as the next thing she knew, she was outside the apartment where she had left Michael studying. He was in high school and a lot more responsible than he had been. She could leave him home alone and not worry about him, even though he wasn't a legal age to be left alone. She trusted him.

She locked the car and went inside. She didn't need to shout on Michael as he was in the kitchen working away. He had just started high school and wanted to do well. She walked over to him and wrapped her arms around him as he studied at the table.

"What's up sis?"

"Nothing, just wanted to give you a hug."

"Well ok, but if I don't get this assignment finished you are going to tell Mrs Esposito the reason for it was because my sister was hugging me." Abby laughed and was glad that he was moving on. The loss of their mother was still raw, but she tried to shield him from the parts she didn't want him to know.

He knew she had been ill for a long time but what he didn't know was that she had tried to kill herself a few months before as she couldn't take the pain anymore. Abby had a feeling that she made herself sick enough to go into hospital then just gave in to the disease that had been with her for so long.

The last few years had seen Abby grow up a lot quicker than other eighteen-year olds due to her circumstances, but it has made her the person she is today.

"What are you studying anyway?"

"Biology. It's not too bad but if I don't get this photosynthesis paper finished, then I'll need to stay behind after school to make it up and I really don't want to spend anymore, time than necessary with Mrs Esposito. Class is enough time."

"Ok, I'll leave to you it. Have you eaten?"

"Yeah, I had one of those meals. How's Cat? When can I see her again?" Abby hesitated before answering.

"About that, she is moving to another family soon and I don't know if we will be able to continue seeing her. I'll need to see what her new guardians say about it."

"You mean I may never see her again?"

"It's a possibility."

"Damn, I wish had gone with you tonight. I would have suffered the extra time with Esposito if I had known that it could have been the last time, I saw Cat." He was so sad looking that Abby pulled him up from the chair and hugged him tight. She didn't even scold him about swearing.

"I'm sure it won't be the last time you see her. There will be times in the future for you to meet up again." She let him go and he went back to his studying, whereas Abby didn't know what to do. She felt at a loss even though she had college work to do she didn't have any inclination to do that. She went into the kitchen and opened the bottle of wine that had been in the fridge for a few weeks. She poured herself a glass and wondered what else could go wrong in her life.

Abby stopped talking and looked at Cat. There were tears in her eyes and when she looked at Rose, she had them as well. What a group they were. They had done nothing but cry since they started down this road but strangely enough, it was cathartic, especially for her. She was letting go of the past and moving on with her life even though it had all happened twenty-five years ago.

"Well, I think that's enough for now. Lunch is about to be delivered." Rose said. We looked at her trying to work out how she could know that lunch was about to arrive when there was a knock at the door. As

Rose moved to answer it, we heard her talking to someone then the door closed, and she came in laden down with bags.

Both myself and Abby stood, taking some of the bags from her as we headed into the kitchen and Rose started emptying the bags. She started naming dishes as she pulled cartons from the bags and that was when my stomach started to growl at me, and I realised that I was hungry. I looked at Abby as it made the noise and she laughed as they continued to empty the bags.

"How much did you order Rose? There are only three of us."

"I wasn't sure what you would like so I ordered a bit of everything. Wan Tong's is the best Chinese restaurant in the district." I moved around the table getting plates out. I know you usually eat Chinese from the cartons, but I wanted to be polite. We started helping ourselves to the food when I remember the drinks.

"What would you both like to drink?"

"A beer please." Abby said. I should have known. Beer is always drunk with Chinese.

"Rose, beer ok for you?"

"Well, I am driving but I'm sure one won't hurt." I pulled three bottles from the fridge and opening them and handed them out.

"Anyone want a glass?" They both shook their heads. I took a drink then looked at all the food wondering where the best place would be to start.

About an hour later, we were all stuffed with food and feeling better. I began to close the containers and putting them in the fridge. There was enough food left over for dinner and lunch tomorrow if I wanted it. When the table was clear again, we moved back into the living room and we were so chilled that I really didn't want to start back where we left off, but I knew it needed to be done.

"Right, let's get started again. Aunt Abby, please continue from where you left off." I waited, holding my breath to hear what was to come. So much had been told so far but I had a feeling that there was more to come.

"Ok, where was I?" Abby took a breath and as she started talking again, she kept her gaze on me.

Abby went back to see Cat a couple of days later only to be stopped before she got out the car. She had pulled up outside the Watson's and before she could get out, Susannah got into the car and turned to look at her.

"You can't be here Abby."

"Why not? I'm not doing any harm."

"I know that you have been coming here for a few years and as I hadn't noticed any changes for the worse in Cat, I let it be, but circumstances are changing. You can't keep doing this."

"Why not? I'm not hurting anyone. I'm the only connection she has to her parents." Abby could feel her heart racing and the thought of never being able to see Cat again was shattering her heart. "I only want her to be happy and to know where she came from."

"I know but the adoptive parents do not want you to have any contact with her again. They want a clean break from you so that she can grow and move on with her life. They see you as a reminder of what she has lost, and they don't want her to be sad."

"I'm not a reminder of what she's lost. I'm the only link to her parents, where she came from. Everybody has the right to know where they came from." Susannah kept looking at her and Abby could feel her stare right into her soul. She had nothing to lose.

"I only want her to be happy. She has been over the last few years and you can see the progress that has been made. Susan and Raymond don't mind me visiting. They even said that they noticed the change in Cat when she knew I was coming by. That is proof enough that I am good for her not bad. Is there anyway, I can talk to the adoptive parents and explain my case to them." Susannah shook her head.

"No. They know about you and although they appreciate what you have done for her, they don't want you to contact or see her in any way. They want a clean break. They are even prepared to move away from the area to ensure this if you do not stay away." Abby didn't think she could hurt any more. Just the thought that Cat would be in a different district was crushing to her.

"I'm sorry. I tried to speak to them, but they wouldn't listen. Make this your last visit and if she wants to search you out when she is older, then so be it." Susannah reached across and put her hand on Abby's arm. "I am truly sorry about this. I know how much you love that little girl and that you would do anything to make her happy. Stay away." Susannah got out of the car and left Abby going over what she had said.

Everything seemed to be falling apart and there was nothing she could do to stop it. She sat there for a few minutes before trying to decide if she should stay or leave just now before anyone else saw her. The decision was taken out of her hands when she looked across and saw Susan standing at the door.

Her pregnancy was showing but she looked worried. Abby couldn't leave without speaking to her, so she grabbed her bag and got out of the car. Her mind was going in all directions and she felt as if she were floating with nothing to tie her down. As she got closer to the door, she could see that Susan looked about as bad as she was feeling. She stopped in front of her and just looked. Before Abby knew what was doing, she felt herself being pulled into a hug that was the last straw and the tears began to fall.

Chapter Fifteen

The door closed behind them, but Abby wasn't aware of it. She stood wrapped in Susan's arms feeling the bump of her pregnancy and let the tears fall. They must have stood in the hallway for some time before Abby felt herself being moved away from the door and sat down on a chair.

She tried to wipe the tears away with her hands but there were too many of them. She was handed a box of hankies and she used them to mop up her face. She heard movement around her, but she couldn't place what it was until she could focus properly.

Susan was making tea and they were in the kitchen at the table where only a few nights ago, the news had been dropped. She looked at the huge bundle of soggy hankies on the table and lifted them to put them in the bin.

"Sorry about that. I thought I had gotten over the crying." Abby sat back down and let Susan sort things out.

"It's to be expected. You've been through a few hard years and it needs to come out somehow. Keeping it bottled up inside is not good for you. You need to think about yourself, and Michael. He needs to be your priority right now." Abby just sat and stared. Susan seemed so calm and put together despite what she was going though, with her pregnancy. She moved back and forth getting mugs out and sorting them for tea. They had dispensed with using a teapot and teacups shortly after they met, and they now used mugs.

When Susan sat down, she looked as if she had something on her mind and Abby was afraid to ask but did so anyway.

"What's wrong? Is there something wrong with the baby?"

"No, no. Everything is fine with the baby." As she spoke, she moved her hand to her stomach and gently rubbed it as if to reassure herself that there was someone in there. "I've been thinking about the situation and I have an idea. It may not be possibly and I wasn't going to say anything until I knew but you need to have some hope just now."

Abby say up a little straighter in the chair and wondered what she was going to say.

"I've spoken with Susannah who says it may be possible. She has spoken with the Smythe's and there is a possibility that we can keep in contact with Cat. I'm waiting to hear if they will agree to it, but I think there is a good chance that it will."

"How? I didn't think it would be possible."

"It's not for you but for us, there is a chance. We have fostered quite a few kids over the years, and we have stayed in touch with as many of them as we could. You know that from the get togethers we have. It is only because of this, that they may, and I stress may, allow us to stay in Cat's life. If that is so, then I am offering you the chance to keep in her life in a way."

Abby couldn't take in what she was saying. Susan moved her chair so that she was sitting closer to her and took her hands in hers forcing Abby to look at her.

"I'm not promising anything, but it looks good. As soon as I know for sure, I'll let you know. It may be that you can't see Cat, but you can be around and know how she is getting on. You can give her birthday and Christmas presents. Be there for her at the big events in her life. I know you would prefer to actually spend time with her, but this means you can still be in her life."

Abby was trying to take in what she was being told. Yes, it wasn't ideal but if it meant that she could still see Cat grow up, then she would take it.

"When will you know?"

"Tomorrow. Susannah was going to speak with them today and she would call tomorrow and let us know. Cat is going with them tomorrow so tonight is the last night we have her." Abby looked away and that was when she saw the bags packed at the front door. She had been oblivious to them early and it was now hitting home that this would be the last time she was see her for a while.

"When will she be home?" As she spoke, the front door opened, and Cat came running in.

"Aunt Abby, Aunt Abby. You're here." The little girl ran at her and Abby had just enough time to move the chair away from the table to catch her before she hurt herself.

"I'm here." She held on tight and looked at Susan over her head then moved to meet Raymond's gaze as he stood in the doorway. He nodded and watched the three of them at the table.

"You're squeezing me too tight Aunt Abby." Abby let up on the pressure and Cat moved away. She stood in the kitchen/diner and looked at the three adults.

"What's wrong? Why are you all looking sad?" The adults looked at each other and it was Raymond who moved and crouched to the same level as her to tell her the news.

"Cat, we have something to tell you. You know that Auntie Susan is going to have a baby and that we have been looking after you for the last few years." Cat nodded. "Well, there is a family that wants you to go live with them permanently." A puzzled look crossed the little girl's face.

"Why?"

"Well, you know how we are a older than all your other friends parent's at nursery." She nodded again. "This means that it takes us longer to do things. The baby that we are having is something that we have been wanting for a long time and we thought it was never going to happen but there are problems. As we are older, it is harder for us to keep up with you and make sure that the baby is safe."

"I'll be good, I promise. I'll help around the house as well." Raymond smiled.

"It's nothing to do with you not being good. You help a lot when we need it, but you are only a child. We want you to have the best childhood that you can and if that means that someone else needs to raise you, then we will do that." She looked around at the adults trying to work out what she had done wrong. When Susan spoke.

"Cat honey, you have been a blessing in our lives and for us a good luck charm. We have never been able to have a baby all these years until you came along. You are the only thing that has changed for us. We want to thank you for helping us to get what we have been wanting for an awfully long time." The tears were shining in Susan's face and Abby could see them in Cat's as well.

"Will I be able to see the baby?"

"Yes. And you will be the best big sister to him or her when they arrive. We will never forget you at all." The tears were starting to overflow Cat's eyes as she turned to look at Abby.

"Will you still visit me?"

"I don't know if I can, but I will always be watching over you through Susan and Raymond. Never doubt that for a moment." Abby watched as the little girl was taking in what had been said to her. In the last few years, she had grown up a lot, but she was still only a child that was about to start school. Abby caught a breath as she realised that she wouldn't be there to see her go to school for the first time.

"Ok, but I want lasagne for dinner tonight." The three adults laughed as she asked for her favourite meal as if that was going to be the thing that sorted everything out.

"Ok, lasagne it is. Raymond can you check to see if there are enough pasta sheets. I can't remember if I picked them up in the last shop. If not, then you will need to go and get some. Abby, you will stay for dinner."

"I can't I'm sorry. I need to get home as Michael is going to something after school and I need to pick him up." She stood from the chair but didn't get far as Cat came over and wrapped her arms around her body.

"Bring Michael back here then. I haven't seen him in ages, and I like it when he plays with me." How could she say no to that especially as Michael felt bad at not being able to see her the other night.

"I'll text him just now and ask. He should be out his last class." Abby pulled her phone out and dropped him a quick text. She hadn't long to wait for a reply that said he would be there. "Ok, he says he'll be here. I'll go and pick him up and bring him back here. Do you need anything brought back?"

"We have enough pasta so the only thing we need is bread. Could you pick that up on the way back?"

"Not a problem. I'd better go. I'm going to hit rush hour traffic, but I will be back as quick as I can." Abby gave them all a hug before she left and headed back to her car to go and pick up Michael. She hadn't expected this after the conversation with Susannah. She thought that this would be the last time she would ever see Cat. Ok, maybe it would be in the flesh, but she would still be able to know how she was doing through Susan. That was something that she could never repay for.

They had opened their home to her and Michael when they needed it and she would never forget that. They had been through a time of it trying to conceive for the last ten years with no luck until they all came into their lives. It was as if it had all been destined to happen this way.

She unlocked the car and headed out to get Michael. She had known what his answer would be even before she had texted, but she wanted to hear it from himself and not assume that he would. For a pre-teen, he was not like all the others. Yes, he had the normal hormonal urges that they all had, but he was more in control of himself and less likely to carried away with things.

That night was one of the best nights that Abby had had in a long time. The last six months had been hard for both her and Michael. This felt like a new beginning even though it also felt like the end of one.

When she arrived back with Michael, he could hardly contain himself. He was out the car before she had even got it into park. The door was open, and Cat came running out.

"Michael." She ran straight to him and he caught her and lifted her up. Abby felt as if someone had stolen her breath from her as watched them. They were as close as brother and sister and she wanted that to continue but she didn't know if it could.

Abby spotted her over Michael's shoulder and waved at her. She got out the car and walked towards them. She wanted to tell Michael that she could walk herself but looking at the grip he had on her, he wasn't going to let her go just yet.

They headed into the house and she could smell the lasagne cooking away and her stomach grumbled at the smell. She headed to the kitchen as Cat took Michael into the living to play until dinner was ready.

She stood watching them from the kitchen doorway knowing that this would be the last time for a while they would all be together.

"She is one lucky little girl to have him as a big brother." Susan came to stand next to her as they watched them play. Abby's gaze moved to Michael and as she watched him, she could have sworn that his look turned from one of watchful to something else. Something that she had never seen in him before. It was as if he had aged ten years in front of her and the love shining out his eyes was so tangible that she couldn't take it in.

By the time she had blinked again, it was gone and in its place was the twelve-year-old playing with what could have been his younger sister.

"Come on, let's set the table." Susan turned away and Abby followed trying to work out if she had imagined the look or not. Soon after, they were all seated at the table and tucking into homemade lasagne. They looked like a family and the love that was between them was showing and Abby felt something shift inside her as if things had moved and that everything was going to be alright.

Chapter Sixteen

Abby had been talking to Cat more than Rose and she was okay with that. Rose seemed to blend into the background as if she knew that this was between the two of them. She just sat back and jotted some things down as she spoke, but she knew that it was all being recorded. She had to have something to focus on otherwise, she would be lost in her memories.

"I really had no idea how much you had done for me when I was that young. I have a few memories here and there, but the first consistent ones were when I was started school. Before that, it was nothing until you started talking then things seem to come to me. I remember that night. Everyone seemed so sad then when Michael turned up, everything seemed to change. I didn't know the reason for it at the time but now it all makes sense.

"It's as if something has been unblocked and I can't stop the memories coming back in flashes." I felt the tears fall from my eyes knowing that this was what happened when you found out where you came from. I had always known that my parents had died and that I had been put into foster care then adopted. It had never been hiding, from me but knowing how much Abby had went through for me was something that I could never repay.

She had been the adult in my life for as long as I knew even when she wasn't there, I knew she was looking out for me. I couldn't explain it at the time but now it all made sense. Knowing that someone had felt so much for me was humbling and it was beginning to make me think about how I had treated Michael before the accident.

I had to put it from my mind as I had more to get through before I could think about that anymore. It was going to come out later, so I wasn't going to think about it until I had to.

"Cat, what else do you remember about that time?" Rose asked. I thought about it but there were flashes of memories flying through my mind that I was trying to organise.

"I remember not wanting to let them go when they tried to leave. I know I fought the tiredness and the only way they could get away was when Michael put me to bed. He read me a story then the next thing I knew it was morning and I was being taken away with my things with Susannah Croft."

Rose looked across at Abby for confirmation. She nodded.

"That's right. You were ready to go into a full-blown tantrum when we tried to leave until Michael said he would read you a story and wouldn't leave you. You calmed down then and allowed him to put you to bed. When you were asleep, we left knowing that you would be ok. We were there the next morning when you were taken away, but you never knew. We had parked down the street in my neighbour's car so that you wouldn't see us, and we watched as you were taken away. You were looking about for us and for a moment, I thought you spotted us then you kept moving and got into the car and drove away. That was the last time I saw you until just before your sixteenth birthday."

I could see that Rose wanted to say something, but she kept quiet. I knew that it was getting to the point that it would be my turn to talk about my memories and I was trying to get them into some order as there were now more there than before. My mind kept drifting back to the new memories that had arisen, but I kept pushing them away as I had enough to get through without them.

"Ok, I think it is about my time to start talking. It may be in bits, but I can tell you what I can remember about my life until I met up with Abby again. If you give me five minutes, then I'll start." I wasn't giving them an option, just stood and headed upstairs to the bathroom. I needed some time alone to process all that had come out so far. I knew that the more that came out, the more therapeutic it would be for both me and Abby, but it was hard going.

Exposing yourself like that was hard to do, even with someone you trusted and loved. I knew that I had lived through it and it couldn't be any worse telling someone about it, but it was still hard going and exposing the raw parts of my life was going to hurt. Up until now, Abby was telling from her perspective but now it would all be from me and no-one else. I had to be truthful to myself about what was going to be said as there was no taking it back once it was out there.

I washed my hands and face then headed back downstairs to continue from where we stopped. I could hear Abby and Rose talking and the pain could be heard in Abby's voice. She had lived through what she had said whereas I couldn't really remember it. In some ways I was glad but in others I felt as if I had missed something.

I walked back into the room and they stopped. "Anyone like a refill?" I asked holding up the empty bottles that were on the table. She hadn't even been aware of them drinking them, but they must have. Abby nodded and as she waited for Rose to answer. "You can leave your car here tonight if you wish. I know we will probably have another day or so to go over everything." Rose nodded and I lift her empty and headed to get three more bottles. I wasn't sure if alcohol was a good idea, but I needed something to give me the courage to talk about what happened next.

Once I had the three bottles opened, I headed back in and handed them out before sitting back in the chair where I had been. I took a drink from the bottle and held it before looking at both then I put the bottle on the table.

"My turn now. If there are any parts that I am a little vague on, Abby please fill in any blanks if you can." She nodded and I took a deep breath before starting.

When I woke up the next morning I felt as if I had lost something. I looked around my room and saw my stuffed animals around me and the book that Michael had read to me was on the bedside table. I grabbed Bunny and held on tight as I felt the tears fall. I couldn't explain it but I knew I had lost him.

I lay there until my bedroom door opened and Susan walked in rubbing her tummy. The baby must be causing her discomfort. I sat up in bed and she came over and sat on the edge and just opened her arms. I went into them and held on. The tears had stopped but I knew within myself that things were going to change, and I wasn't sure what it was going to mean for me.

Just as I was puling away from her, I felt something hit my body. I looked down but saw nothing except Susan's stomach. I looked up at her and she smiled.

"That was your little brother or sister letting you know that they are there for you no matter what." I tried to take in what she was saying but I was too young. I knew that it was a big thing but at the time I didn't know.

"Come on, let's get up and get breakfast. You have a big day ahead of you." Susan stood and I pushed the covers back and got out of bed. I went over to the get some clothes out. I pulled out my favourite jeans and top and laid them on the bed. I then went and got my underwear and shoes out, lying them on the bed and the floor respectively.

I looked at Susan who was standing watching me. It seemed as if she wanted to hug me and knew that if she did, she wouldn't be able to stop. I walked past her and out into the bathroom. Even though I was only six, I was very independent and wanted to do things on my own rather than have people help me. When I came back out, she was still standing where she had been before.

I went back to the bed and stripped off my night clothes and got dressed in normal clothes. When I had my shoes on, I went over to my dresser and lifted my brush.

"Could you braid my hair for me?"

"Of course, I will. What bobble do you want to hold it together?" I looked at the vast array I had on the dresser and pulled out one of the oldest ones I had and held it up to her. I went and sat on the bed and waited for her to come in behind me to fix my hair.

I knew this was a big occasion and I wanted it to last for as long as I could, but I knew it would come to an end at some point. Soon enough, my hair was part braided and the rest flowing down my back. I stood and turned to her.

"It's going to be alright. Everything is going to work out." I leaned in, giving her a hug and a kiss on the cheek then left her sitting there and headed out into the kitchen for breakfast. I stopped at the end of the hallway as I saw my suitcase waiting beside the door. I headed into the kitchen and saw Raymond making pancakes. He didn't turn as I came in but he knew I was there.

"How many do you want, two, three?"

"Two please. Do we have chocolate sauce?" Even before I finished, the sauce bottle was handed to me from the counter. I put it on the table and started putting the plates out for the food. I could just reach the table but not the counter, so they were sitting at the edge and I put one out for each of us.

Soon after, Susan appeared back, and the pancakes were made. We all sat down, and I watched as Raymond took Susan's hand giving it a squeeze as if to reassure her that everything was going to be alright.

I stood and reached out for the sauce and began to squeeze some onto my pancakes. I wasn't really that hungry, but I ate them as they had been made by them. I wanted to remember everything I could about this day as I knew it was a turning point in my life.

Soon enough, breakfast was over, and the table was being cleared. Around nine o'clock, the doorbell rang, and Susan went to answer it. I knew that the time had come. I had to leave now. I put my coat on and headed to the door stopping next to my case. I knew the moment they had seen me as they stopped talking and I could see them looking me over.

"Is it time to go now?" Before I got an answer, Raymond appeared next to me with another bag and in it I could see Bunny sticking out the top. I had completely forgotten all about him. I couldn't leave without him. I took the bag from him and stepped away and tried to lift my suitcase but couldn't. Raymond lifted it for me and stood behind me.

"Let's go Catriona." I recognised the lady from before, but I didn't know her name. I knew that she was the one who was taking me away from home to somewhere else. I stopped at the door and turned to Susan.

"Will you let me know when he or she has arrived?" I could see her looking over the top of me then back down to me.

"Yes, I will. It won't be for some time, but I will let you know."

"Ok. I want to come visit, them as well." I turned to the other lady and gave her a look that I hoped she could tell that I meant business. If they didn't allow me to visit them, then I would find a way to see them myself.

"Let's go. They are waiting on you." I turned back to Susan again and gave her a hug before going to Raymond and hugging him as well. I walked behind the other lady as she taken my case from Raymond and headed down to a car that was sitting at the kerbside. She put my case in the back then opened the back door for me to get. I climbed in and got the seatbelt on and waited. I turned my head back to the open doorway and I felt something break inside my chest. I didn't know how I was going to get through this, but I would.

The lady got in and started the car then pulled away. I kept my gaze to the house I had lived in for the last few years until we had turned the corner and it was out of sight.

"How far is it to the other place?" I asked.

"Not far about twenty minutes." I sat back in the seat and looked out the window trying to take in the direction we were going so that if I needed to find my way back there I could.

Chapter Seventeen

We pulled up to a house that was larger than anything I had seen before, and I couldn't stop myself from sitting forward to get a better look. I didn't know where I was, but I knew that this was where I would be staying going forward. The car came to a halt and the lady got out and came around to open the door for me to exit.

I unclipped the seatbelt then pushed myself out the door bringing my backpack with me. I stood a few feet away from the car and waited to see if someone was going to come and meet us or if we were going up to that huge door. It was the latter. As we walked up the pathway, I looked around and I could see movement inside the house, but I tried not to think about it.

We stopped at the front door as the lady rang the bell. We didn't need to wait long before the door opened and standing in front of us was woman who was unlike anything, I had ever seen before. She was tall, thin and very beautiful. She looked like a princess. I couldn't speak and I couldn't even imagine what my face looked but I just stood there. I could see their mouths moving but I didn't hear what was being said.

Soon after I was gently pushed inside the house and I went. I stopped in the entrance way and just gawked at what was in front of me. The hallway was huge with a sweeping staircase upwards. It was all done in creams and gold and everything looked expensive. I pulled my bag closer to me as I didn't want to break anything.

I had ignored the adults and was trying to keep myself together with what I was seeing in front of me and what I had left behind. It was hard but I kept it going. I hadn't realised that I had stepped away from the door and was now standing in the middle of the entranceway looking about to see everything that was there. It was too much for me to take in.

I felt the tears prick behind my eyes and I squeezed them shut with the hope of stopping them from falling but it didn't work. I kept my back to the adults but that only helped a little as the lady that had brought me here appeared in front of me and it was only then that I knew I had re-opened my eyes.

"Catriona, this is Julie, she is going to be looking after you from now on. I wiped my eyes before turning to look at the woman who had opened the door. Her face was kind and gentle. She stepped towards me and crouched down to my level.

"Hi. I know this is a lot for you to take in, but I am here for you." I looked at her then around at the surroundings again before looking back.

"I'm Catriona Mont-Clair. I'm six years old and I have no parents. My aunt wanted to look after me, but she wouldn't let her." I stood waiting for any reaction to what I said. The lady's, Julie's, face sagged a little and gave me a sad smile.

"I know all about you Catriona. That is why I wanted you to come here. I want to look after you. I want you to have a happy life here with me and my husband John. We are not replacing the parents' that you lost. Think of us as family that want to take you in."

"I had a family that wanted to take me." I watched her gaze go to the lady then back again. She couldn't respond to that.

"How about we go and find your room so that you can get settled." She straightened and stepped towards the bottom of the stairs waiting to see if I would follow. I knew I wasn't going anywhere but I didn't want them to think I was too eager. I stepped forward slowly and started climbing the stairs. I was a few up when I heard the lady speak again.

"I'll get her suitcase from the car and just leave I here then I'll leave you both alone." I didn't turn around, just stood staring upwards to where I was going. I heard the door closing and waited for Julie to come up beside me. When she did, she didn't try and take my hand only motioned upwards and I started climbing again.

When we got to the top, I stopped as I had no idea where we were going. We turned left and headed down a hallway that was long and looked to have expensive things on the walls and in the little alcoves along the way. I thought we were never getting to the end of the corridor when we stopped at the second last door on the right.

"This is your room." The door was opened and as I got my first look at where I would spend the rest of my life, I couldn't really process what I was seeing. I stepped into a room that looked like something out of a fairy-tale. There was a bed with curtains all around it and many stuffed animals lying on top. To the right, there was a door that was open slightly and I could see clothes hanging there. I stepped towards it and pushed the door open further.

There were rows and rows of clothes hanging. It was as if I had my own shop. I turned back to the main room and took in the dresser that had a brush set on it along with a box of some kind. I stepped closer and looked at it. It was so shiny that I was afraid to touch it. Julie was still standing at the doorway letting me explore on my own.

"Through the door to the left of your closet is your own bathroom. Through the other side of that is your playroom." I couldn't understand what she was talking about and she must have known. She came in and opened the door to allow me to see my own bathroom. At the other end of it, there was another door which she opened and as I followed her through, I couldn't believe my eyes.

The room was filled with toys of every description that I could dream of. I stepped inside and just looked around. There was so much that I couldn't take it all in. I just stood in the room and turned around trying to take it all in.

"I know it's a lot, but I wanted to make sure that you had something to play with. If you want something else, let me know and I will see what we can do." I didn't know what to say so I said the only thing I could think.

"Thank you." I turned to her as I spoke and waited to see what her reaction would be. It was happiness tinged with a little sadness but considering she was taking in an orphaned six-year-old girl, how could it not be tinged with sadness.

"I'll leave you to settle in. I'll bring up your suitcase and give you some time alone. If you need anything, just press star on the phone and I'll be here."

I didn't know what to say. She was being nice, and I could tell she meant everything she was saying. I knew it wasn't going to be plain sailing for us, but we would get through it.

"Do you live here alone?"

"No. I live with my husband John, Sophia our housekeeper and Bonny, our dog."

"You have a dog?"

"Yes. She's four years old and full of energy. John has taken her out for a walk, but he should be back soon." As she finished talking, I heard a noise from downstairs then footsteps coming closer along with the dog.

A man appeared in the doorway but kept back whereas the dog that was with him didn't stop just came right at me and began to try and lick my face and climb over me. I couldn't help myself, but I started laughing.

"Bonny, come." The dog stopped and looked away from me to the man that spoke then back at me as if it was torn between going to his master and staying with me. He started walking away from me with the head down and tail between its legs. I couldn't stop myself.

"Bonny, come here." The dog turned to me and looked between the two of us as if it was having an internal conversation with itself. One side won as she came back to me. I began running my hand over her back and I started to laugh as she tried to climb on top of me.

"Well ok then. I can see who is in charge here." I looked up at the two adults who were going to be looking after me and I had a feeling that everything was going to be alright. For now.

It took me time to settle into the new house and I never forgot the Watson's. When Susan had her daughter, they allowed me to go and see her in the hospital. They allowed me to keep in touch with Susan and Raymond and their daughter Tracey and I was happy. I had a sister but every now and again, I still missed the brother that I had. Through the years, I forgot about Michael but never Aunt Abby. I never knew why until years later. I had been protecting myself by not remembering the one person that I loved like an adult.

I gradually settled into a new routine and began school. I made new friends and Julie and John quickly became the only parents that I could remember. They were always up front with me about being adopted. I never lost touch with the Watson's until they moved away just before my fifteenth birthday. Soon after that, Bonny died, and I fell apart.

That was the point when something changed in me. I don't know what it was whether it was hormones, them moving away or things getting tougher at school, but something made me change. I suddenly felt as if I was floating away with nothing to hold me down and I didn't know how to deal with it.

I started getting into trouble and hanging out with the wrong crowd. I never went so far as to cross the line, but that year was mostly a blur to me. Julie and John tried to help me out, but I wouldn't listen to them. I said some hurtful things, but they were there for me through all the years regardless. I wouldn't have the strength to do that if it had been me.

A few months before my sixteenth birthday I started to change again. I didn't go back to the way I had been, but I mellowed a little and began to listen more to the adults. It was as if something inside me knew things were going to change and I had to step up and make the most of what I had before it was taken from me.

I looked at Abby as she listened to what I had said. I could see that she was struggling to hear what I was saying but I knew it had to be put out there. This was nothing to what happened later, but I had to show where I was coming from.

"I remember that. I was always there for you even though you never saw me. I watched when you went a little wild and I wanted to step in and help but it wasn't my place to do so. I could see that you were about to get out of control when I made the decision to speak to your adoptive parents about you."

I stared at her taking in what she was saying. I had no idea that she had been there through the years for me. I had a feeling at times as if someone were watching me, but I never let it get the better of me and now it seemed that

I was right. There had been someone watching me but not for nefarious reasons, but for love.

"You spoke with Julie and John?"

"Yes. I had to do something." I sat back and allowed Abby to talk.

Abby couldn't stand back any longer and watch what Cat was doing to herself. She knew that her parents would have tried to get her back on track, but it didn't seem to have been working. She had to do something. She took time off from work and made the journey to their house.

This was the first time she had been here at her home. She had been around the area but never at the home. When she saw the house, she knew that this had been the right move for Cat. She would have given her a good life, but the Smythe's had given her a great life and that was all that mattered. She parked the car and headed up the driveway to the front door. She knew that Julie would be in as she worked from home.

She knocked on the door and it was opened by an older woman in a black dress that was more like a uniform.

"Yes?"

"I'd like to speak with Julie Smythe please."

"Is she expecting you?"

"No. But please tell her that Abigail McIntosh is here to see her." The woman looked at her before stepping back and allowing her to enter the hallway.

"Please wait here and I'll see if she is available to speak with you." The woman walked away to the right and left Abby standing there. She looked around at the grand entranceway and knew that it had been right to let her go. A few minutes later she heard heels on the marble flooring, and she turned to them. The woman that stopped in front of her was guarded and Abby knew she only had one chance.

"I'd like to talk to you about Cat."

Chapter Eighteen

Abby stood waiting for a reaction that she didn't know would come. She could tell that she was being assessed but she stood tall and tried not to look as uneasy as she felt inside. Julie just looked at her before motioning for her to follow her back down the hallway that she come from.

Abby stopped inside a home office and debated about closing the door but left it and came forward and stood on the other side of the desk gathering her thoughts before she spoke.

"We need to talk about Cat."

"We don't need to do anything. You shouldn't even be here. I know you have been keeping up to date with Cat's life through Susan and I let it go as you hadn't actually appeared but you have no right to walk in here and demand that we talk about her when she is perfectly fine."

Abby felt the anger build inside her.

"She is not perfectly fine, and you know it. For the last year or so since Susan moved away, she has become a different girl. She has been acting out, skipping school, hanging about with the wrong crowd. She needs help."

"You have no right to tell me how to deal with my daughter."

"I only want her to be happy and right now, she's not. She needs help and it seems that she is not getting it at home. Let me help her."

"How can you help her? She doesn't even remember you." Abby couldn't hide her reaction to that comment.

"I know, but sometimes, a stranger can be better than those at home. You can tell others, things that you wouldn't tell you parents. Please, let me try. What have you got to lose?"

Abby waited to see what Julie would decide. Yes, she was correct in that she didn't know this Cat, but she did know what it was like to be a teenager and everything seem out of control about them. She had lived through it and came out the other side of it. She could tell that Julie had come to a decision and she could only hope that it was the one she wanted.

"Ok, but I have to talk it over with John first. He may disagree but we will see. He should be home soon. Would you like something to drink?"

"Coffee please." Julie nodded and stood leaving her in the room. She had no doubt that she could have called through the order to the housekeeper, but she left needing some time to herself. She heard whispering outside the room and had to force herself to remain where she was. She doesn't want to eavesdrop, but she knew it would tell her how things were going to go.

The decision was taken from her when the door opened, and Julie came back in.

"Coffee is on its way and John will be home in shortly." Julie walked back around the desk and sat down as if she needed it as a barrier between them. "I know you have watching over Cat whenever she received a gift from you even though it didn't say your name, she seemed to know that it wasn't from us. She has been indifferent, and it is hurting us not being able to help her. We have tried everything we can to pull her out of this, but nothing seems to work. We are running out of ideas." Abby kept her gaze on Julie and watched her emotions as she spoke. It was hurting her at not being able to get through to her.

There was a knock on the door and the housekeeper came in with a tray of coffee.

"Thanks Sophia." The tray was put down on the table to the side of the desk and Julie stood going around to it and began to pour. "Milk? Sugar?"

"Just black please." Abby replied. She stood and went to the chair that was at the opposite side of the table. As she took the cup from Julie the door opened again, and John came in. He stopped when he saw Abby.

"What is she doing here?"

"John, she only wants to help. We need all the help we can for Cat." Abby waited to see if he would sit down but he doesn't. He crossed to the desk and leaned against the side of it watching the two of them drink coffee.

"Well?"

"I want to see Cat and see if she remembers me. I know it has been nearly ten years since I last seen her and she may not even remember me, but I want to try. As I said to Julie, it can sometimes be easier to talk to strangers than to family about things. It can't hurt for me to try but only if you both agree." Abby waited to see what they would decide.

"I don't know if that is a good idea. She has been doing better recently and she is almost the same girl she has been for years. We don't need someone from her past coming into her life and taking her away from us."

"I am not here to take her away from you. I only want her to be happy and currently she isn't. We need to sort that out so that she can move on. I do not know what has happened to make her like this, but we need to find out. I am willing to be the person that she takes it out on and allow you two to be there to pick up the pieces that are left. It is better for me to take the hit than you two. You are her family and she needs, to know that you are there for her no matter what."

"If you excuse us for a moment?" John walked to the door and Julie followed him. Abby took a drink of coffee for something to do whilst they were away discussing what they were going to do. She put the cup down and stood and walked around the home office looking at everything that was there to kill time until they returned.

She was that inside of herself that she had not heard the door open behind her and as she turned, she froze when she saw who it was. Cat stood just inside the doorway and was staring at her as if she were trying to place who was in the office without her mother.

"Who are you? Where's my mom?" Abby had to clear her throat before she spoke. It had been so long since she had seen her in the flesh.

"She is talking with your father somewhere. I'm .." Abby did not know how to respond as to who she was. "I'm a client of your mother's." She did not know what else to say. She moved from where she stood at the bookcase back to the desk and waited to see if she would say anything else. Abby watched the expressions on her face as she looked to place her. She knew the moment that she recognised her.

"Aunt Abby?" Abby could only nod as she watched the teenager seemingly fold into herself at the recognition. She only had a moment to brace herself as she came at her and held her so tight that she thought she was not going to breathe again. She held on herself and did not want to let go. They were standing holding each other when Julie and John came back in. When they caught sight of them, it seemed to change their mind about whatever decision they had made.

Abby pulled back and tried to let go of Cat, but she would not have it. She turned them to where her parents were standing to see how she would react. She just had a big smile on her face, and she seemed at peace.

"I can't believe you are here. How did you find me?" Cat turned to her parents. "This is my Aunt Abby. I haven't seen her in a long time. I thought she had forgotten about me." She hugged her again before looking back to her parents. "Can she stay for dinner?" Abby could see the warring expressions on their faces. They wanted to appease their daughter, but they did not want her stepping in where she didn't belong.

"I can't stay. I have to get back to work."

"No, you can't you need to stay. Please tell her she has to stay." Abby was about to speak when Julie spoke first.

"Of course, you have to stay Abby. I can't let you go without spending time with Cat after all this time, isn't that right John?" She looked at her husband who nodded slowly not liking where this was going but knew that he could nothing about it. Cat gave a squeal of delight then started dragging her out of the room.

"You need to come and see my room. It is the best." Abby could do nothing but get pulled along with her. She did see Julie nod as she went passed as if to say it is ok. Her husband was a different story. He looked as if he had lost her and would never get her back.

Later that night, after dinner and Abby had heard all about Cat's life at school even though she knew about it before hand, the teenager went to bed drained but not without extracting a promise from her that she would be at her sixteenth birthday party next month.

When they were left alone, Abby formed the words in her head as to what she was going to say but before she could, John spoke.

"Thank you for bringing out little girl back to us." Abby looked surprised at him. "It has been a long time since we have seen her so happy and outgoing. It is as if you were the key to changing her back to her old self."

Abby didn't know how to reply to that, so she kept quiet. She looked at Julie who had said nothing but had tears in her eyes as she looked at her husband.

"Yes, thank you Abby. I never imagined the effect you had on her. If I had known, I would have asked you here before now. I never knew how strong the bond was between the two of you. I regret not allowing you into her life, but I know that you have been watching out for her."

"I only wanted to make sure she was happy. That was my only goal through everything. Whether it was me looking after her or someone else. I just wanted her to be happy and that if she wanted to know about her biological parents, I could tell her."

"I think I understand that now. She has never been interested in a birthday party until now so please come next month. I'm not sure what it's going to be like, but I think as long as you are there, she will be happy."

"I'll be there. I do have one request though."

"What?"

"I would like to bring my younger brother with me. He spent a lot of time with Abby when she was younger, but I do not know if she will remember him. I will not force her to remember him, but I know he misses her and would like to see her again." Abby could see them hesitating about allowing Michael to come. "I promise that if she doesn't remember him, I will not force it. I will tell Michael that if she doesn't remember him, then he is not to say anything."

"Ok. If she remembers fine but if not, then I don't want to force it. How old is he?"

"He's twenty-one and away at university. He's due to come back on a break next month."

Julie nodded agreeing to it and Abby felt relief. She couldn't wait to tell Michael that he would be able to see Cat again. She was wondering if what she had seen the last time, they had been together would still be there. She half hoped that it was, and it wasn't, but she would need to wait and see.

Chapter Nineteen

The next month flew past as Abby got ready for the birthday party. When she had told Michael about it, he was surprised but happy. She could hear him in his room getting ready and she smiled. It would be good to all be in the same room again. She finished putting her earrings in and lifted her bag from the bed. The dress she was wearing was new and different to what she would normally wear.

She had bought it on a whim knowing that there would be times when she needed to appear professional and business like at parties. The deep blue colour suited her, and she was glad that she had bought it. It was the most expensive thing in her wardrobe, and she felt a little uneasy at wearing something that cost so much.

She stepped out of her room and went into the living room calling for Michael to get a move on. She woke her laptop up and checked how many more emails had come in since she had last looked at it. There were too many. Her business had taken off and she was struggling to keep up with everything. She had just taken out a bigger lease of office space that she was hoping wouldn't be a mistake.

Since she started her marketing business after leaving college nine years ago, it had gone from strength to strength. She now had a staff of about a hundred and fifty and she had clients ranging from the local store to big brand names. She was lucky to be where she was, and she was going to make it a success.

Cat wanted to come work for her, but she wouldn't allow it until she finished school. She had to concentrate on her studies before thinking about working. Abby fired off some replies to some of the emails then closed it down otherwise she would never get away from it. She stood and lifted the present that she had got for Cat and looked at it.

She hoped that she would like it as she had pulled together a photo album of her and her parents. She could have put more photos in there, but she wanted this to be all about her and her heritage. She closed the album and wrapped the tissue paper around it again and put it in the gift bag and put her bag next to it.

"Michael, we need to get a move one. What's taking you so long?" She started walking back to his room to see what was taking him so long. Normally, he was ready in ten minutes flat but not tonight. He had taken longer than her in the shower and now he was still getting dressed. She knocked on his door and pushed it open. He was standing at the mirror fussing with his tie.

"Here let me." Abby walked over and stood in front of him and fixed his tie. He looked so handsome in the navy-blue suit. She could also see that he was nervous.

"What's up?"

"What if she doesn't remember me? How do I take that?"

"She was only little when you last seen her. I didn't expect her to remember me, so I was surprised. Just take it as it comes and if she doesn't remember you at the beginning, then it may come later. Take it as an opportunity to get to know this Cat as the one that we both knew no longer exists." Abby watched her brother taking in the nervousness in him that she had never seen before. She could only hope that it would disappear when they got there. She didn't want him to freak out if she didn't remember him.

"Come on, we need to get going or we'll be late." She moved away from him and knew when he followed. He stopped in his bathroom and came out with a huge bouquet of flowers. He looked them over so seriously that she knew then that the look that she had seen all those years ago would appear again tonight. She could only hope that he kept it together if she didn't recognise him.

They locked up the house and got into the car and headed to Cat's for her party. When they pulled up to the house, there were parking valets there to take their car from them. Abby handed the keys over and headed up to the door. Before they could knock, it was opened by Sophia who had a smile a mile wide on her face.

"Welcome, please go into the front room to wait whilst everyone arrives." They handed over their coats and headed into a room that was filled with people and a lot of teenagers. Abby could see Michael fiddling with his tie again and she patted his hand away as she looked through the crowd looking for Julie. She spotted her across the room, and she waited where she was until she came to them.

"Abby, I'm glad you are here. Cat has not been able to stay still all day waiting for tonight. She was worried that you wouldn't make it."

"I wouldn't have missed it for the world. This is my younger brother Michael." Michael moved the flowers to his other hand and shook Julie's.

"I'm please to meet you Mrs Smythe. You have a lovely home."

"Thank you, Michael. You are a handsome young man." Before he could respond, with the exception of the blush that had covered his face, Cat came running up to them.

"Aunt Abby, you came." Abby held on as she pulled into a bear hug that would have been a line backer proud of.

"I wouldn't have missed this for anything. Now, let me look at you." Cat stepped back and twirled. "Looking good. Are you sure you're only sixteen? You look at lot older in that dress." Cat laughed.

"Yes, I'm only sixteen. Have you reconsidered about me working with you?"

"No. we'll talk about it when you've finished school." Abby knew the moment that she saw Michael. She stepped back and began to fuss with her hair. "Cat this is my…."

"Assistant. Happy birthday." He held out the flowers he had been holding and Cat took them and tried to hide the blush that was showing on her face. They stood awkwardly for what seemed an age then Julie took the flowers from her.

"Let's get these in some water. Cat, why don't you show Abby and Michael around." Julie walked away and Cat seemed to stumble to get her words out. Abby flicked her gaze between the two of them and knew that Michael was being courteous by not saying who he was. She would find out later. She could tell by his look that he had not forgotten his feelings for her.

"This way." Cat led them out the living room and gave them a short tour of the ground floor. She only mentioned where her room was but nothing else. As they were heading back to the living room, the front door went again and as they were there, Cat answered it and let out a squeal when she saw who was there.

Abby looked over her shoulder and smiled when she saw Susan. She couldn't see Raymond but there was someone in front of her and as Cat moved back, she saw Tracey standing dressed up holding a present for her.

Abby had to turn away as she could feel the tears pooling in her eyes. She excused herself and went to the bathroom before she started crying in public. By the time she came back out, everyone was in the living room and the music was pumping loud and the teenagers were having a ball. The adults started gravitating towards the room across from where the younger ones were, and she headed in that direction.

When she got there, she scanned the crowd and found Susan standing at the fireplace talking with Julie. She crossed to them lifting a drink from a passing waiter as she went.

"Susan, it is so good to see you again. How's have you been?" She leaned into her and gave a kiss on her cheek and stepped back. Now she could see her face more clearly, she could see something was weighing heavily on her. "Where's Raymond?"

"He's in hospital."

"What's happened?"

"It's cancer. He's not doing well. He's on his third round of chemotherapy and I don't know if it is going to work this time. He seems to have given up all hope. I wasn't going to come tonight but he made me promise that I had to. He misses Cat as much as I do, and he didn't want Tracey to miss out this."

Abby struggled to speak. She didn't know what to say so she said nothing. She only put her arm around her and hugged her letting her know that she was there for her if she needed it.

"If there is anything you need, let me know." Susan nodded and then she seemed to pull herself together.

"Michael has turned into a handsome man." She was looking across the room at him. He was standing at the door and looking across the foyer into the other room where the teenagers were having fun. "Does she remember him?"

"No. He introduced himself as my assistant not my brother. I'm letting him take the lead on this. If he doesn't want her to know that they knew each other then, that is up to him. It's strange as was worried that she wouldn't recognise him but he hasn't told her who he is." They stood looking at him and he must have felt them looking as he turned to them at that time. Abby just smiled and waved at him. Before he could move from the doorway, Cat came up to him.

Abby looked on as Michael tried to keep his distance, but Cat kept trying to get closer to him until he could go no further. She took pity on him and walked over.

"Michael, I need you to re-check the Dougan contract before we sign the papers tomorrow. Can you go and do that tonight?" Abby stood and watched as Michael swallowed a few times then nodded.

"Yes Abby. I'll get that done for you. If you'll excuse me Catriona I need to go. I hope you enjoy the rest of your party." He moved himself away from where he was trapped and headed to the door. Abby looked at Cat as she followed him away. She heard a click and glanced down to see her phone pointed in the direction that Michael had gone in. She smiled to herself thinking it was great to be young and in lust.

Julie started getting the attention of everyone and was ushering them into the entranceway for the presentation of the cake that they had gotten Cat. Abby marvelled at how much she had changed since last month. It was as if there was a different girl in front of her now.

Chapter Twenty

"Oh god, how embarrassing. I remember that party and what a fool I made of myself." I fell back in the chair and covered my face with my hands to hide the embarrassment. When I think about it, I had thrown myself at Michael not knowing who he was, but he was courteous enough to rebuke my advances. Ok, there was a five-year age gap that wouldn't have been appreciated by the parents', but it was the first time I have felt like that in a long time.

"I can't believe I acted like a lovesick fool in front of him. I wasn't even careful to hide my intentions. I am so embarrassed. He never even mentioned that night when we met up again all those years later. I was glad as I just wanted to forget about it."

"You affected him more than you know Cat. That night when I got home, I found him shivering in the bathroom trying to cool his body down as you had heated him so much that if he hadn't left when he did, he wouldn't have been able to walk straight." I looked at Abby as what she said sunk in.

"He has loved you for a long time. That night was when he realised what it was for himself and he was struggling to control his emotions. He had thought he could handle it, but when you crowded him like, it was like putting a match to dynamite. He had to get out there and fast. I could see it and that is when I gave him the escape route."

"I never realised that he had loved me for so long."

"It's even longer than you think. I first noticed something different about him when you were being moved to the Smythe's. That last night at the Watson's I noticed how he was looking at you and it wasn't something I had ever seen in a child his age. I could tell he was confused by how he was feeling but I let it go as I thought it would be the last time you saw each other. I thought that his feelings would have diminished over the years, but I was wrong. It was that night that I knew he was head over heels in love with you and that no-one else would do for him. If it wasn't you, then he didn't want to know."

"But he'd had girlfriends before, he told me so."

"Yes, there were others, but his heart wasn't in it and they knew that from the start. If they started getting ideas about changing him, then he walked away. That day when you walked back into his life after that party, I could see the change in him. He seemed to come to life again after so many years. You did that to him."

I sat back and dropped my hands back into my lap as I listened to what Abby was saying. I was struggling to take in that I had such an impact on one person, but I suppose when I thought about it, he had made a big impact on my life as well.

"Ok, I think that's enough for today. We're getting through it quite well but it is emotional so we need to take breaks when we can." Rose said. I nodded and glanced at the time. It was early evening and the time seemed to have gone by so quickly. Rose clicked off the recorder and gathered her things together.

"Is ten o'clock tomorrow ok for you both?" She looked from me to Abby and back again.

"Yes, that's fine. Do you want me to call a taxi for you?"

"No, it's fine. I need some fresh air, so I'll walk to the train station and catch a train home." She pulled her jacket on and lifted her bag and crossed to the door. "You are doing really well. I know this is hard for you finding out things you never knew about your early life. It takes a lot of courage to be open to hearing this stuff and getting through it. Having Abby with you is a good thing. She only has your happiness in mind with everything she has done. Give her a break over what she did to protect you."

I nodded and said goodbye to Rose and watched as she walked down the street to the station. She closed the door when she started shivering thinking what can we talk about tonight? There has been so much going on that I feel as if there is nothing left to say. As I turned back to the living room, I saw Abby lifting the empties and putting them into the bin before lifting her coat and putting it on.

"Where are you going?"

"Home. You need some time alone. There has been a lot aired today and you need time to think over it all. I want you to know that I am here for you whenever you need me. Michael is as well. I can only hope that you forgive him and let him back into your life again. He has been broken these last few weeks without you and I don't know how he is going to recover."

Abby came over and hugged me before leaving me standing alone as she closed the door. She was right. When I think back over everything, Michael had always been there for me no matter what. I had never realised or understood the depth of his feelings for me until now and I can only imagine how he must be feeling now.

I walked into the kitchen and noticed that there was a mug sitting out with a teabag in it. I laughed to myself thinking that Abby knew exactly what I was needing. I put the kettle on to boil and stood waiting for it to stop. As I let the tea steep, I went back into the living room and lifted my phone from the table.

I scrolled through the photos and found all the ones that I had taken when I had been sixteen. I had saved them and then downloaded them to my phone a few months ago. It is only now that when I scrolled through them, that I could tell by his expressions how he felt about me. It was there on his face plain as day, but I never saw it.

I went into my contacts and found his. I hesitated for a second before pressing the dial button. I held the phone next to my ear and waited for him to answer. I was praying that he would answer. The longer it rang, I felt the tears in my eyes thinking that he didn't want to talk to me. As I was about to hang up, he answered.

"Cat?"

"Hi."

"Thank god. I'm so sorry about everything. I should have told you who I was before now and not let you find out that way. I am so sorry. Please can we talk."

"I don't know if I can forget what you did. I am finding out more than I expected, and it is shining a light on the reasons for you doing what you did. I am trying to accept it, but you need to give me time."

"I'll give you as long as you need. I'm here for you and I always will be." His voice sounded hoarse and broken as if he had accepted that he would never see me again. I felt my heart break again and I don't know how many more times I could take that.

"I know you will be. I am working through some things and once I have, we need to talk more seriously about where we are going to go from here."

"Ok. Whatever you want. Just know that I am here whenever you need me. No matter what the time, I will be there for you."

"I never knew you had loved me for so long." Michael was quiet on the other end of the phone as if he were trying to work out what I was meaning. "I never knew that you felt that way at my sixteenth birthday party. I made a fool of myself over you and you were the perfect gentleman."

"I wouldn't say I was a gentleman. If you had any idea as to the thoughts that were going through my head watching you in that dress dancing, then you wouldn't have called me a gentleman. I would more likely have been arrested."

"I wouldn't have had you arrested I would have been with you all the way." I heard a groan through the phone and knew that I had pushed him too far. "Give me a few more days and we can meet up. I don't trust myself with you just now, but I will soon enough. I'll let you know when."

"As I said anytime, anywhere." There was silence on both ends of the phone and it was like when we had first started dating. Neither of us wanted to be the one to hang up first. I could hear his breathing and it made my breath quicken. I really wanted to hold him, but I had to remain strong to get through the rest of my history before I could do that again.

I knew now that he would always be there for me. I just had to get myself into a good place to speak to him face to face.

"I love you. I don't expect you to say it back to me just now but please know that I do, and I always will. Sleep well." Michael ended the call, and I was left holding my phone listening to the dial tone. I put the phone down and stood heading into my bedroom. As I sat on the bed, I lifted Bunny, holding it close and lay down on the bed and let myself go.

I forgot all about the tea, the interview, the story, Abby and Rose. The only thing that was in my mind was Michael. I held Bunny wishing that it were him and that this was all over with and we could move on.

Chapter Twenty-one

When I awoke the next morning, I could feel every bone in my body. Even though the injuries had healed, I still felt sore all over even though the accident had been a few weeks ago. I knew it takes time to heel but I just wanted to feel normal again. Well, as normal as I can be in the current circumstances. Yes, I had been, but it was a while ago and I shouldn't be feeling it this bad now. I groaned as I swung my legs out of bed and it took all my strength to force myself to stand.

As I did, I lost my balance and when I looked down, I saw Bunny lying on the floor and it was him that I had stood on. I bent down and lifted him up and put him back on the bed. Last night came back to me as I remembered talking with Michael and I could still hear the sadness in his voice and that hurt more than the rest of my body.

I tried to walk but ended up limping to the bathroom and started the shower. As it heated up, I looked at myself in the mirror. I looked the same on the outside but inside was a different story. I felt as if I had been ripped apart and was only now trying to weave myself back together again. When the shower was hot enough, I stripped off and got in and felt my muscles ease as the hot water ran over me.

I could have stayed under the hot water all day but knew that I had to get out. I decided then that I would go for a bath later and soak in the hot water to help ease my aching body. I switched the shower off, got out and grabbed a towel and wrapped it around myself. The bathroom was humid with the steam and I knew as soon as I opened the door, it would get colder. I braced myself and did just that.

The cold hit me, and I shivered but kept going and pulled out clothes to wear. Once dressed, I brushed my hair then dried it. It felt good to be clean even though I hadn't been dirty. As I headed downstairs, I felt the coldness in the house but knew it would warm up once the heating clicked on.

I went into the kitchen and switched on the coffee machine. As it warmed up, I got a mug out and picked what type of coffee I was wanting. Once the machine was warmed up, I put the capsule in and pressed the button to allow it to flow into my mug.

I leaned against the counter waiting for it to finish and thought about what was to come. Yes, I had told part of the story the day before, but not all of it. It was now going to be my side of things. No doubt aunt Abby would add to it, but it was all going to be from my point of view from now on.

So much had been aired before now and I was still struggling to take it all in. I knew that things had been tough for her, but I never knew just how much. She had handled it a lot better than I could have. I don't know if I would have been strong enough to deal with everything she had been through. I stopped myself there as it had been me that had lived it.

Yes, I was young when it happened and so much of it, I hadn't remembered but it had been me that had lived it. I was the one who had lost my parents when I had been young. It was me that had been put into foster care then eventually adopted not Abby or Michael. It had been me. Some people would say that it had been a blessing as I hadn't remembered any of it, but I wouldn't say that when it felt like a part of me had been missing for so long and only now it had been found.

I would agree that somethings are best left unsaid and unknown but something like this, I think it is better to know than not know but only if that is what you want. The coffee stopped and I lifted the mug and sat down at the kitchen table. I had about an hour or so before Rose would be back. I wondered when Abby would be back. She had been quick to leave the night before, but I had been glad when she had.

I knew what the next part of the story was going to be, and I knew that it was going to hurt. There was nothing I could do to stop it, but I had lived it and came out the other side stronger. If could do it, then others can as well. I want people to realise that there is nothing that you can't get through whether you are on your own or have people who love you.

I know everyone has their own limits and how much they can cope with but there is always a way through if you want to see it. Some may not want to see the way out and block it, but others can and take the path that will lead them to the other side. Having help along the way is a bonus and, in my case, necessary as I was too young to fight for myself. Others had to do it for me until I was old enough and that was about to come to light.

I lifted my mug to take a drink only to find out that I had already drank it all without realising it. I stood and went to make another cup. My body was still sore but not as bad now. I can imagine how I'll be when I get back to the gym, this will seem like a cake walk compared to how I'll feel then but that was some time away yet.

As I waited on the coffee pouring, my phone rang, and I answered without looking at who was calling.

"Hello."

"Cat, how are you?"

"Michael." My breath quickened as I listened to his voice. He hadn't said much but it seemed to ground me in a way I had never imagined. "Why are you calling me?"

"I wanted to hear your voice and after speaking with you last night, I wanted to know if I could see you."

"Michael, I can't just now. I need to get through things before I see you. I can't be strong enough if you are here. I need to do this on my own."

"No, you don't need to do it on your own. Abby has been with you when I wish it were me. I can hold you up through what you are doing."

"I need to do this on my own. If I could do it without Abby, I would but she needs to be here. I need a little more time and then we can meet. I will be able to tell you everything."

"I know about the article. I know what you are doing, and I want to be there for you. I want to be able to hold you through the tough parts and let you know that I will always be there to pick you up."

"I know but that is the reason why I don't want you there. I need to get through this on my own. There are things being aired that I knew nothing about, and I am too raw to go through this with you. You were there, you were behind the deceit and I need to wrap my head around the reasoning for it so that I can forgive you. If the last few weeks have shown me anything, it's that I need to rely on myself first before anyone else."

There was silence on the other end of the phone, but I knew that he was still there. I could picture him sitting clenching his hand wanting to take over and protect me like he has done all his life. A little part of me wanted to tell him to come over now and we can move on but there was still stuff to go through and it would only be then that I could feel strong enough to see him again and not collapse.

"I need to go. I'll call you when I am ready. You said you would be there for me anytime, anywhere, I will hold you to that. Goodbye Michael." I hung up on him and had to take a few deep breaths that didn't make a difference as the tears fell from my eyes.

This wasn't what I expected this morning, but it looked like today was going to be the same as the last few days, heart wrenching. As I stood in my kitchen with the tears falling, I told myself that I would see him again. We will get through this even though I knew it was myself that was causing the obstacle.

I jumped when there was a knock at the door and I quickly tried to brush the tears away but with not much success. I lifted the towel and rubbed my face before going to the door. I assumed that it would be Rose, but I was wrong. It was Abby and as she stood on the other side of the door, I looked to the bottom of the driveway and saw Michael behind the wheel.

He looked as bad as I felt, and it was good for a little while then I had to step back before I found myself running to him. As Abby came in and I closed the door on him, stopping to try to pull myself together. That had been the first time I had seen him since that night and however bad I had felt previously, it was a hundred times worse now.

I felt a hand on my back and I just broke down and turned into the arms that were open and waiting for me. Abby held me as I cried for everything. I had thought I had no more tears left to fall but how wrong was I.

She guided me to the sofa and sat me down just holding on and letting me set the pace. Her hand was rubbing my back gently and I felt like a little girl again and it was comforting.

I knew it wouldn't last but I wanted to hold onto it for as long as I could. I felt the arms go from around me and I sat back on the sofa. I heard voices and it was only then that I realised that Rose had arrived. My sense of time was completely off, and I couldn't keep track. I sat up and wipe my face but stopped when I knew it was a hopeless exercise.

"Excuse me a moment." I said and headed to the bathroom to try and clean up a bit and be more presentable. As I closed the bathroom door, I leaned against it and wondered if I was ever going to be whole again. Yes, telling my story was therapeutic but it was also nerve wracking and opening wounds that I never knew existed.

I understand the reason why Abby and Michael did what they did, but it was hard to take in and think that they could have handled it some other way. I was trying to hold myself together to get through the next part of the story and this had made me unravel and wonder how I was going to get thought it. I had to and I would, but it was going to be hard.

I dried my face and left the bathroom going back to the living room and found Abby and Rose sitting in what was becoming their usually seats with coffee cups in front of them.

"Are you up to this today?" Rose asked.

"Not really but I want to keep going. I need to keep going and finish what I have started. I need to be able to move on soon." I sat down on the sofa rather than the other chair and took a few breaths. I could feel them looking at me and it was unnerving me.

"Ok. We finished at my sixteenth birthday party where I made a fool of myself over Michael. Now for the rest." I sat back and took a breath before beginning to speak. I knew that it was going to be hard, but I would get through it.

Chapter Twenty-two

It took me a few days to come back down to earth after my birthday party and I was still going back through the photos I had taken of him. He was so unlike anyone I had ever met before that I couldn't stop myself from swooning at him.

Me, swooning, I would never have thought that in a million years but there was just something about him that pushed my buttons. I lay on my bed and scrolled through the photos giving a huge sigh every now and again as I took him in. I had even been able to capture him in a video.

It was only a short one, but never less it made me remember that he was alive and not some figment of my imagination or some fantasy man that I had picked out from somewhere. As I played the video, I felt myself get hot all over and I didn't bother to contain it.

I lay watching it repeatedly wishing that I had been able to get another chance to meet this man. He was way too old for me, but I didn't care. In a few years, the age gap wouldn't make a difference and I could do anything I wanted. I had no idea if I were going to see him again but as he was Aunt Abby's assistant, I could only hope.

I began planning how I could drop by her office to see her and hope to catch a glimpse of him at the same time. He must have loads of women throwing themselves at his feet. He probably had a girlfriend, or fiancé hidden away somewhere. She would be tall and beautiful to match him, and they would make a striking couple.

I didn't care. I knew that it was probably just a teenage crush, but I held onto it until someone else came along and caught my attention which would be soon. I looked at the time and knew that they would be home soon. I put my phone down and got changed. We were going out to celebrate the end of the school year.

I changed into my favourite jeans and top pulling on my new heeled boots. I was looking good. I had never had much interest in how I looked until my birthday. Now, I was going to take my time to ensure that I was always looking my best just on case I met him again.

I waited downstairs for Julie and John to come home. I never called them mum and dad as they weren't. It had never felt right saying that. I knew that it hurt them at times when I called them by their names but to me, they weren't my parents. My parents died when I was little, they had been looking after me until I was old enough to do it myself.

I was busy scrolling through social media sites when there was a knock at the door. I glanced up and wondered who was knocking. I then noticed the time and that they were late, very late home. I got up, finishing the comment I was typing until I got to the door. I could see shadows on the other side and opened the door without thinking.

Standing on the other side were two police officers. My brain seemed to fritz out a little and I could see their mouths moving but the words were not registering with me.

"Sorry, can I help you?"

"Are you Catriona Mont-Clair?"

"Yes."

"Is there anyone else at home with you?"

"No. I'm alone."

"Is there someone you can call?"

"Officer, what is going on? What's happened?"

"May we come in?" I stood back and let the two officers in. I was automatic pilot as I closed the door and walked past them. I had wrapped my arms around myself as I suddenly felt very cold despite it being summer. I watched as they looked around them at the house, but I was screaming inside. I knew something had happened and that it was bad.

"Officer, please tell me what has happened?"

"Miss, I am sorry to tell you that your parents have been involved in a car accident."

"What hospital are they are?" As I waited for the answer that I knew was coming, the older officer, looked down at his hat them back up at me.

"Miss, they didn't make it." Everything seemed to close in on myself. I didn't hear what they were saying, only that I was struggling to catch a breath. I felt myself being guided to a seat and my head being forced downwards. I felt a hand on my back rubbing and being soothed. A few minutes later, I sat upright and saw a glass of water sitting on the table next to me. I lifted it and took a drink for something to do.

"What happened?"

"Miss, is there anyone we can call for you? Someone to come sit with you?" My mind seemed a jumble of things and I struggled to sort them out. I must have said something as the response I got back took a while to sink in. "Who's Abby?"

I looked down at my phone as my brain tried to get into gear to unlock it. I put my finger on the screen and it unlocked. The phone was taken from me and the officer stood and walked away. I heard his voice in the distance, but I stayed where I was.

"She's on her way."

"Who?"

"Her aunt. She'll be here in about ten minutes. She must have been close by." I knew they were looking at me, but I couldn't get myself to look upwards. I was still trying to take in what was happening. Soon after, I heard knocking at the door and the younger officer answered it. Through the dimness, I could hear a voice that I recognised. I looked up and when I saw Aunt Abby, I ran to her and held on allowing tears to fall. I held on so tight that I felt her trying to push me away, but I wouldn't let her.

We moved back to the sofa and we sat down together. I lifted my head from her chest and looked at the officers. It was only then that I noticed one looked just out of the academy and the other looked as if they had been on the force for a while. The older one had a strange look on his face but before I could say anything, Abby had spoken.

"Officer Gordon. It's been a while."

"It has indeed, and I am sorry that we meet again under these circumstances. I assume this is the little girl you had been looking after?"

"Yes, this is Cat." I looked from the officer to Abby and the expressions on their faces. I gave them a questioning look but neither of them answered. They knew each other but I didn't know from where.

"She has grown up into a fine young lady."

"She has but for this to happen again to her, it's not fair. What has she done to deserve this?"

"I don't know but if she has you behind her, she will get through it. You fought for her before when she couldn't do it. Now, you can stand by her as she fights for herself." I felt as if I was in a film watching everything happen to someone else and not me. I wanted to walk out as I didn't want to know what happened next, but life wasn't like that.

Abby stood and left me sitting on the sofa as she walked away with the older officer. I watched as they spoke quietly and every now and again, they looked back at me. I felt fragile but I wanted to feel strong. I had to stand up for myself but at that moment in time, I was struggling to hold it together.

The officers left soon after and I was left alone with Abby. I had so many questions in my head, but I couldn't form the words to ask any of them. I knew that it was shock, but I had so much I wanted to know. What happened to John & Julie? How did Abby know that officer? What was going to happen now? I looked up at her and her expression was something that I never want to see again. She was so sad and heartbroken that I didn't know what to do.

She came back over to me an wrapped her arms around her. I heard her talking but I couldn't quite make out the words. They were soothing regardless of what they were, and I let myself sink into that as I didn't want to think of anything else at that moment. My world had been ripped apart and I needed time to sort things out and put a mask on so that the world didn't know how broken I was inside.

The next few days were a blur for me. I don't know much of what happened except Abby was there for me. She moved in for a few days and I was grateful for it. I didn't know what was going to happen to me as I was only sixteen and couldn't live on my own. I didn't know what to do.

The day after the funeral, someone from Child Services came by and told me that I had to pack a bag as I was going to a group foster home. She told me straight that the chances of me being adopted again, were slim and that I should get used to living the next two years in the home until I turned eighteen then I was on my own.

I had no chance to say goodbye to Abby or anyone else as I was taken to a group home in a different city. I had thought I would stay in the same city but there weren't any spaces, so I had to go where I was sent.

I walked into that home the first time and knew that this was not going to be easy. The place was run down and the kids that were hanging around were the kind that you would avoid if you could. I was numb from everything and I could tell by the looks that it was not going to be easy. I had just put my bag down on the bed that I had been assigned to when two girls appeared at the door.

"Don't get too comfortable, you won't last long here." The one that had spoken looked hard and I was afraid of her. They smiled then left me alone. I sat on the bed and tried to make sense of the last week. My stomach growled at me and I looked at the time. It was dinner time. I stood and headed back down the corridor and followed the sounds of plates being passed about and people talking.

I walked into a large dining hall that reminded me of the school cafeteria and I quickly got the lay out. I lifted a tray and headed to the end of the queue and waited until it was my turn for food. I didn't really want to eat anything but knew that I had to. When I had gotten my food, I looked about for an empty seat and found one, I walked towards it but didn't get anywhere near it.

About halfway there, the girl from earlier stood in front of me.

"Where do you think you're going? This area here is only for those in the group. Not you."

"Sorry, I'll go somewhere else." As I turned away, the tray I was holding was knocked out of my hands and there was silence in the hall.

"It's too late for that now. You have to pay the price."

"What price is that? I have no money."

"Who said it the price was money." I stood terrified looking at her wondering how I was going to get out the situation. Before I could move, a fist came at my face and I landed on the floor. I lifted my hand to my mouth, and it came away with blood on it. I looked up and could tell that she wasn't expecting me to fight back. I stood and braced myself as I watched her eyes. They widened at the sight of me standing up to her.

"What is the price?" As I waited for an answer, I was shaking inside, and it was taking all that I had not to show it. Before there was an answer, one of the guardians came in and broke everything up.

"What's going on here? Are you up to your usual tricks Selena? You know that you have one chance left then you are out."

"Everything's fine here Miss Roper. I was just giving the newbie the lay of the land." I kept my gaze on Selena and we seemed to come to an agreement as she nodded her head slightly and walked away. I knew then that the next two years were going to be a test of my strength, but I would get through it.

Part Three

Living

Chapter Twenty-three

The next two years were tough, but they made me who I am today. I fell in with the wrong crowd and it took another death for me to wake up to reality. It was easier to go with the flow than fight back. Selena and I became not exactly friends, but acquaintances. We were together a lot and I was involved in some things that I knew I shouldn't have been, but it was easier that way.

I knew that it wasn't right, but I stuck with it. Life was easier in the home that way and I was one of the lucky ones as I only had a couple of years to stay there whereas, others had been there most of their lives.

The turning point came a few months before I turned eighteen. Selena had left the home six months before when she had turned eighteen and had been living wherever she could since then. Her addiction had risen to another level after that point and despite trying to talk her out of each of her fixes, but I knew it wasn't going to work. We were always trying to find Selena's next fix. I had remained strong in not turning drugs but not her. We had found her dealer just as she was going into withdrawal symptoms. She had been shaking so much that she couldn't get the needle in.

I watched her and knew that she needed it, but I didn't want to give it to her. When I could stand it no longer, I took the needle from her arm and looked into her eyes. They were desperate and hopefully that once the rush came, it would solve all the wrongs in her life. I plunged the needle into her arm quickly and depressed the plunger so that the drugs could enter her system and give her the relief that she had been craving.

I sat back and watched as her eyes had closed and a smile appeared on her face. The rush had hit, and she was going on a ride that she had been craving. Things changed quickly soon after. Selena began to convulse and shake. I tried to stop her, but she was flailing about too much. We were in an abandoned building where they all went to take their fix.

I pulled out my phone and dialled the emergency services. As I answered their questions, I knew that it was too late for her. She was going to be gone by the time they arrived. I stayed by her side until they turned up. They did what they could, but she was gone.

I gave the authorities whatever information they were looking for automatically and as soon as I could, I left there and headed back to the home. I couldn't stay and watch them take her body away. It had been cold that night and I didn't have a heavy coat on. As I walked, I thought back on the last two years or so and how my life had changed. It had been myself that had put me where I was at that time. No-one else. I had known that what I had been doing wasn't the right thing to do but it was the easiest.

I kept walking until I came to an all-night café and went inside and ordered a coffee. I sat at the window and took out my phone. I knew that if I didn't do something now, then I could end up the same as Selena before long. As I took my phone out and made the call, I felt like I was a little girl again asking for forgiveness. I spoke when it was answered.

"Aunt Abby?"

"Cat! What's wrong? Where are you?"

"Can I see you?"

"Of course. Where are you? I'll come and get you."

"I'm at an all-night café on Union St."

"Stay there. I'll be there soon." As she hung up, I felt as if everything was out of control and out to get me. I had pushed everyone away especially her and for her to come when I asked is proof that she won't leave me. I wouldn't have blamed her if she had said no but I had to try. I didn't want to end up like Selena.

About thirty minutes later, the door opened, and I felt someone standing next to me. I looked up and saw Abby. It was as if a dam had burst and the tears started flowing. She just pushed me further into the booth and sat down next to me and wrapped her arms around me and held on.

I don't know how long we sat like that but by the time I sat upright again, I felt as if a huge weight had been lifted from my shoulders. I wiped my eyes the best I could, and it was only then, that I noticed how she was dressed.

"I'm sorry. You were out tonight." I could see her looking confused then she looked down and back up.

"It was a work thing. Don't worry about it. You are more important than anything. Now, how about we get out of here and go home."

"I don't want to go back there."

"I meant with me. For tonight anyway. I'll call the Guardians and let them know where you are. Afterwards, we'll see what we can do." I sat looking at her and couldn't believe that she was still there for me after everything I had put her through, she came when I needed her. I nodded and she stood waiting for me to exit.

I walked out and suddenly stopped as I didn't know what car belonged to her.

"This way. I only have this car because of the work thing otherwise I would be in my own car." We walked down the street and I began to shiver. An arm came around me and I felt the warmth come from the body next to me. We walked in sync down the street before I stopped when a large man got out of a car a short distance away from us.

"It's ok. He's with me." Abby pulled me on again and the man stood at the side of the vehicle and opened the back door to allow us to enter. I was still nervous and on edge, but I trusted her. I slide into the back seat first then Abby came in behind me.

"Where to Miss?"

"Home please." I sat frozen in the back seat watching the driver as he started the engine and pulled away from kerb. I turned to Abby and saw that she was looking through her phone then she held it to her ear.

"Miss Roper please." There was a pause where I assumed the person on the other end was transferring the call to the head. "Miss Roper, I just wanted to let you know that Catriona will be staying with me tonight. I will bring her back some time tomorrow afternoon and then we will be having a conversation. I will see you then." I stared at Abby as I had never heard her sound that cold and hard before. She seemed to change in front of me and I didn't know how to take it. As she slipped her phone back into her bag, she turned to me.

"Now, how about we get you home and into some warmer clothes before we talk. Have you had anything to eat tonight?" Before I could say anything, my stomach let out a growl in answer. Abby smiled and took her phone out again. I zoned out as she spoke to someone ordering food. Soon enough, she had hung up again and she reached across and took my hand. Feeling her warmth in mine did more for me than anything. Being able to feel the warmth again was amazing and I didn't want to let it go.

Soon after, we stopped behind a restaurant and I began to panic as I couldn't go in dressed like I was. I would stick out too much. Before I could say anything, the window was rolled down, and bags were handed inside the car. The smell was fantastic, and I wanted to open then all and start eating immediately.

As the bags were put in between us, I had to hold myself back from opening them and eating whatever was inside. I was so focused on not digging in, that I didn't see the bread that was in front of me.

"Eat up. This will keep you going until we get home." I looked between the bread and Abby thinking that it was going to disappear but gave in and took the bread. It was still warm and crusty. I knew I was making a mess, but I didn't care. I had eaten the first piece without taking a breath and then another one was held out to me. I look to the owner of the hand and told myself to slow down.

The sadness on her face was hard to take in. I began to eat the second piece more slowly and before long; we were pulling into a driveway that I had never seen before. The car stopped and the driver got out and opened the door for me to get out. I glanced to Abby who nodded, and I stepped outside into the cold but held the bread close to me as if it were a shield.

I looked around and saw a house that was as big as the group home and I felt my mouth fall open.

"Where are we?"

"My home." Abby had come around the car and stood beside me as she looked up at the building. "I only moved in last month, so I am still getting used to the size of it. I needed more privacy and this place has it." I turned around and saw that there were trees all around the property and I could just make out the sounds of the road. It was as if they were in the middle of the countryside with no-one around for miles. I could see a glimpse of the gates closing at the bottom of the driveway.

"Come one. Let's get you inside and warmed up." She took my arm as I was still trying to process the surroundings. We walked up to the front which opened before we even got there.

"Evening Miss Abby. You're back early."

"I had to pick up my niece. Cat, this is Lydia, the housekeeper." I took in the other woman who didn't look old enough to be a housekeeper. I had always imagined them to be old, spinster types who had no family. As we walked into the house, I tried to make myself smaller. I tried to hang back, but Abby was having none of it. The man who had driven us home came in behind us with the bags of food.

"I'll take these through to the kitchen." I kept my eyes downwards and tried to walk backwards. This was not the same Abby that I had known from years ago. This was a stranger who lived in another circle to me. I couldn't allow her to pull herself down to my level.

I was nearly back out the door when I heard the old voice.

"Cat, come here." I froze not wanting to hope that the owner of the voice was there. I slowly raised my head and in front of me was the old Abby. I could see past the fancy clothes and surroundings and saw the person that I had known all my life. Everything went blurry and it was only then that I knew I was crying again. Abby came forward putting her bag on the table next to the door and took her coat off and wrapped it around me. I breathed in the smell and it felt like home.

Chapter Twenty-four

I don't remember moving from the doorway or making my way up a grand staircase but when I felt myself again, I was in a bedroom that looked homey and comfortable. I was sitting on a bed that had a mountain of pillows on it and it felt like a bed of feathers.

I still had the coat around my shoulders, and I pulled it closer even though I was beginning to feel warm again. I heard voices outside the door, but I couldn't make out what they were saying. The door opened shortly afterwards, and Abby came in dressed in what looked like pyjamas. I kept my gaze away from hers as I didn't want her to know how much this meant to me.

I had felt so alone since John and Julie had died which had caused me to push everyone away except for Selena. She got me and we stuck together. I knew somewhere deep inside that it wasn't right, but I couldn't stop myself. I had to have the feeling of control and that is what I got with her.

I had been feeling sorry for myself and was putting more on me than I had deserved. I had begun to feel that I was destined to be alone my whole life as my biological parents left me when I was young. My foster parents didn't want me anymore and the adoptive ones left me as well. I was better off on my own with no one to rely on but myself.

I don't know when it began to change for me but somewhere it had. The final straw had been seeing Selena die and I had a feeling that it could just have easily been me. I didn't do drugs like Selena, but so many things could have taken their place. I knew I was going to be on the street in a few months and I had no idea how I was going to survive.

I knew I had brought it all on myself, but I couldn't stop myself. I wanted to be the owner of my own destiny regardless of where it took me. I was the only one who had the control, and it was me who decided where I was going. Until now.

Abby came over and sat beside me on the bed but said nothing. She was close enough that I could feel the heat from her body, but she still wasn't touching me. I knew she must be disappointed in me and I didn't know how to tell her that she was right to feel that way. I had let everyone down.

"Why don't you grab a shower and a change of clothes. I'll bring the food up for you coming out." I still couldn't look at her but nodded. As I stood from the bed, I held the coat close to me. "The bathroom is through that door and there will be a change of clothes sitting just outside for when you are finished. Take your time." I walked across the room to the door that she meant and opened it. I switched on the light and had to close my eyes against the brightness of it. When I felt I could open them, I saw a bathroom that had a walk-in shower cubicle, and a huge separate bathtub.

I crossed to the shower and opened the door and switched it on. It was like being in a fancy hotel and I was scared to touch anything else. I knew it was getting warmer as I could see the steam hanging about. I looked around and saw a chair in the corner and went over to it and folded the coat up and put it on it. I then stripped quickly leaving my clothes on the floor and got into the shower.

It was so good to feel the hot water on my body. At the home, the water was barely warm at times so having this much was a pleasure. I could have stayed in there for a long time, but my stomach growled at me again and I made myself switch the water off and wrap a towel around myself.

I crossed to the door again and opened it slowly and saw clothes sitting just outside it. I picked them up and stepped into the main bedroom again. I felt the cold over my body after the heat in the bathroom. I quickly dried off and put the clothes on. I was looking about for somewhere to put the wet towel when the door opened.

"Your dinner miss Catriona." Lydia, the housekeeper came in pushing a trolley that looked as if it had come out of a hotel. She gave me a smile and then backed out the room. I looked at the food as if it were going to attack me then I took a step closer. I had just reached out to lift one of the covers when the door opened again, and I jumped backwards as if I had been caught stealing something. It was only Abby.

"Help yourself. Please." I watched as Abby came closer and pulled a chair up to the food feast. She began lifting all the covers off and putting them on the floor. She said nothing only began to help herself from the plates. I stepped back to the food and began to help myself as well. I looked about for somewhere to sit when Abby gave me her chair.

I sat and began to eat the food. I had taken a few mouthfuls of it before the taste registered. Before I could say anything, Abby did.

"Yes, it's from Franco's." It had been so long since I had been there, but the food was just how I remembered. I gave in and started eating more heartily. I didn't know how long this was going to last but I wanted to take as much as I could. They did feed us at the home, but it was usually only what they could spare. The younger kids got more of the food, which is fine, but it was hard when you were hungry, and you had nothing to eat.

Soon after, I began to feel sleepy and I knew I was struggling to stay awake. I felt the plate being moved from my hands and then I felt myself being pulled up from the floor. I tried to open my eyes, but it was as if they were glued shut. I was moved backwards until I hit something then I fell back onto a soft bed. My brain was just connecting with reality and with one last effort, I was able to open my eyes. I saw Abby leaning over me and tucking me in with tears in her eyes.

"Thank you." I was able to get out. I don't know if she heard or not as the next thing I knew, I was out cold in a deep sleep. When I awoke again, I was disorientated trying to work out where I was and what had happened. It came back in a rush. Selena. Abby. I sat up quickly in bed and felt the room spin a little. As it stopped, I glanced at the time and was taken aback at what the clock said. It couldn't be right.

I pushed the covers back and got out of bed. I crossed to the door and opened it listening for sounds in the house. I heard none. I walked back down the corridor that I had no memory of traveling before and stopped at the top of the stairs. I heard voices below me and I looked down. They were talking too quietly for me to hear what they were saying.

I could see Abby talking with a man, but I couldn't see his face. There was something about him that was familiar, but I couldn't place it. Before I could step back, Abby glanced up and saw me. Her expression was one of happiness. The man went to turn around, but she stopped him. He must have said something, but she shook her head and frowned at him.

I hesitated for a few seconds then began to descend the stairs. I wanted to get a closer look at the man. By the time I reached the bottom of them, he was gone.

"Who was that?" I asked as I stopped in front of her.

"Just a business colleague. Now that sleeping beauty is awake, how about something to eat?" Abby took my arm and began to walk towards the kitchen. She was talking away, but I wasn't really taking it in. As we entered the kitchen, I saw a tv on in the corner and I stopped suddenly when I saw the date.

"Why didn't you wake me?" Abby turned to me.

"I tried to, but you wouldn't wake. I was going to call a doctor if you didn't wake soon. You must have needed the sleep otherwise you would have woken before now."

I still couldn't believe that I had slept for nearly twenty-four hours. I have never slept for so long in all my life.

"Come, you must be starving. Lydia, what can we rustle up for a growing teenager?" I moved towards the large table and sat down in the nearest chair.

"How about blueberry pancakes with maple syrup?"

"Sounds fantastic. Let's get to it. Cat, do you want to help?" I looked at the woman in front of me and knew that she was the one that had been keeping me tethered to the ground. Not my biological parents or adoptive parents. It was this woman here who had been the one constant thing in my whole life.

I didn't know how to repay her, but I was going to work out a way to do just that. I would finish school, get a job and try to be the half the woman that she was. I sat back and watched as Abby worked with Lydia to make pancakes. They were like friends rather than employer and employee. It was a good feeling. The door at the back of the kitchen opened and in came the man that had driven us home. I was a little scared of him, but I had to get over it.

"Cat, I never introduced you the other night. This is Lance, Lydia's husband. He does all the jobs around here that we can't." I looked at the man and saw that he had a kind face and he smiled at me.

"Hello again Miss Catriona." I found myself smiling at him.

"It's Cat. I only get called Catriona when I am in trouble."

"Ok, Miss Cat it is then." I felt as if I had finally come home. I wrapped my arms around myself as if it would stop myself from exploding outwards. I finally felt safe again even though I had never felt in danger.

"Now Miss Cat, do you drive?" I shook my head. "Ok, we'll start lessons when you are feeling more like yourself. How about self-defence? Do you know any?" I shook my head again. "Right. We'll start on a plan so that you know how to take care of yourself if the need ever arises. I hope not but you can never be too careful."

I looked at Abby as she was measuring out the ingredients for the pancakes. "Don't look at me. He's tried to teach me, but I seem to always go the opposite way from what I should. I think he has given up hope on me."

"Never Miss Abby. Maybe with the help of Miss Cat we can get you a little more co-ordinated. You wouldn't want to be shown up by a teenager, would you?"

"No, I wouldn't and that is a challenge that I accept." A thought suddenly burst into my mind.

"Wait, what about Miss Roper? She'll be expecting me back."

"Don't you worry about Miss Roper. I have spoken with her and she is happy for you to remain here until you reach eighteen. It's one less person she needs to be concerned about."

"What about the authorities? They won't let me stay here?"

"You'll be fine. We are keeping the arrangement between us and Roper. The authorities need never know. We can give an excuse if they ask too many questions. It's only for six months anyway. They have enough to deal with, without worrying about a teenager who is about to become a legal adult."

I didn't know what to say to any of them. They were making me feel at home in a place that I had never seen before. It was true what they said. Home was not a place but the people that you surround yourself with. This was going to be my new home.

Chapter Twenty-five

I found myself settling into life at Abby's quite easily. I had to take extra classes so that I could graduate school, but I didn't mind. Lance took to me to and from school whilst Abby drove herself. He had started teaching me to drive on the way home and I was getting the hang of it.

With regards to the self-defence lessons, that was something else. I was struggling with them, but I gave it my all. I don't know where Lance came from, but his knowledge about a lot of things was substantial and the way he taught was easy to pick up things except defending myself.

I didn't feel as bad since Abby was having the same problems as me in trying to get the hang of it. The two of us persevered with it and eventually, it seemed to click with me. I don't recall what happened, but everything seemed to fall into place.

The day before my graduation, I had made my mind up as to what I wanted to do. I had been too late in applying for college, but I wasn't interested in that. I wanted to be out in the world living life not stuck in a classroom. I hadn't told Abby yet and I was going to tonight.

I put on my comfiest clothes and headed downstairs. We were going out for dinner tomorrow night, but tonight was a night for staying eating things that were bad for you and watching movies. I headed into the kitchen and found the popcorn, chips and dips sitting on the counter. I snagged one of the chips and dipped it in the sour cream and ate it. I went to the fridge to see what there was to drink when I heard Abby's voice.

I turned around to see her coming into the kitchen whilst talking on the phone. She seemed upset about something. She hung up quickly when she saw me.

"Is everything alright?"

"Everything's fine. I was just sorting out a problem at work. I want to ensure that I can spend the day with you tomorrow without any interruptions."

"Don't you have an assistant to help you?" Abby froze as I spoke.

"I used to. He left a couple of years ago and I decided that I was better off on my own. I could get things done quicker."

"Oh, ok." I told my insides to calm down there was nothing there for them to get excited about. He wouldn't remember me anyway.

"Now, what order do you want to watch the movies?" Abby came closer and lifted two of the bowls from the counter and headed back into the living room. I followed with the other two and put them in front of where we would be sitting. "What would you like to drink?" Abby pointed to some bottles on the table. "Wine, beer or soda? You are eighteen now so you can drink."

I was trying to work out why she was trying so hard to hide the fact that she was hurt by her assistant leaving her.

"I shouldn't really as I have to on the ball at the graduation tomorrow, but a glass of wine would be great."

"Then that's what you'll have." I sat down on the sofa and pulled my legs up under myself and watched as Abby opened the wine. When she had poured two glasses, she handed me one of them and lifted the popcorn. "I know beer would be better with the popcorn, but I really prefer drinking wine. I only had beer in the house for M...." she stopped herself before she said his name and I knew that she wanted him back.

"How about this one first?" I nodded not really taking in what movie she had held up. I let her go knowing that she had to get through this. I began to wonder if there was more to their relationship than just boss and assistant. There must have been as she wouldn't still be so touchy about him after all this time. I would need to see what I could find out.

We settled down to watch the movie and I began to work out how I could find out more about Michael and not just for Abby's benefit.

I awoke the next morning with a headache that felt like a jackhammer was going to work on my brain. I shouldn't have drunk that wine. I pulled the covers over my head and hoped that the pounding would stop. No such luck. Another pounding started up and I just slide further into my bed.

The covers were pulled from me and the blinds were wide open letting the glorious sunshine in and making my eyes burn.

"Close the curtains." I mumbled and tried to get the bed clothes back over my head.

"Come one lazy head, it's your graduation day. The end of one part of your life and the beginning of another."

"I really, really hate you just now. How can you be so cheerful this morning? You drank most of the wine."

"I'm used to it. You're not but after a shower, coffee and food, I promise you will be feeling more human again. Come on, up you get." I opened my eyes to slits and could see Abby moving about my room getting things out. She disappeared into the bathroom and I heard the shower being switched on.

I knew I couldn't stay here all day even though I wanted to. It was my big day and I wanted to show the others at school that it can be done.

"Come on. I'll meet you in the kitchen when you are dressed." Abby left like a whirlwind and I was reeling from her going about my room. I knew that if I didn't get up, she would be back with reinforcements in the shape of Lydia and then the big guns of Lance if I wasn't up in half an hour.

I smiled to myself thinking back over the last few months at the change in my life. Some people have more to get through than others and I feel that I've had my fair share. It was time for someone else to get kicked when they were down. I was standing up and climbing away from all that had gone before this day.

I dragged myself into the bathroom and when the humidity hit me, I began to relax my body that I hadn't known was tense. One thing I was glad about, was that I didn't feel sick. A headache this bad I could deal with but throwing up over and over no thanks.

I stripped off my pyjamas and got into the shower. The hot water seemed to revive me a little and made the jackhammer sound a little quieter. By the time I had washed myself and my hair, I was feeling almost normal again.

As I wrapped a towel around me, I went to the sink and wiped the condensation from the mirror and looked at myself. I had bags under eyes which were a little bloodshot. I could only guess if I was still legally drunk. I was going to have to be inventive with my makeup today.

After I had brushed my teeth and dried my hair, I went back into the bedroom to get dressed. I saw a godsend on the bedside table in the form of a glass of water and two painkillers. I took them and sat on the bed for them to kick in.

Soon enough, I felt the numbness come with them working. I stood again and crossed to where my dress was hanging. It was the most expensive thing I had ever owned, and I was nervous about wearing it. The shoes were high heels that I wasn't used to, and the underwear was little scraps of lace that I thought wouldn't hold anything in.

I pulled the towel off and put everything on. I was struggling to get the zip up at the back when I heard my door open.

"Can you help me with this zip? I'm not able to bend my arm enough to get it all the way up." I was standing with my back to the door and when no-one was forth coming, I turned around to see Abby standing looking like a proud mother.

"What is it? Have I ripped it?"

"No. You look beautiful. So, like your mother." I froze when she said that. I had no memories of my biological parents and I was envious of the fact that Abby had known them, but I hadn't had the chance to. "Here allow me."

She came over to where I was standing and turned me about and pulled up the zip. She looked at me over my shoulder in the mirror and it was giving me a freaky feeling the way she was looking at me.

"What were they like? My parents?"

"Your mother was beautiful just like you are. She was kind, considerate and always looking out for others. Being a doctor, she helped others when they needed it. She helped me out a few times as well with my mother. Your father was a scientist and ran his own department. I never could understand exactly what he did, so he gave up trying to get me to understand. One thing I can say with one hundred percent certainty was that they loved you. They would never have left you if they had a choice. They would be proud to see all grown up and graduating high school. They would have been beside you all the way. As they aren't here for you today, I want to give you this."

I looked down and saw a box sitting on my dresser that I hadn't noticed before now.

"What is it?"

"Open it and see." I reached out with shaky hands to open the box that I couldn't think what would be in it. I glanced back up to Abby in the mirror, but she was standing strong behind me. Her hands were on my shoulders as if she were grounding me.

I opened the box slowly and when I saw what was inside, my breath caught. Inside the box was a locket and photo frame. In the frame, was a picture of a young couple with a baby looking at the camera with huge smiles on their faces. I knew who they were instantly as the woman was like as if I was looking in a mirror.

"How…?"

"I took that photo the summer before they died. It was one of your mother's favourites. I wanted to give it to you before now, but it never seemed to be the right time. Now I know I was waiting for this day to give it to you."

I could feel the tears as I looked down at the happy family. I put the frame back down and lifted the locket. It was engraved on the back with initials that I knew were my parents and mine. Inside, was a picture of both my mother and father on either side so that I could carry them with me wherever I went.

I turned and hugged Abby fiercely. She held on to me as well as if neither of us wanted to let go. I pulled back slightly and looked at her. She was crying as well, and I had a feeling that this day was going to be filled with tears but happy ones rather than sad.

"Right, we need to get a move on, or we will be late. Now, would you like a hand with your makeup?" I didn't know what to say so I nodded. I was turned back around and sat down on the stool as Abby got to work pulling out my stuff to hide the bags under my eyes and hopefully hid the bloodshot in my eyes. Although how she was going to do that, I had no idea.

"Could you put it on for me?"

"Of course." She took the locket from my hands, closed it over and draped it around my neck and fastened it. "They will always be with you now. No matter what."

Chapter Twenty-six

By the time we got downstairs, we had little time to spare if we were going to make it on time. Lydia and Lance were waiting for us and I went over and hugged each of them. They both had tears as well as being proud looking.

"Come on, we need to go. Your coffees are in the travel mugs. You can drink it on the way." We grabbed the mugs and headed out to the front of the house. Sitting there was a limousine and I stopped suddenly when I saw it.

"What's this for?"

"It's your big day and you are going in style. Allow me ladies." Lance opened the back door and we climbed in. It was huge inside and there was a holder for coffees. I was speechless at what they had organised. I knew we were going to dinner tonight, but I didn't expect this.

I sat in the back of the limo and held onto the locket hard. I never wanted to let it go but I knew I had to. Before long we were pulling up to a high school and I could tell that people were staring at the car. Not many turned up in a limo to a school graduation. I was suddenly nervous. I had kept to myself at school and no-one knew that I was staying with Abby. She had climbed the ladder in the corporate world and now owned her own marketing business that was the best one around. I hadn't wanted people to think that just because I had someone like her behind me, that I was entitled to a free pass in things. If anything, it made me want to prove to her and others that I could stand on my own two feet and fight for myself.

After all that had happened, I felt as if I were finally turning a corner that I had thought was so out of reach that I would never get there. I was wrong. Here I was on my graduation day, taking a step forward into the adult world on my own terms and under my own steam. Yes, I had people behind me to hold me up if I needed it, but I was determined to do it on my own. I slide to the edge of the seat and stepped outside and looked around. I could see people staring and I also noticed when they saw who it was. The disbelief on their faces was something that I would remember for a long time. I had gotten where I was today through my own hard work. Yes, there had been help at the beginning but after that, it had all been me. I stepped forward and allowed Abby to exit behind me. Lance closed the door behind her and smiled at us both. I could tell that he wanted to give me a hug, but it wouldn't do.

We stepped forward and Abby put her arm through mine, and we headed into the school. We signed in at the desk and were told where we were sitting. I stopped suddenly and turned to Abby.

"My robe..." She was holding out my graduating robes in front me.

"I had Lance put them in the car for us as I had a feeling you would forget all about them. Come on, let's go find where I'm sitting. I want to make sure I have a bird's eye view of the ceremony." I put the robe on with help then we headed into the gym where the ceremony would be held. It was bustling with all those who were leaving the school that day and never coming back. There was shouting and laughing. I could see tears on the faces of the parents who were proud that their kids had finally made it to this day.

I gave Abby a hug and headed to where my seat was for the ceremony. As I sat down, I took hold of my locket and found myself wishing that they were here with me today.

"Cat, I didn't think you were going to make it." I turned to the voice and saw my one and only friend that had stuck by me just like Abby.

"Michelle." I stood and was soon enveloped in a hug that took my breath away. "I am so sorry about the way I have cut you off."

"Don't be. You have been going through a hard time and you were entitled to let off some steam. I can't say it didn't hurt. It did. But I am glad you are back on the straight and narrow. I have missed you."

"I didn't think I would graduate. But I'm glad I did. I don't want to lose our friendship." I was an emotional wreck talking with Michelle. I had so many feelings going through me that I didn't know what to focus on first. "Where are you sitting?"

"Right behind you." I turned and saw her name on the chair directly behind me.

"Are your parents here?"

"Yeah. They're over there with my little brother who had to come." Michelle rolled her eyes and I smiled at that. Even though she put on a show of not liking her little brother and always going on about how annoying he was, she would never treat him the way I had treated her. "Is there anyone from the home here with you?

"No, but my Aunt Abby is."

"She's here!" I nodded.

"I have been staying with her these last few months."

"She must be happy to have you home." I smiled at that thinking she was right. Abby was happy to have me home. I looked past Michelle and saw Abby staring over at me. She smiled and nodded at me as I stood next to my friend.

"We are all going out tonight to celebrate. Come with us."

"I can't. I'm going out with Abby. I don't want to let her down."

"Ok, but we are going out this weekend. No excuses. I want my friend back." Michelle climbed over the chair and sat where she had been told. I sat down again and for the first time in a long while, I felt happy again.

I was running on a high by the time the ceremony was finished. They had told us what to expect at it, but I never really thought about it. It was so long for such a simple thing. I knew that it was a milestone in our lives, but I just wanted it over with. I had looked at Abby when it had been my turn to collect my diploma. She was sitting clapping along with everyone else and I could see the tears on her face.

As soon as I we were dismissed, I pushed my way through the crowd to find her. I knew I had a silly grin on my face, but I couldn't stop it. I ran to her when I saw her.

"I did it. I finally did it."

"Yes, you did." I threw my arms around her and hugged her tight. I stepped back but didn't let her go just yet.

"I wish Lydia and Lance could be here as well. They have helped me get here as well."

"Of course, we're here, we wouldn't have missed it for the world." I turned around and saw them standing behind me. I let go of Abby and hugged both. "I thought the school wouldn't let you come."

"They didn't want us to come as we were not family but that wouldn't stop us. You have worked hard to get here, and nothing would keep us away. Let them try and kick us out and you will see what happens." I felt my face hurting from all the smiling that I was doing but I couldn't stop myself. I was happy and I was going to keep this feeling for as long as I could.

I saw Michelle with her family behind them and I waved to her. She started to come over with her family. Lance moved to the side of Abby and stood behind them slightly and I saw his eyes scanning those coming closer to them. When they stopped in front of them, I hugged Michelle and turned to introduce them to my family.

"Aunt Abby, you remember Michelle?"

"Yes, I do. It's good to see you again. Congratulations on graduating top of the class."

"Thanks Miss McIntosh. It's good to see you again."

"This is Lydia and Lance, they are family."

"It's nice to meet you both. This is my parents Sofia and Miguel, and that little squirt is Javier, my little brother."

"I'm not a little squirt. I'm ten years old." Michelle laughed and her parents held out their hands to my family.

"We are going out to celebrate tonight, please join us." Abby asked them.

"That is a generous offer, but we have a family celebration to go to. All Michelle's cousins are coming over as it is a double celebration as her grandmother turns ninety today as well."

"Ok. Please give her my warmest wishes on this big day. We need to leave soon Cat if we are to make it on time."

"Ok. I'll just say goodbye and I'll catch up with you." I watched as Abby, Lance and Lydia walked away from me and towards the limo that was waiting for us all.

"I am so happy for you. Having her back in your life has changed you." I turned back to Michelle to find that we were alone and that her family had moved away as well. "What are you going to do now? College?"

"No. I'm going to find a job. I'm not going to sit in a classroom for another four years learning theory when I could be out learning on the job. I've not told Aunt Abby yet and I don't know how she will take it."

"I'm sure she will be fine. She will be behind you helping you get to where you want to be. She doesn't seem the type to sit back and let you fail. For someone who owns one of the most successful marketing firms in the country, she didn't get to where she is by sitting back."

"I don't want her to pave the way for me. I want to do it on my own, under my own terms. I want to prove to her that I have changed, and I can forge my own way in life without relying on others to bail me out when I fail.

"I think she will be that person. She will be what you need her to be and nothing else. Listen, I need to go or else I will get an earful from my abuela when I get there. She may be ninety, but she acts as if she is fifty years younger." Michelle gave me a hug then pulled back. "I'll call you tomorrow and we can go out this weekend. Is your number still the same?"

I nodded then she went back to her family. I turned and headed to where Abby was waiting beside the limo. They hadn't told me where we were going yet, and I was a little nervous about it. I had planned on telling her that I wasn't going to college tonight but as I didn't know where we were going, I didn't want to cause a scene.

I didn't think she would be too upset with me, but I was still getting to know this new Abby. As I walked towards them, I heard my name being called and I turned to wave at some students who had been in the same class as me. Everyone seemed to be different today. It was the end on an era and things were never going to be the same again.

"Ok. Where are we going?" I stopped in front of them and waited for them to speak. "I know we are going out for dinner, but it is mid-afternoon, and we have plenty of time until dinner."

"We don't. We have an hour to get to the airport and we should make it on time."

"Airport? Where are we going?" I was moved into the limo and Abby and Lydia got in beside me. Lance got in the front and drove away from school. "Aunt Abby, where are we going?"

Chapter Twenty-seven

They still hadn't told me where we were going even after we had taken off. I had known that Abby had money just by the house she had moved into. Not to mention having Lance and Lydia working for her. Not just everyone could afford that. But when we drew up to the airport and was directed through to the where the private planes were sitting, I knew then that she was wealthier than I had ever imagined.

We were escorted from the limo to the plane and I was trying to take it all in. As I stepped up into the plane, I stopped as Abby made herself at home.

"Sit down. Would you like something to drink?" I moved as if I was in a daze trying to take in the wealth that she had.

"Is this yours?"

"Yes. It's easier having your own plane than flying commercial when you need to go places quickly."

"We'll be leaving in ten minutes Abby." I turned to find Lance leaning out of the cockpit.

"Cat sit down, and we'll talk. We have about an hour's flight." I moved and dropped into the first seat I came to. My mind was struggling to take in where I was and what I was living in now. Lydia came forward and put down two drinks for us both then disappeared to the back of the plane and left us alone.

I felt the plane begin to move and I fastened the seat belt across my lap and took a drink. I choked a little as I didn't know what it was, but I drank more of it. I felt it go through my body making me feel relaxed despite being tense about the situation I was in.

"When I formed my company, I never imagined that it would be as successful as it has been. Yes, I dreamed of it being like this, but I never thought that I would make it. Triple M is something that I have held dear to myself for the last ten years or so. Even when I was thinking of a name, it had to be something that meant something to me. There are very few people who know what the initials stand for and I aim to keep it that. As far as the world knows, my company's name is MM Marketing or Triple M as it is also known. The double M stands for McIntosh Mont-Clair." I stared at her in disbelief as she spoke. I heard what she said but my mind was not really understanding it. Abby sat forward and touched my knee. "I named my company after the people who gave me a chance when I was young and helped me become the person I am today."

"My parents." I whispered.

"Yes, your parents. Stewart and Isla made me feel part of their family and well, their daughter melted my heart the moment I saw her. I couldn't get her out of my mind, and I would do anything to protect her." I reached over and took another drink and held the glass close to me. I knew what she said made sense but finding out the truth is something that I feel is too much for me now. I felt the tears begin to fall and Abby reached over to hug me. I wanted to hold on and never let go but I was an adult now. I had to stand on my own two feet. I pulled away from her and undid my seat belt.

"Is there somewhere I can freshen up?"

"The bathroom is back there." I stood and walked to the back of the plane. I pulled back a curtain I hadn't noticed and found Lydia sitting there. She pulled headphones from her ears.

"Are you ok?"

"Bathroom?" Lydia pointed just behind her and I walked past her. I closed the door behind me and closed my eyes. I let the tears fall as I felt as if a piece of me was missing. I grabbed the locket and held on tightly as I felt the loss of my parents all over again. I sobbed as quietly as I could and wrapped my arm around myself as I held onto to my parents.

I lost track of time and it wasn't until someone knocked on the door that I realised how long I had been in there.

"Are you okay Cat?"

"I'm fine. I'll be out just now." I moved to the mirror and looked at myself. I was a mess. My makeup was smudged, and I felt undone. My little bag didn't carry much make up and I looked around the bathroom and stopped when I saw a stocked makeup shelf. Abby really had thought of everything. I used what I could to repair the damage then headed back out. Lydia was sitting in the chair I had been and stood when she saw me coming.

"We'll be landing in about fifteen minutes. You'd best buckle up." I sat down and fastened the seat belt again.

"Are we ok Cat?" I looked at her sorting out my emotions as best as I could.

"We're fine. Now where are we going?" My voice didn't sound as strong as I thought but I could do nothing about it.

"You'll find out when we get off. It won't be long now." I turned and looked out the window. I could see a city below us, and I tried to make out where we were. We hadn't been flying long so there were only a few places that we could get to. I watched as the plane banked and then began to drop in earnest. We were about to land. The plane touched down without so much as a bump and I felt the brakes as it slowed the plane down.

Once we had slowed enough, I looked through the small window still trying to work out where we were. As the plane turned towards a hanger and a waiting limo, I knew where we were. I turned to Abby with disbelief on my face. She stood as Lydia came from the back and stood at the door until we had come to a complete stop. I heard movement outside then the door was unlocked and opened. The hot air came inside as I stood. Lance was standing outside the cockpit as I got to the door.

"Have fun tonight Miss Cat. We'll be here when you are ready to go home." He wrapped his arms around me then let me go. Abby was already down the stairs and waiting on me outside.

"Are you not coming with us?"

"No, we have other plans tonight." He wrapped an arm around his wife and smiled down at her. "We will be here to take you home when you are ready to leave. Go on now, Abby is waiting on you." I hugged them both then stepped down the stairs carefully. I felt the excitement building in me at the thought of where we were going.

"Are we really going there?"

"Yes, we are. We have half an hour to get there before we will be late now let's get going." Abby put her arm through mine and began walking to the limo. The chauffer was waiting with the door open and we slid in the back. The door closed and soon after, we were moving away from runway. There was a bottle of champagne in the back and two glasses. I watched as Abby opened this and poured a glass each and handed me one.

"Here is to the rest of your life. To whatever you want to do in life I will be there to help you if you need it." We clinked glasses and drank.

"Aunt Abby, I'm not going to college. I want to work."

"Ok. What do you want to do?"

"Well, I was wondering if you had any vacancies in triple M?" I was nervous as saying that as I wanted to work in her company so much.

"I don't have any vacancies in my department, but I think there may be something in the mailroom."

"That's fine. I'll start there. I don't want to jump ahead of others who deserve to be working there before me. I want to be able to make it on my own. I don't want anyone to know that I am living with you. I don't want them to think that I am there just because I am staying with you." I could see the hurt cross her face, but this was the only way that I could do this. I had to prove to her and everyone else, that I can do this on my own merit.

"Ok. I'll make some calls and see what there is available. Now, let's drink as we have a long night ahead of us."

We drove for about half an hour or so before we pulled up outside a restaurant that I had always wanted to visit but it was so far out my price range it was in the atmosphere. Holly Malone's is the best place in the country and with a waiting list a mile long to get in. I ask Abby how she got a table, but she remained silent and kept it to herself.

The décor was something I had never imagined seeing. Chandeliers hung from the ceilings, tasteful gold furnishings throughout. The tables were covered with the softest material I had ever felt. I took one look at the volume of cutlery and nearly passed out. How can you use all that for one meal?

The head waiter seated us when he saw us entering and I felt everyone staring as we walked through wondering who we were. Yes, it was mainly rich and famous people, but still, seeing the head tend to customers was something.

Dishes were put in front of me that I couldn't pronounce but I ate them and had a wonderful time. When we were finished, I didn't want to leave but Abby insisted. We headed back into the limo and I couldn't keep the smile from my face. We pulled up an alley way and stopped outside a door. Before we could get out, the door opened, and a bouncer stood there.

We walked past, him and I was wondering where we were going. I didn't even know where we were. We stopped at another door which was opened after the bouncer spoke into a comms device. Abby stood back to let me go first. My eyes couldn't understand what they were seeing at first them they widened in disbelief when they did. I turned to look back at Abby and could see that she was happy.

I walker further into the room where there must have been about a hundred people partying but what caught my attention, was the person on stage. My favourite artist was performing. When he had finished the song, he caught sight of us and came down from the stage to greet us. My stomach was in knots that I was going to meet him.

I stood quietly as he greeted Abby.

"Miss A, how are you doing?"

"I'm doing fine Jeff. Thank you again for doing this."

"No problem. When a friend of Lance's asks for something, I help. After what he did, I owe him. Where is he?" I watched as they spoken hoping that he would and wouldn't see me.

"He and Lydia had other plans tonight. This is my niece Cat that I was telling you about." He turned to me and I felt the butterflies start up again.

"Hello beautiful." He lifted my hand and kissed the back of it. I felt myself blush all over as he did. I couldn't find my voice to respond.

"Don't mind her, she's just in awe of you."

"Well, we need to see what we can do to get her talking." He tucked my hand in his and led me away from Abby. I turned to look at her, but she just shooed me away. "Cat, I'm assuming that is short for something?"

"Yes. Catriona."

"Beautiful name." We had been making our way through the crowd to the bar. "What would you like to drink?"

"Just a water please." He nodded to the barman and two bottles of water were place in front of us. I didn't know what to think. Thoughts were running through my head in all directions and I was trying to make sense of it all. We drank our waters then he pulled me onto the dance floor. I tried to refuse but didn't succeed.

I felt self-conscious out there with all these skinny beautiful women and handsome ripped men. I couldn't stop looking around, but Jeff caught my attention and kept me in the moment. From then on, we spent most of the night on the dance floor and I found out he is really a nice guy. Not like what the papers say.

I looked around for Abby and found her standing at the door on the phone. I made my way to her and I could see that she wasn't happy with whoever was on the other end of the phone. She hung up when she saw me getting close.

"Everything ok?" I asked her. She gave a smile before answering.

"Everything's fine. Are you ready to leave?" I nod and she turned and made her way back the way we came. I followed feeling a little bad for not saying goodnight to Jeff, but I wanted to make sure Abby was ok.

Chapter Twenty-eight

I turned to look at Abby then Rose as they listened to what I was saying. I could see by the expression on Abby's face that she was still hurting over what had happened.

"Was that Michael you were arguing with on the phone that night?" I waited for her to answer.

"Yes. You can probably take that anytime I was arguing with someone whom I didn't tell you who it was it was probably Michael. I didn't agree with not telling you. I wanted to but he wouldn't let me. I knew that whatever I did, I was going upset one of you when I didn't want to upset either of you."

I knew that she had my best interests at heart, but it still hurt that they had both lied for so many years. I was coming to terms with it, but I needed to get this out first before I spoke to Michael in person. The fact that it hurt so much meant that I still loved him.

"What did Lance do for Jeff?" I saw her take a breath before speaking.

"Lance was part of Jeff's security team when he first became a star. They became friends but Jeff wouldn't listen to what he was told. There had been some serious threats against him from maniac fans, but Jeff thought it was all talk, that there was nothing behind them. Lance tried to get him to listen but failed.

"After one of his first big concerts, there were some fans waiting on him at his hotel. Lance had been checking all the threats that had been received and there had been one that had caught his eye. He tried to get him to pull out but failed. As they were exiting the car to go into the hotel, one of the fans opened fire. Lance was able to get Jeff down to the ground, but he had taken two bullets for him."

"It was touch and go whether he would survive or not, but that night changed Jeff and he became the man he is today. He has never been able to repay Lance for saving his life and keeps trying. Lance quit after and took time out to recover. He and Lydia had been trying to start over when I came across them. They started working for me about a couple of years ago and when I moved into the new house, they came with me."

I didn't know what to say. I can vaguely remember something in the news about a shooting but never gave it a second thought. Now everything seems to make more sense.

"How are they?"

"They miss you. They wanted to come to the hospital to see you but didn't want to intrude."

"Did they know about the lies?" I held my breath waiting on her answer. I didn't know if I wanted the answer to be yes or no.

"I didn't tell them, but I have a feeling they would have guessed when Michael stopped coming around. They never said anything just played dumb."

"Ok. Where was I?"

"Your graduation with Jeff." Rose said.

"Right." I began to talk again.

I crashed out on the flight home and felt myself being lifted from the plane and put into a car. I assumed it was Lance as he and Lydia were waiting on us at the plane. When we got home, I as lifted out again and took inside to me bed. I felt so heavy as if there was a tonne weight lying on me.

I was put on my bed and a cover thrown over me. I snuggled down under it a little more and fell into a deep sleep. Just as I was going under again, I thought I felt something brush my face but before I could do anything, I fell fast asleep.

When I woke the next morning or afternoon as it was when I looked at the time, I felt stiff and I raised my hand to my cheek and held it there as if holding something tight to me. I threw off the cover and stood, my body aching with all the dancing I had down last night. I was still in my dress and I struggled to get the zip down. I went into the bathroom and took a shower to waken up.

When I came out, I felt a lot more awake, but my stomach was now growling at me looking for food. I put on my slippers and headed downstairs to see where everyone was. I came down the stairs listening for voices but finding none. I went into the kitchen and found Lydia there baking quietly as Lance sat reading a book.

"Afternoon." I said and they both looked up.

"Did you have a good time last night?" I crossed to the breakfast bar and sat down.

"Yes, it was great. Thank you for arranging it Lance."

"It's no problem Miss Cat. Mr Jeff is a different man to what he was years ago and now will do anything I ask of him. This is the first time I have done so."

"Thank you." I move from the stool and give me a hug and kiss on the cheek. He pats my hand and I move away.

"Would you like some coffee?"

"Yes please." I move to get it, but Lydia stops me and just waits for me to sit down. A few minutes later, I'm drinking my coffee. "Where's aunt Abby?"

"She went out about an hour or so ago saying she has some things to do at the office. She shouldn't be too long until she is back." I nod wondering what I am going to do next.

"Do you want to go for a run?" Lance asked me.

"I'm not very good at running."

"Well, let's see what we can do about that." I look at him uneasy knowing that I am bad at running. He stood up and put his book on the table. "I'll go get changed and meet you back here in ten minutes." He walked away leaving me sitting there watching after him. I turned to Lydia.

"Don't look at me, when he gets an idea in his head, he doesn't let go. Maybe you'll enjoy it. You better get a move on or else he will be back in chasing you." I finish my coffee and head back upstairs. I look at the weather and see that it is fair, so I change into shorts and vest top and dig out my trainers from the wardrobe.

I was back downstairs about fifteen minutes later and saw Lance waiting for me at the front door.

"Ready?"

"As I'll ever be." He opens the door and motions for me to go for first. We walked down the driveway and stopped just before the small gate. We started doing some stretches to warm up before we headed out. Once we were out Lance started at a slow pace, so I was thankful for that.

We must have run for about an hour or so and I was glad to get back. I was feeling the effects of the run and the late night. I could feel myself shaking as we slowed outside the gates and once, we were inside, I wanted to sit down but Lance pulled me up again and took me through some stretches to cool down. Finally, he allowed me to go and it was only when I got to front door, that I noticed Abby's car was back.

I opened the door and shouted. "Aunt Abby, are you there?" I walked through the ground floor to her office as I knew I would most likely find her there. I opened the door and walked in to find her sitting behind her desk finishing up a call. She motioned me to sit down but I didn't want to as I was all sweaty from my run. She hung a few minutes later.

"I see Lance had you out running. He keeps trying to get me to go but I refuse. How was it?"

"Better than I thought it would be. I enjoyed it. I'll never be a professional athlete, but I might do go again." She smiled at me.

"Why don't you go and get showered. I have something to tell you." I watch her trying to guess what she has to say. I feel a shiver and know that I am cooling down too much after my run. "I'll get you in the kitchen."

I nodded and headed upstairs to get showered and changed. When I came back down, Abby was sitting alone in the kitchen and I could smell the baking that Lydia had been doing. I went around to see what she had been making and could feel my mouth watering. Lemon drizzle cake, cupcakes which I know will not just be plain and a mixture of scones.

I look at Abby waiting to see what she is going to say. I grab myself a drink from the fridge motioning to her if she wants one, but she shakes her head.

"I've spoken with Frank Somerston and he says you can start a week on Monday at 8am." I looked at her blankly not knowing who she was talking about. "Frank is the mailroom manager and he is giving you a chance to prove yourself." I felt the smile on my face at the thought of getting my first job. Ok, I had help with this one, but from here on out, I was going to prove to him and her that I can do this on my own.

"Does he know our relationship?" I ask.

"Yes, but I've told him, and he knows to keep if quiet. It will only be the three of us who know the truth." I could tell that she was a little hurt by me wanting to keep it a secret, but I know how some people can be and I don't want to add anything else to her. I want to prove that I can do this on my own.

"Now, how about we cut up this cake?" I nod and move to get a knife. I cut a couple of slices but before I can sit down, Lydia is back.

"Are you cutting my cake?" I smile at her trying to hide the knife. "Why didn't you tell me. I want a piece as well."

"Did someone say cake?" Lance came in behind her. I smiled as I held the knife up over the plate. "Make sure mine is the biggest piece please." We laugh as it is one of Lance's weaknesses. He can never resist lemon cake when it is about.

The next week flies by as I am making the most of the last days of freedom before I start working. I spent some time catching up with Michelle and we fell back into our old routine as if we had never been apart. The day before I look at my wardrobe trying to decide what to wear. I want to make an impression, but I don't really know what the job entails so I don't want to be too dressy.

I pull out a pair of navy trousers that I haven't worn yet and lay them on the bed. I check the dresser looking for a top to go with them. I search through and find a cream top with capped sleeves that will go well with them.

I then go through looking at shoes. I don't want to wear heels as I could be on my feet all day and don't want them to hurt. I find a pair or soft leather boots that have a small block heel that will be perfect. Dressy but practical and comfortable. I'm sorted for the next morning. I head downstairs for dinner and can smell the food before I enter the kitchen.

"Mmmm, something smells good. What's cooking?" Lydia looks up from the veg that she is chopping.

"Roast chicken with thyme, roast potatoes and veg. For dessert we have lemon cheesecake." What she had said was my favourite dinner.

"What's the special occasion?"

"To celebrate you starting your new job tomorrow. I would have done it tomorrow, but I don't know if you will be up to it when you get home." Abby said as she came in. "We need to leave early to make sure you are there on time. If you are ready for quarter to seven, we should have enough time." I opened my mouth to say something, but she held up her hand to stop me before continuing.

"We are going to drop you at the train station a few stops, away so that you can travel in just like everyone else. I want to make sure you get an early enough train to be on time." I feel the tears gathering in my eyes, but I push them back at her thoughtfulness. Not many people would do that.

"Now don't just stand there, help me set the table." I move from where I was to pulling out plates and cutlery to set the table.

Rose spoke bringing me out my memories.

"Why don't we take a break just now?" I nod and take a few deep breaths. Each day I talk about what has happened, the weight on my shoulders gets a little lighter. Many one day it will be away completely. I stand and head to the kitchen to make coffee. When I return, Rose is talking with Abby, but they stop quickly when I enter.

"What is it?" I ask. Rose wouldn't look me in the eyes and Abby looked unsure about what to do. "Abby, what is it now?"

Chapter Twenty-nine

I wait holding, the tray with the coffee and biscuits waiting for her to speak. I moved slowly and put it on the table waiting for her to speak again.

"Rose, what's going on?" My gaze moves between them both wondering who is going to speak first. It was Abby.

"You weren't alone." My eyebrows draw down trying to work out what she means. "That first day you went to work on your own, you weren't on your own. I had someone watching you."

"Why?"

"I wanted to make sure you were ok. It was a big step for you and even though I knew you could handle it, I wanted someone close by just in case you faltered somehow."

"How long were they watching me?"

"The first week then I called them off as I knew you were doing fine and would be ok." I didn't know what to say to her. I felt as if she thought I couldn't do it and I will admit there were a couple of times that I didn't think I could but I got past them and came out on the other side stronger. I thought back to those who worked around me at that time.

"It was Jeremy, wasn't it?" I waited for an answer. She nodded. Jeremy was someone who also working in the mailroom but gave most people the creeps. There was nothing wrong with him just that he was the typical geek.

I sat down and lifted my coffee to drink. I began to wonder how many other secrets she may have bene keeping from me.

"Was it only him?" I could tell from her expression that it wasn't. "Who else?"

"Simone." Simone had befriended me the first day I walked in. She had only started a few months before me so was still finding her feet.

"Why don't you pick up from where you stopped now that you know this." I nod and began talking again.

I was trying to keep myself calm as I walked from the train station to the office where I would be working. It was only a ten-minute walk and I arrived at Mackenzie Tower at quarter to eight. I walked in and headed to the reception desk where the security guard was on.

"I have an appointment with Frank Somerston." I wait as he checks the computer before handing me a visitor's pass.

"If you want to take a seat, I'll let him know you are here." I move away but I'm too full of nerves to sit so I wander around the reception area looking at the artwork on the walls. I didn't need to wait long as an older man came out from the bank of lifts and came towards me.

"Catriona Mont-Clair?" I nod. "I'm Frank Somerston." He holds his hand out to me and I shake it confidently. "If you come this way,"

I follow him back the way he came passed the lifts and into a corridor at the other side. We took a few turns and went through a few doors that I was completely lost. I never realised how big this place was.

We walked into a large room that had many desks and shelving units set up everywhere. We walked past them all to a small office at the back. Frank gesture for me to sit and I did as he closed the door and went round to the other side of the desk.

"Miss Mont-Clair, I don't appreciate being told to hire people just because of who they know. I am doing this reluctantly as I don't believe an eighteen-year-old can handle the workload that we have here."

"I don't understand, I thought there was a vacancy here?"

"There was but it was filled a few weeks ago." I sat there feeling defeated as he didn't want me there and that Aunt Abby had forced him into taking me on.

"I don't want any charity so if there is no position, then I'll leave." I stood to go even thought I had no idea how to get back to the exit.

"Sit down Miss Mont-Clair." He waited until I had sat again before continuing. "I am willing to give you a chance as we always have more work than we can handle. The youngest person here is twenty-eight so having you here may make some people feel as if they are babysitting."

"They won't be. I'll work hard and you won't regret hiring me." Frank looks at me and I feel his gaze. I know he is trying to work out if I will succeed or not.

"Miss McIntosh said that you don't want anyone to know of your relationship?" I nod my head. "That's for the best. Some people may not take too kindly to know who you are related to." He stood and I stood as well.

"Let's get you orientated so that you know where everything is." He opened the door and I walked through taking in what he said. I didn't notice that there were now other people around.

"Simone." A tall blond came towards us. She looked like she had just stepped out from the cheerleading squad.

"Yes Mr Somerston."

"This is Catriona who is starting here today. Show her where everything is and get her a permanent pass."

"Yes sir." She turned to me. "Hi, let's get you a locker." Before I could say anything, I was following her through the room to a door at the back that I hadn't noticed before. She opened it and I saw a small kitchenette, some tables and a wall full of lockers. Simone headed to the lockers looking them over.

"Here's an empty one. You can put your stuff in here. Just remember to keep the key on you at all times." I walked over to her and took my bag off and put it inside the locker then hung my jacket up on a hook inside it as well.

"We are all friendly here except Jeremy. He gives everyone the creeps, but he wouldn't harm anyone. Just keep away from him and you'll be fine. He's not in today so you will need to wait until tomorrow to meet him. He'll probably stare at you as you are new and gorgeous, but he won't do anything." The door opened behind us and I turned to see who it was.

"That's Graeme, John, Loretta and Simpson." They each nodded their heads when she said their names. I hoped I could remember them later. "Guys, this is Catriona."

"Just Cat please." Simone smiled.

"Ok this is Cat she's just starting." I smiled at each of them as they came to the lockers and put their things in them.

"How old are you?" Loretta asked.

"Eighteen." She slammed her locker and walked out leaving the others standing. "What did I say?"

"She jealous cause you are young and beautiful and will have all the men lusting after you rather than her." I blushed as Graeme spoke.

"I'm not interested in anyone. I just want to work."

"She'll get the message eventually just hang in there." Graeme walked away with John following him. I turned to Simone with a questioning look.

"Loretta things every male should worship at her feet. Until you came along, she could have her pick of any of the men. She thinks you are going to steal them away from her. Do you have a boyfriend?" I blush again as the first thing in my mind was Michael.

"What's his name?"

"I don't have a boyfriend."

"Well there's someone who made you blush like that and if he doesn't notice you then he must be blind. Come on, we need to get a move on otherwise Somerston will be on our backs." At the mention of his name again, I stand straighter knowing that he doesn't want me here, so I need to prove him wrong.

The rest of the day goes by in a whirl and before I know it, it is finishing time. I've never had a day go by so quick. Through the day, I could see Frank watching me to see if I were up to muster and I was going to prove him wrong.

After Simone showed me around in the morning, I began to fill in the HR forms in the afternoon and getting my picture taken for my ID which should be ready in the morning. I waved goodbye to Simone at the doors and headed down to the station to get the train.

As I got to the entrance, a car pulled up beside me, but I was so exhausted that I didn't register it at first until someone was standing in front of me. I bumped into them.

"Sorry." I went to move around them when I felt them grab my arm and my instincts seem to kick in. I moved as Lance had taught me, but it wasn't enough. I found myself with my back to the man and his arm around my throat. I felt the panic build in me before I heard a voice breaking through.

"Miss Cat, Cat. It's me Lance." I felt myself sag at recognising his voice. He let me go and I turned to see him. I must have caught him in the face as it was turning red.

"Sorry, I didn't see you and I reacted on instinct." He smiled at me.

"Good, that's the point of the training."

"What are you doing here?"

"I thought you may want a ride home after your first day."

"Thank you. I'm sorry about your face." He put his arm around me and ushered me into the car.

"Don't worry about it. I've had a lot worse. I'm only glad that you remember what to do even in your current state." I looked at him puzzled. He motioned to the side mirror and when I saw myself, I can understand what he was meaning. I looked drained and ready to fall over from just one day of work.

"All I want to do is go home, shower and go to bed."

"You need to eat something."

"I don't think I have the energy for that." He smiled and put me in the car. I must have dozed off for the next thing I knew, we were pulling up to the house. I dragged myself out the car and into the house. I made my way to my bedroom as all I could think of was showering and getting the sweat washed off.

I felt marginally better after the shower and when I came out the bathroom, there was a tray with food on it. Lydia, I thought to myself. I wonder what Lance told her about his face. I put my pyjamas on and ate the food that was left. When I finished, I put the tray on the dresser and got into bed. I was out cold within a few minutes and I wondered how I was going to do it all again the next day.

"So that's how Lance got the black eye that day. He told me that the car door hit him." I looked at Abby and saw her smiling.

"I don't remember it being that bad."

"It was bad enough to see but not too bad that people would stare. I think Lydia covered it with makeup so that you wouldn't know. He didn't want you to feel sorry for him. I think deep down, he was proud of it knowing that it came from you defending yourself even after the tough day that you had."

"I wish they were here."

"They are but they are letting you have your space. When you are ready, you can call them to come over. They are anxious to see you and the little Jay is missing you." I smile at his name.

Jay was an unexpected arrival for them and since then, they have stepped back in some of their duties. The little boy was two years old and I felt a little sadness at the thought that I was only a little older than him when I lost my parents and I started down this road that I was now on.

Chapter Thirty

I kept away from Jeremy, but he was always there in the background and he did give me the creeps. I don't know what it was about him, but something was just off.

I spent the next few years in the mailroom learning all that there was to learn. After the first week, I think Frank was impressed with me as he always smiled at me when he saw me. Some people thought it was creepy, but I knew different. He was giving his acceptance that despite my age, I could do the work.

I did little except work and sleep. Everyone used to tell me that I needed to get out more, have a life as I was still young, but I didn't really listen. I wanted to prove to them all that I could stand on my own two feet without help anymore.

Just before my twenty first birthday I was stopped on my usual rounds delivering the mail by one of the new consultants. She had only been with us for about six months but had been making waves in her work. I remember Abby talking about her, but I had never really spoke to her except in passing.

I had just dropped her mail off outside her office when I heard my name being called. There weren't many people around as this was the early drop. I glanced around and saw that it had come from her office.

"Yes Miss North?"

"Please come in Cat. I want to talk to you about something." I froze as we never go into offices. We stop at the doors and go no further. I glanced around to see if anyone could see me then stepped in. I moved slowly towards the desk where Miss North sat behind. I took a quick glance around the office and liked what I saw before I brought my gaze back to her.

"I've heard a lot of good things about you."

"You have?"

"Yes. I've heard how the mail room has never been so organized or running as smoothly as it does now." I lower my head as she speaks. I know I made a few changes since I came in, but I never thought they were that outstanding. "I've also heard how you stepped up to run the room when Frank was off ill when no-one else wanted the job." Frank had taken ill last year and had been off for four months. There had been no-one wanting to take on his role so I just kind of fell into it. I loved it.

"I was just doing my job Miss North."

"No, you were doing more than your job. How old are you?" I felt her gaze staring right through me, but I pulled myself up to stand tall.

"I'll be twenty-one next week." I waited for her response, but I couldn't read her face. I knew I was young, but I work hard at whatever I do.

"Do you like working in the mailroom?" I nod before speaking.

"Yes. Every day is a challenge. Most people think it is easy to work in a mail room but there is a lot more to it than just delivering letters. You need to make sure they go to the right person, pick up mail to go out, sort out deliveries that come and organise staff."

"Do you see yourself working there for ever?" I stopped myself from responding straight away. I hadn't thought about it as I loved my job. I knew that it wasn't what I wanted to do but I hadn't yet found where I wanted to be.

"I've got a big project coming up and I need someone who can help me organise things and make them run smoothly." I just stared at her. "I want to offer you the chance to move out of the mail room and do something more." I didn't know what to say. I knew that there was a big project coming up as I'd heard Aunt Abby talking about it, but I didn't know much more than that. She kept things quite close to her about future projects.

"I...I...I don't know." I answered her. I knew that it was going to be out my comfort zone, but I had a feeling that I would be up to the challenge.

"You don't need to make a decision just now. I'll email you the details of the position and salary and you can let me know by the end of the week. If you're not wanting it, I'll need to look for someone elsewhere. I want whoever it is to be in from the ground up so that they know everything."

I nod at her, but my mind is whirling at this chance. Yes, I want it but I don't want to let the others down.

"I'll think about it. Thanks for the offer." She nods at me and goes back to the paperwork on her desk. I turn and walk slowly out the office closing the door behind me. I was glad to reach my trolley as I needed to hold onto something. I finished my rounds and headed back to the hub. When I walked in, Simone was the first person I saw.

"Cat what's wrong?" I looked at her but not really seeing her. I felt myself being moved then sat down and something put into my hand. When I looked, it was a glass of water. I looked up to Simone and saw the concern on her face.

"I've just been offered a job." Her face light up.

"That's fantastic. I knew you wouldn't be her for the long term. Where is it? Who's it working for?"

"Isabella North and I don't know what the position is exactly. She's going to email me the details."

"Well let's go then." She pulled me and headed to my desk to logon to see the details. I didn't think anything would be there just now, but I was wrong. I opened the attachment and began to read knowing that Simone was reading it as well.

"Oh my god!" I could feel the excitement brimming from her, but I felt numb. I had to read it twice before it sunk in. I felt myself shaking my head at what I had read.

"This can't be right."

"It's right ok. You are moving up in the world girl, and you deserve it." She hugged me and I was still trying to take it all in. Before long everyone in the mail room knew about my job offer and told me I would be stupid not to take it. Even Frank told me to go for it. I wanted to go for it, but I began to doubt myself about taking such a different role on from what I had been doing.

I closed it down and tried to take my mind off it all day, but it kept drifting back to it when I saw everyone in their business suits as I did my work.

By the end of the day, I had decided to go for it, but I was going to wait until the morning to give her my acceptance.

When I passed her office the next morning, it was empty, and I asked around to see when she would be back. I was told that it wouldn't be until the end of the week. I felt a little deflated, but I kept going. I would rather tell her face to face that I'll take the job rather than telling her via email If I don't see her by the end of the week, I'll do it that way.

I was working late later that week when I heard someone come in.

"I'll be there in a minute." I finished off what I was doing then went to see who it was. We had a little counter where staff could come and drop of letters and parcels, they wanted to go out quicker than the normal post route. I stopped when I saw Isabella North.

"Evening Cat. How are you?"

"I'm fine Miss North. Working late again?"

"Not late, this is just my normal time." She glanced behind me to see if there were anyone else around. When she saw no-one, her gazed fixed back on me. "Have you made a decision?"

I took a deep breath before I answered her. "Yes, I have." She waited for me to say more. "I'd like to take you up on your offer." She smiled as I spoke as if she had known all along that I would take it.

"Good. I'll speak with HR and get the paperwork sorted out for your transfer. You can start Monday and I'll get you up to speed on where we are now."

"No." I said. She had been going to move away but stopped. "I can't start Monday. I need to work my notice here and make sure they have someone to replace me. I can start in two weeks." My heart is racing as I tell her. Her face tightens a little before relaxing again.

"Ok. Two weeks then you start. I'll be sending you documents to read over to get familiar with the project so that when you start, we can hit the ground running." I nod at her as she walks away. I could feel myself shaking inside as what I am going to be doing.

I move away from the counter and decide that enough is enough and I was going home. I packed up and switched everything off. I knew Lance would be waiting on me as he often did that when I worked late. I really needed to take my driving test so that I could drive myself about. Aunt Abby had bought me a small car of my own which I had been learning in, but I now needed to get this down so that I had a little more freedom. I hadn't been bothered about driving as I liked to take the train but I had a feeling I'd be needing my own transport with this offer.

I walked out switching lights off as I went. When I got to reception, I said good night to Doug then left the building. I started walking towards the station knowing that Lance would be waiting. I kept my head up and walked purposefully as I thought about my new adventure that was coming.

I didn't see him at first as I was lost in thought, until his arm came around my neck and I felt myself being dragged into an alleyway. I let out a scream before a hand covered my mouth and then there was a voice in my ear.

"Keep quite bitch or I'll slit your throat." I felt fear running through me. At first, I thought it was Lance making sure that I knew what to do but I knew it wasn't him. He wouldn't use a knife. Now that it was really happening, my mind went blank. I felt his other hand move down my body grasping my chest and squeezing tight. I let out a whimper.

His hand moved down further as it got closer to my crotch, I felt something awake in me. I stopped struggling and let myself sag. He loosened his grip and that gave me time to elbow him in the gut before I stamped hard on his foot then brought my fist up to his face. I turned on him and kneed him in the groin before stepping back.

I was breathing hard and I just looked at him on the ground groaning. I heard someone call my name, but my eyes were fixed on the man on the ground. I felt a hand on my arm, and I flinched moving away until a face stopped in front of me. It was Lance.

"Cat, Cat are you ok?" I could feel the shakes coming on, but I nodded to him. He stood watching me for a few more seconds before bending down to the man on the ground. I saw him pull out his phone, but I couldn't hear what he was saying. I felt my body shaking more and I suddenly felt so cold. He stood and put his arms around me and moved me away from the guy and to the car which was sitting at the front of the alleyway. He put me inside and turned the heating way up. He sat with me until the police arrived.

"Stay here." He got out and spoke with them telling them what he knew. I knew that I would need to make a statement, but I could hardly talk just now so it would need to wait. I don't know how long I sat there until he came back and said nothing and drove me home.

As we turned into the driveway, both Abby and Lydia were waiting on us. Lance helped me out the car and Abby just put her arms around me and took me upstairs. My brain seemed to kick in again then.

"I need to make a statement."

"I've told them you will be there in the morning." I looked around Abby to Lance who was standing in the doorway. "I'll drive you when you are feeling up to it. We are also going to get your licence so that you won't be walking alone again at night." I just nod knowing I had been thinking the same earlier.

They left me alone to shower and change but they came back, and I couldn't stand their sadness, so I pretended to be asleep and they left. I felt bad about it, but I needed time to process what had happened.

Chapter Thirty-one

I kept my gaze on Rose as I didn't want to see what Abby was thinking but knew that I needed to at some point. I moved it slowly to her and I was right. It was full of sadness and regret and I didn't like it.

"I never knew what really happened that night. Lance wouldn't tell me, and you had shut down."

"I didn't want you to worry or start to smother me just because of what happened. What Lance had been teaching me kicked in and I was able to help myself. Even if I couldn't have, Lance was there soon after so I knew he would have stepped in." I was amazed at myself at talking so plainly about the attack. I knew it hurt Abby not to know what happened, but I didn't want her to. I wanted to deal with it on my own.

I know that it may have been wrong, but so much had happened in my life so far that I wanted one thing that I could control who knew what, and that was it. I saw the tears in her eyes, but I could see that she accepted the reasoning for me doing what I did.

"If you remember, that was when Lance stepped up my training so that I had more knowledge in case anything like that happened again. I also sat my driving test so that I didn't need to walk any more. I know it gave Lance a bit of a comfort and yourself when I did.

"I had all the gadgets in the car so that if anything happened, I had something to hand and could let someone know when I was in trouble. Fortunately, I never needed it, but I felt safer knowing that it was there if I did." I let myself look at Abby and could see the weight on her shoulders and I knew that I had put that there. I wanted to take some of it away from her, but she wouldn't let go. She was what I always thought a mother should be.

"You've certainly been through a lot Cat and I am amazed that you are still standing strong over it." Rose said. "I have reported on many attempted rapes and attacks and the women just seem to pull into themselves not wanting anyone around. I try telling them that it wasn't their fault, that they didn't ask for it to happen to them but some of them don't seem to listen. There are the few that are like you and stand strong and are determined not to let it happen to them again. Some have even gone on to set up support groups for others to help them." I looked at Rose.

"At the time, I wanted to forget about it and get on with my life. I know that may not have been the right thing to do but for me, it was what I needed to do. Thankfully, the guy confessed to the charges and he served jail time. I was only glad that it didn't need to go to court as I don't know if I could have handled that."

"I am so proud of you." I turned to Abby and saw her trying to hold back the emotion. As I did, I caught sight of the time.

"How about some lunch?" Both nodded and I headed into the kitchen to gather myself before looking to see what we had to eat. I checked the fridge to see what I had then I popped back through to see if they would be ok with my suggestion. "How about frittata?" I waited for a response and when I got two nods, I headed back to start preparing.

Soon after both Rose and Abby came through.

"Can I help with something?" Rose asked. I looked at what I had pulled out them gave her over some peppers to chop. I looked at Abby who smiled and I gave her the onions. We all stood quietly chopping when I couldn't stand the quietness, I turned and put the radio on. I just wanted something to cover the quietness.

Both looked up when the music came on and then there were smiles. I looked to see what station it was on and saw that it was an old station. Soon we were singing along to the songs and by the time we sat down to eat, the mood and lifted and we were all smiling. I had forgotten how much fun it was listening to the radio whilst preparing meals.

When we had finished, I really didn't want to go back to what we were doing before but I knew that the sooner we get back to it, the sooner we can be finished and I can then deal with Michael.

We moved back into the living room with our drinks and I waited for Rose to get set up again. I don't know how she is going to put all this together, but we will see.

"Ok, back to moving on." I said.

The next week moved by fast as I was tying up loose ends in my current job. I had a date for my driving test later that month, so I was still on public transport. Lance, Abby and Lydia weren't happy about it, but I was able to talk them into it. They still dropped me off at the station in the morning and I walked to the office when I got off. Even though I never saw him, I knew Lance was there watching me and I felt comfort at him being close by should I need him. I knew it was only going to be for a short while until I passed my test.

My first day working with Isabella North was something that I will never forget. I had to buy some clothes as what I had wasn't smart enough to work beside her. I looked young enough as it was that I didn't want people to think I shouldn't be there.

I appeared at her office at eight sharp my first morning and the nerves were kicking in. I could hear her from outside and she didn't sound happy. I debated about knocking or waiting until she finished so I sat down and waited until she had stopped talking. No-one came out the office so she must have been on the phone.

When it was all quiet for a few minutes, I stood and knocked on the door.

"What?" I hesitate briefly before opening the door and stepping in.

"Miss North, it's Catriona Mont-Clair."

"Yes, I know. You are late. I told you to be here at eight sharp and it is now nearly half past." I stood a little straighter.

"I'm sorry Miss North but I was here on time, but I heard you shouting at someone, so I didn't want to interrupt." Her eyes narrowed at me not believing me. "I didn't know if you had someone in with you or you were on the phone. I assumed the phone when no-one came out."

"You should have knocked and come in. I don't like to be kept waiting."

"Miss North, I would not come in when it sounded as if someone were being fired. I did not want to embarrass both myself and whoever it was. I wanted to give them their privacy." I hadn't realised that I had been moving as I had been talking. I stopped in front of the desk as I finished. She sat back in her hair and smiled.

"I can see I was right to pick you for the job. You have what it takes. I don't like people who cower from me and not tell me the truth. Now let's get started. Joanne should be at nine, so I'll get her to show you where your office is." I nod trying to take in the dramatic swing of her moods. "Do you drink coffee?" I nod as she stands and comes around the desk.

"Good, you will need it to keep up with me. Let's go and I'll show you where the most important machine in this building is the coffee machine." I followed her out the office and down a corridor to the kitchen area. I saw the machine sitting and wondered how the hell you used it.

"It looks more complicated than what it really is. You fill this with water to the max level, switch in on and once it stops flashing, it is ready. You select a pod from the selection available." I watch what she is doing trying to keep track. When she opened the cupboard, there seem to be hundreds of coffees.

"They go in order of strength from one to twelve with twelve being the strongest. I normally take a ten but anything below a nine is too weak for me. What would you like?"

"I don't know. I've never seen as many coffees before." Isabella just laughed.

"Well, how do you like your coffee. Strong, medium, black, with milk, with cream or sugar?" I stuttered trying to say what I wanted.

"Black but not as strong as you like it."

"Ok. Let's start you on this and see where we go from there. You can take a mug from the cupboard if you don't have your own, but I would advise getting your own. Not everyone cleans them all properly." I lift a blue one out and hand it to her. I watch what she does next. "You pull this handle and the drawer pops out. You put the capsule in foil side out and then close it. Once in press this button and away we go." She was doing it as she spoke, and I watched as the coffee poured out.

I could smell the strong coffee smell and it made me feel good. I was looking forward to trying it. It stopped just in time so that the mug didn't overflow. She lifted it and handed it to me.

"What do you think?" I took a small sip hoping I didn't burn my mouth and my eyes opened wide and the taste. "You like that?" I nodded and watched as she sorted her own out. When hers was ready she took a sip. "Ahhh, that's better. I get cranky in the morning if I don't get my coffee. Let's go."

We walked back to her office and when we got there, Joanne was in and setting up for the day.

"Joanne, this is Catriona Mont-Clair. She will be working with me on the Hamble Project." She stood and held out her hand.

"Hi, you used to deliver the mail, didn't you?" I nod. I don't know where my voice is, but I needed to find it soon otherwise everyone would think I was mute.

"Show her where she will be sitting and where everything is on the server. I'll leave you two together and I'll catch up with you later Catriona." Again, I nod. I feel like a nodding dog today. I watch as Isabella goes back into her office and closed the door. I turn to Joanne.

"Well, I see you've found the coffee machine. Give me five minutes 'til I get mine then I will show you where everything is." I sit down in the chair next to the desk and wait until she comes back. I sip away at my coffee wondering what I have let myself in for.

"Ok, let's go." I stand with my mug and follow her. We didn't go far only to an office just down the hall. "This is where you will be working." She opened the door and stood back. I stepped in and my mouth dropped.

"This can't be right." I was only an assistant; I shouldn't have my own office. I was too young to have my own office.

"Yes, it's right. The Hamble project is one of the biggest we have taken on and a lot of it is being kept under wraps until further into it. You need privacy for this, and this is where you will find it. That door leads to the conference room which is in between you and Miss North." I turned to take in what was around me and I saw the door that she was talking about. I never imagined that I would have my own office. I thought I would have desk outside along with everyone else. Joanne kept moving about the room talking to me. I had switched off and I needed her to repeat what was she saying.

"Everything that you may need is here. There is a little fridge for you to use but unfortunately you need to use the same coffee machine as the rest of us." She smiled as she spoke. She seemed nice and upbeat. She looked to be around mid-twenties but then, everyone here was going to be older than me. I moved to the desk and sat down behind it. I ran my hands over it and looked to the laptop that was sitting closed on the top.

"This is your laptop that you need to keep on you at all times. It has good security, so you don't need to worry about someone hacking it. You can either use the laptop screen or you can link it to the monitor. There is also a wireless keyboard and mouse for you to use as well." She came around beside me and opened the laptop and started it up. When the login screen came up, she stepped back.

"If you want to put in your ID, we can then get your password set up. I warn you now, the password guidelines here are strict and it can be hard to come up with one to accept." I typed in my ID and waited for the next screen to come up. Joanne had opened the drawer and pulled out a booklet and put it in front of me. "This is the guidelines for passwords and access to all systems. I have marked up the systems that you will need access to so we can get your requests put in today. It shouldn't take long but, in the meantime, you can read up on where we are with the project so far."

I looked at her as she pulled another larger book from the bottom drawer and put it in front of me. It was thick. I didn't know if I could remember all it.

"Ok, let's try a password." I looked at the screen then at the paper showing the guidelines. I had a think then typed in what I hoped would be acceptable. I hit enter and waited. It liked it and I was up and running.

Chapter Thirty-two

The next couple of years flew passed as I found myself emersed in the project work. I coped better than I thought I would, and I found that I enjoyed it. I was dealing with people from all departments in the company and many people outside. I felt my self-confidence grow immensely and I knew that I could take on anything that was thrown at me.

Isabella, or Bella as she told me to call her, left when the project was completed and tried to take me with her, but I wanted to stay where I was. I had been able to keep under wraps my relationship with Abby and I know that it hurt her, but she could understand my reasoning behind it. Anytime we saw one another in the office, we were professional and sometimes, it was hard to keep the smile from my face as I knew she would be talking to me about it that night.

I didn't know what was going to happen after the project was complete, but I was surprised when Abby called me into her office. I walked up to her secretary trying to calm the butterflies in my stomach. She had never called me up here before. Her secretary called through to her and told me to go in.

I knocked on the door then opened it when someone answered from inside. I heard voices as the door opened and wondered who else was there.

"Miss Mont-Clair, I'm glad you could join us. Please have a seat." I could tell by her face that she knew how I was feeling, and she was loving it. I would be having words with her later.

"Miss McIntosh. What can I do for you?" I stood next to the chair and a man whom I hadn't seen before.

"Catriona, may I all you that?" I nodded. I couldn't very well say no could I. She was the top boss. "This is Scott Jameson head of our ongoing business." I reached my hand out to him and he stood to shake mine. He kept standing until I had sat down. I was puzzled at what was going on.

"Catriona, I've had raving reviews about your work on the Hamble project and I am impressed. For someone so young to have dealt with something so huge and important, it is a credit to your upbringing. Your parents must be proud of you." I felt tears in my eyes but held them back.

"My parents died when I was little."

"Oh, I am so sorry for your loss. If I had known I would never had said. I do hope I haven't upset you?"

"No, it's alright. My adoptive parents raised me, and they would be proud of me." I said no more as I didn't want to get into it in front of a stranger.

"I'm sorry for your loss Miss Mont-Clair." Scott said to me. I turned to look at him and could see a look on his face that told me he had suffered a loss in his life as well.

"Ok, let's move on. The reason I asked you here today Catriona is because there is an opening in Scott's department, and I think you would be ideal to fill the position." I looked at her, but I couldn't tell from her face what she was thinking. I turned to Scott to see what he was going to say.

"I spoke with Isabella before she left, and she couldn't praise you enough for all your hard work. She even said that in a few years' time, you would rival her for her work ethic, and I didn't think that would be possible. Not many people can keep up forty to fifty-hour weeks along with a life outside of here."

"Well, the project involved a lot work that needed to be done and not always possible in the normal working day. I wouldn't want to work like that forever otherwise I would be dead by the time I hit thirty. What is the position you have available?"

"It's helping with the transition of new business to ongoing business. As you know we have teams that specifically deal with new business then it's handed over to us for ongoing work. I want you to be one to oversee these transitions."

"Don't we have someone doing this at the moment?"

"We do but it is put out across a number of different managers and they all have their own way of working. While at times this is okay, I want to be able to put in a more streamlined process so that we are all working in the same way."

"Oh. How many people will be working on this?"

"At the moment only you as it is a new position. Once it is up and running, there will be a team of people dealing with it. This is going to fall into the restructure process that is about to go out. There will be some people who will be upset about it but I am hoping that most will be accepting of it."

I think over what he has said and know that this is a big step for me. I wasn't sure what I was going to do as the project was finished but handling these contracts, that is something completely different.

"May I think about it?"

"Of course. I wouldn't expect you to accept on the spot. I will send you the details for you to review but I must stress that this needs to be kept in secret until it has been officially announced."

"I will. And thank you for thinking of me for the position. Is there anything else?" I turn from Scott to Abby who both shake their heads. I stand to leave but shake Scott's hand again before leaving the office. I keep myself together until I reach my office where I check to make sure there is no-one in the conference room before I let out a little scream of joy.

I was finally moving up under my own steam. I can't see Aunt Abby having anything to do with this, but I will check with her later. I do a little dance in my office and let the feeling wash over me of the acceptance I have been given here.

When I got home that night, I went straight to find Abby. She wasn't in her office, so I went looking for her. I found her in the kitchen with Lance and Lydia who looked to be hiding something.

"What are you up to?" They turn guiltily and I see what they have been hiding.

"Congratulations." They all say. I walk towards them and see the massive cake with my name on it.

"What's this for?"

"Your new job."

"About that, did you have anything to do with it?"

"Nope, it's all on you. I don't think I've had someone work for who was basically head hunted by management before. I've done it from other companies but not in my own. Scott came to me a few months ago about you but you were still on the project. I knew that you wouldn't leave not this close to the end. He told me his proposal and I thought it over. What he suggested was a good idea and I was mad that I hadn't thought of it myself.

"It wasn't something that could be done quickly so we did a review of that area and found out the best way to streamline it. It means that there will only be one or two job losses and I think I know who they will be. The rest will be re-organised and eventually they will be working for you."

"You more than deserve this Cat. You have worked for it over the last few years and have shown what you are capable of." Lydia said. I looked at her and there seemed to be something different about her.

"What's up Lydia?" She froze and her look went to Lance who put his arm around her and hugged her.

"Well, I was going to tell you both in a few days but since we are celebrating why not. I'm pregnant." The squeals that came from me and Abby were load as we both went to them and hugged them both hard. I hadn't realised they had been trying.

"It's not something we had been expecting so it came as a surprise to us. It does mean that I will need to cut back on somethings eventually, but I will find someone to fill in for me after I have the baby." I could see tears in her eyes at the thought of becoming a mother.

"This is definitely a celebration now. Don't worry about anything, we'll get by. Now I would say that this calls for champagne but since one of us can't drink, how about some sparkling non-alcoholic wine?" We all nod and Abby heads to get the bottle.

"When are you due?" I ask.

"Late January." I smile and hug her again. She can't keep the smile from her face, and I am so happy for them. Later that night I went in search of Abby. I found her in the living room reading.

"Aunt Abby, can I have a word?"

"I've been waiting on you all night. Come, sit down beside me." I crossed and sat beside her on the sofa. "What's up?" I didn't know how to begin so I just came out with it.

"Am I ready for this job?" I knew my voice sound small and quiet, but I couldn't stop it.

"Cat, you are ready for this. I have been keeping an eye on you over the last few years and I can see that you are more than capable of doing this job. You have impressed not only me but anyone you have worked with. You don't know this, but I have a file of reviews about your performance from external parties. They all loved working with you. They knew where they stood and what they were getting. Some even tried to poach you but I knew you wouldn't leave."

I lifted my head from where it was bowed slightly to look at her directly. She was telling the truth. She wasn't hiding anything from me.

"I had thought that your age my put some people off, but you have proved them wrong big time. You have shown that even though you are so young, you can handle whatever is thrown at you." She stopped and let what she said sink in.

"I'm sorry I brought up your parents today, but I had to act as if I didn't know you."

"It's ok. I know that. I just didn't expect it." She pulled me in for a hug and we sat there for a while without talking.

"I think I already know what your answer is going to be but don't tell me just yet. Let me find out with everyone else."

"Ok. When is the restructure announcement going out?"

"Next week." I keep quiet thinking over everything and enjoying the peace.

I waited a few days before giving Scott my answer and then I knew what I wanted to do. The following week the restructure announcement came and that was all the talk in the office. Some people thought there were going to be a lot of job cuts whilst others thought that there wouldn't be many.

I listened to what they were saying and understood their fears I had never been through something like this before, so I didn't know how it felt. Even now, I had a new job to go to whilst others were waiting to see what the outcome was going to be.

The new structure was put in place smoothly and I began in my new role a month later. And at first, I thought I couldn't handle until one day I took stock and told those that were pressuring me to step back and give me space. It worked. After that day, they didn't hound me as much and it was good.

By the time it was fully in place six months later, I found myself in charge on about thirty people which included four managers. I never imagined I would find myself in this role, but I found I loved it.

The next big turning point in my life was a few Christmases ago at the office party. I hadn't wanted to go by myself, so I talked Michelle into coming with me when she was home for the holidays. She had gone away to university and was in her final year.

Chapter Thirty-three

"Girls, you need to get a move on, or you will be late." I heard Abby shout to us, but we were having too much fun catching up whilst getting ready.

"Come on, if it's boring then we will find a club to go to." I knew I was dragging my heels, but I really didn't want to go but I had to show face as it was my boss that was hosting it and I needed to be there.

I turned from the mirror after finishing my makeup and knew it was time to put on my dress. It was a new one that Michelle had talked me into buying just yesterday and it was a little bit more risqué than I would normally wear and I thought it was bit much for an office party but I got it anyway.

I took off my robe and went to the closet to dress. I stepped into the emerald green dress and pulled it up. It covered me from neck to mid-thigh but there was a large cut out in the front that showed what little of my cleavage I had off. It was the same at the back so I had to buy special underwear for it as I couldn't go without. It was tight everywhere and I wasn't used to it.

I walked out to show Michelle who was just putting on her jewellery.

"Wow, you look hot." I blushed and looked down at myself. I put my hair half up and half down as I wasn't brave enough to have it all up with the cut outs. I crossed to where I had left my shoes and slipped them on before going to the mirror again to make sure that I hadn't messed up make up.

It was fine. I grabbed my bag and put some lipstick and a small compact in to along with some money just in case. I knew that everything was paid for at the party, but it was for emergencies. I was staring at myself in the mirror when Michelle came up beside me and put an arm around me. We looked very festive with me in green and her in red.

We left my room and headed downstairs where I knew Abby would be waiting on us. I saw her watching us as we walked towards her.

"I am thinking that I may need to send a bodyguard with you two tonight." We laughed.

"Aunt Abby, I think you are being a little overdramatic. We will be fine."

"No, I'm not. I would have sent Lance with you but with him looking after Lydia these last few weeks, I have no-one to fall back on to watch you two." I gave her a hug and stepped back. I felt uneasy for some reason, but I tried not to let it show.

"Are you sure you don't want to come? It is for all employees."

"I don't think the big boss showing up at these things is good for morale. They need to relax, and they can't do that if I am around. Right, are you both ready?" It was only then that I noticed a set of keys in her hand. "I'm driving you both there and you can arrange for a taxi home. I am not going to worry about you driving when there has been drinking going on."

"We don't drink and drive."

"I know. It's not you I am talking about it is everyone else on the road. Let's go." She opened the door and allowed us to walk out to the car. We got in the back and drove away. My apprehension about going had vanished and now the nerves were kicking in. I hadn't wanted to drink before but Michelle had had some wine.

It was a quick ride to the hotel where the party was being held and it was the first time that it had been held here. When the car pulled up to the door, a doorman came forward and opened the door for us to get out. He helped us out and I turned back and leaned down to speak to Abby.

"Have fun girls and stay safe."

"We will and thanks again for dropping us off." She just smiled and as I straightened, she drove away.

"Let's get this party going." Michelle said and we headed inside looking for the signs for the ballroom where the party was. The hotel lobby had been decked out beautifully for the holiday period and I couldn't stop myself from looking around. It was my favourite time of year. We found the ballroom easy and when we stepped in, I looked around the room for someone I knew.

"You have been keeping secrets from me." I turned to Michelle with a quizzical look. "You never told me there were so many hunky men working with you." I turned back to the room and couldn't really see what she was meaning. "Let's go get a drink and you can tell me who you know and who you don't so that I can find out who they are." I watched as her gazed moved around the room looking for someone to select. I shook my head and we headed to the bar.

"What can I get for you ladies?"

"Your finishing times." Michelle said before I had a chance to say anything. I laughed as the barman just smiled as if he had heard it all before.

"Two glasses of red wine." He smiled and nodded heading off to get our order. I looked at Michelle as she watched him walk away whistling. I shook my head and turned back to the room. I scanned again looking for familiar faces, but I froze when I saw someone. Michelle pulled me out my daze and I turned quickly back to the bar. I lifted the glass of wine and drank about half of it in one go.

"Hey, what's up lady?" I kept looking at the bottles behind the bar, but the mirror reflects, the room back to me. Michelle puts her hand on my arm, and I turn to her. "What's wrong?" Her cheerfulness was gone, and it was replaced with concern. I swallowed before speaking.

"He's here."

"Who's here?"

"Michael." Michelle's gaze widened before turning to scan the room.

"Where?" I pulled her back around to me and hoped that he didn't recognise me. My heart was beating a mile a minute and I tried to calm myself down but not having much luck. I drank the rest of my wine and the barman came back down to us. He looked at my empty glass and my face knowing that something was wrong. He poured another glass and set it in front of me. I gave him a small smile and fiddle with the stem of the glass.

"Are you sure it was him? It has been what nine years; do you think he will recognise you?"

"I don't know but I don't want to take the chance. I was just a kid when I last saw him and made a fool of myself over him."

"You've grown-up and changed since then, he probably won't recognise you so you will be safe."

"I don't want to take a chance." I knew I was lying to myself as I hoped that he would remember me but also that he sees me as I am today and not as the child I was when we last met. Over the years he had come back to my memories and seeing him again in the flesh made me realise that my memories didn't do him justice. The reality was a million times better than any memory I could call up. I was so lost in my memories of him that I didn't notice her glancing behind me.

"I need to go to the ladies. I'll be right back." She gave my hand a squeeze then she was away. I stood there by myself feeling safe but on edge until there was a voice behind me that made me straighten.

"Hello." I turned slowly to the voice and knew then that Michelle must have seen him coming over.

"Hi." I looked down at my purse and fiddled with it. Anything to keep my gaze from being lost in those dark eyes. I felt myself getting hot just standing next to him.

"I'm Michael." He held out his hand for me to shake waiting for me to give him my name. I took his and felt the heat in me going up a notch just at his touch.

"Catriona." I smiled at him and when I tried to remove my hand he held on.

"Have we met before? You seem familiar." I could either say that no we haven't met and not bring up my sixteenth birthday party or tell the truth. I opted to tell the truth.

"Yes, we've met before, but it was a long time ago. I was only sixteen." He stared a few seconds longer then recognition crossed his face.

"Cat Mont-Clair. You were staying with A… Miss McIntosh." I stepped closer to him as I tried to keep him quiet.

"Shhh. Yes but no-one here knows that. I don't want them to know that I live with the boss." He smiled and I felt my insides turn to mush.

"Don't worry, your secret's safe with me." At that moment, I felt Michelle coming back.

"HI, I'm Michelle." She held out her hand and Michael dropped mine to shake hers. I felt the loss immediately.

"Well, what are you two lovey ladies doing here all alone."

"Well, we are just waiting on the right man to come along." Michelle was talking away, but I wasn't really taking in what she was saying. I found myself being steered away from the bar and over to a table and sitting down Michael followed with our drinks.

"Are you not drinking?"

"I was going to but now that I see you two, I think I'll stay sober to make sure you get home safe later." I was a goner. No matter what he said, it was reaching inside me and pulling me towards him. I felt like I was sixteen again. I knew I had a smile on my face that I couldn't erase.

We sat and chatted for a while about mundane things and I learned a little more about him. He had a sister who raised him after his mother died. He was close to her but didn't see her as often as he wanted to due to work commitments. He had recently moved back here after working away for the last five years.

That explains why I hadn't seen him around. I wondered what department he was working in now. He froze when I asked him, but he answered.

"I'm in the PR department." I nodded thinking if I knew anyone in that department but came up blank. "What about you two, where do you both work?"

"I don't work here. I'm finishing my last year of Psychology. I'm here to give my girl here moral support as she wasn't going to come on her own." She gave me a one-armed hug as I smiled. I felt as if I had lost my voice as Michelle was doing all the talking. His gaze turned to me.

"I'm in transitions with Scott Jameson." I saw his eyebrows raise a little at that, but I was proud of what I was doing. Before I could say anything else, a song came on and Michelle dragged me up to the dance floor. As I looked back at him, I felt his possessive gaze over my body, and I loved it. I turned away and began to enjoy myself.

By the time we made it back to our table, I was needing a drink. On the table was a bottle of the wine we had been drinking and a large jug of cold water. I lifted the jug and poured a glass and downed it in one.

"Thirsty?" I nodded and sat down. I could see Michelle looking over to the bar at the barman she had been eyeing up all evening.

"I'll be right back." She said as she walked up to the bar and began talking with the barman.

"I think she has taken a shine to him."

"Yeah, when she sees something she likes, she goes for it. I wish I had her courage." I looked back to him and saw him staring at me.

"And what is it that you want Catriona?" I opened my mouth to speak but closed it again. I couldn't tell him that it was him I wanted and had done for the last nine years.

"The bathroom. I need the bathroom." He laughed as I stood and headed to the ladies. I wound my way through the crowd that was getting rowdier as the night wore on. I would never have imagined some of the people so relaxed from dealing with them in the office. After I did what I had to do, I started making my way back but was stopped in my tracks by someone blocking me way.

"Excuse me." I tried to go around them, but they followed me. I didn't recognise them, but they had had too much to drink.

"How about a kiss under the mistletoe?" I looked up and saw his arm above his head holding onto some fake mistletoe.

"No thank you." I tried again to go around him, but he wouldn't let me.

"Come on, it's Christmas, the season of good will." I felt the panic rising in me, but it was short lived as the man was quickly turned around and lost his balance and landed on the floor. I looked up at my saviour and saw Michael standing there with such a look of fury on his face that it was hard to take in.

"She said no. No means no." He put his arm around me and moved me past the man on the floor. "Let's get you home." He said to me. I went with him then as we got to the door, I remember Michelle.

"Michelle?"

"She's outside waiting on us." I nodded and found myself being moved outside into the cold air and then into a car that was sitting idling at the door. Michael made sure I was buckled in then got into drivers' seat and headed away. "Where are we going?"

"Abercrombie St." He was quiet in the car, but I could still see the fury on his face. A short time later he pulled up to the gates and waited for me to punch in the code. They opened and he drove up to the door.

"Thanks for the lift Michael. I hope to see you again." Michelle said as she got out the car and went inside. I saw her stop just inside the door and knew that she would be talking to Abby. Michael got out the car and came around and opened my door. He helped me out and I didn't want to let him go.

"Thank you for earlier and for getting me home safe."

"It was my pleasure. I would never have forgiven myself if something had happened to you." I felt myself start to blush then I felt his hand brushing down the side of my face, I felt myself move my head into it. I looked up at him from under my lashes and could see the heat in his gaze.

"May I kiss you?" he asked me, and my heart skipped a beat as I nodded. He moved in slowly and his lips were soft and gentle against mine. I didn't want it to end but light spilled out over us as he pulled back, but his gaze was stuck on me.

"Cat, is everything ok here?"

"Yes, Aunt Abby. Michael here was kind enough to give us a lift home." I turned to see Abby and was taken aback at the expression on her face. She looked angry about something, but I didn't know what.

"Good night Catriona. It was nice to meet you Abby, but I must go." He let me go and walked back to his car and I stood there like a statue watching him leave.

"Cat, it's cold, come inside before catch a cold." I turned slowly and walked up the steps and inside. The door closed behind me and I kept walking in a daze. "Michelle has gone up to bed."

I stopped and turned to her. The expression was something I hadn't seen in a long time. The anger had disappeared and something between sadness and disappointment was showing, I didn't know what I had done so I said nothing and just headed to bed.

Chapter Thirty-four

As the party had been a few days before Christmas I wasn't back in the office until after New Year's. I spent some time with Michelle before she went back to university. It was a great break and spending time with family was the best thing about it. All through the holiday, Michael wasn't that far from my mind.

For some reason, Abby didn't like him, but I couldn't figure out why. I tried to talk to her, but she clammed up and wouldn't say a thing. I did catch her on the phone the day after the party arguing with someone. I never heard much of the conversation, but she wasn't happy about something.

The first day back was busy as there were a lot of clients transitioning over and it kept me busy for that first week that I didn't have much time to think about anything except work. That was until one night when someone knocked at my office door. I knew everyone else had gone so I was a bit on edge. I reached for the phone and got it ready to call security if need me.

"Come in." I stared at the door as it opened and didn't let go of the breath I had been holding until I saw who it was. "Michael."

"Evening Catriona." He looked as good as I remember if not better. He was a little taller than me and wearing that navy suit, it threw out his eyes.

"Cat. Please call me Cat." He smiled at me and I felt myself blushing hard. "I never did catch your second name." He froze a second before smiling wider and coming closer to my side of the desk. He leaned on the edge of it and I had to push my chair back slightly so that he had space.

"It's McIntosh. And no relation to the big boss." I could feel heat come from him and I felt myself getting warm, but I couldn't tear my gaze from him.

"How did you know where to find me?"

"I have my ways." He reached out his hand and touched mine and I felt as if I was going to explode. I stood quicky and moved away from him to the other side of my desk. I couldn't be that close to him. It was too much. He gave a small laugh as if he knew how it was affecting me. He stood and came around the desk but kept his distance.

"I had a good time at the Christmas party." I smiled before answering him.

"Me too. I hadn't wanted to go but when I had mentioned it to Michelle, she talked me into going."

"Well, I'm glad she did otherwise we would never have met. Did you have a good break?"

"Yes. Spending time with my Aunt and family, it was great. Christmas is time for family and spending time with them is the best thing." He had a strange look on his face. "What about you, did you have a good time? Did you spend time with your sister?"

"No, I couldn't as she had to work but I was ok on my own. I had football and beer to keep me company. I caught up with her after the holidays."

"Oh, I'm sorry. I hope next year's different and you can spend time with her."

"Yeah I hope so. I missed her this year." I didn't know what else to say. I was wringing my hands together and knew I needed to stop. I walked back to my desk and sat down to try and finish off what I was working on. I glanced at the time as I did and didn't realise that it had gotten so late.

"Do you have much more to do?"

"No. I was nearly finished anyway."

"How about we grab a late dinner?" I wanted to shout yes but I held back knowing that I needed to keep myself contained. I didn't want to seem desperate.

"I can't. I have to get home."

"Ok. Some other time then." I nodded as he walked towards the door. He stopped before closing it behind him. "Make sure you get security to walk you to your car. You never know who is out there." Before I could reply, he was gone, and I had to calm my racing heart. I finished up what I was doing then switched everything off. I had always felt safe here but for some reason, Michael asking me to take care, has made me feel insecure.

When I get down to reception, I stop and ask Doug if he would walk me to my car. I had parked a little further away than I normally would as I had something to do at lunchtime and couldn't get back in my usual spot.

We chatted about mundane things as we walked the ten minutes to where my car was parked. I thanked him and got in to head home. I had just pulled away when my phone went. As it was on hands free, I couldn't tell who it was until I had answered it.

"Cat, where are you?"

"Just leaving work. I'll be home in about half an hour, do you want anything picked up?"

"No. Lydia's in labour. We're at the hospital."

"Ok. I'm on my way. I'll text when I'm there and you can tell me where to go." I drove as quickly and as safely as I could to the hospital. It wasn't too bad finding parking space and I texted as I got out the car and started heading to the building. My phone buzzed and I checked it. They were at the maternity waiting room.

I glanced at the signs inside and headed that way. When I got there, I found Abby pacing in the waiting area.

"What's going on? She's not due for another few weeks."

"I don't know. She hadn't been feeling great and was extremely uncomfortable all day. I had to make Lance go out and get some stuff to get him away. She started bleeding and I called an ambulance. It pulled up the same time Lance came back." I took her hands and pulled her over to the chairs to sit down. I had never seen her look so scared before.

"Everything will be fine. She'll be ok." I tried to reassure her, but I was feeling uneasy myself. "Where's Lance?"

"He's in with her but he's not come back. I don't know whether to take it as a good thing or a bad thing." I hold her hands tight and I could feel the coldness in them.

"Ok. I'm going to get some coffee. I'll be right back." I know she heard me, but she didn't answer. I left here there and asked the staff at the desk where the nearest place to get a coffee was. They directed me to a stand in the main lobby saying that the coffee was better than what would come out of the vending machines.

I wait on the elevator to take me back down whilst everything was going through my mind. It had been an unexpected pregnancy for Lance and Lydia as they hadn't thought they would be able to have kids. I know it hadn't been an easy pregnancy, but we were all there for her. She kept trying to work until we finally were able to get her to step back and look after herself. She was worried about her job, but Abby told her that the job was hers whenever she needed it.

I had been so lost in my mind that I bumped into someone as the doors opened and I went to step out.

"Oh sorry."

"Cat?" I looked to the owner of the voice.

"Michael. What are you doing here?"

"I was coming to see my sister."

"Oh, she works here?" I knew I was asking stupid questions, but my mind was on automatic.

"What are you doing here?"

"My… a friend is having a tough time having a baby." It was the first time that I didn't know how to explain my relationship to Lydia. Yes, she worked for us, but she was more like family than an employee.

"What are you doing down here and not in maternity?"

"I'm getting coffee." I started walking towards the vendor to get what I had said I was going to get. Michael followed me and I felt his hand on my back and I wanted to relax into him. We were served straight away, and we fell in step together and headed back upstairs. When we got to the waiting room, I went straight to Abby and gave her the coffee. I could feel the worry coming from her. I didn't notice that Michael had stayed back. It was a few minutes before she noticed him.

"I bumped into Michael downstairs. He's here to see his sister who works here." My gaze flicks between the two of them and I couldn't work out why they didn't like one another. He stepped forward and held out his hand to Abby.

"Miss McIntosh, it's good to meet you but I'm sorry it's under these unfortunate circumstances. We weren't properly introduced when we first met. I'm Michael McIntosh. No relation." He smiled as he held out his hand. Abby stood slowly and took his hand to shake.

"Michael. It's nice to formally meet you." She dropped his hand and turned away from him and began pacing again. I glanced to Michael and saw what I thought was hurt cross his face then it was gone. Before I could say anything, Lance came out to us.

"How is she?" I walked quickly to him and gave him a hug. He hugged me back tight. I stood back and waited for him to speak.

"It's a boy. They had to section her, and it took a while before they could stop the bleeding but she's going to be ok."

"That's great news." I said as I hugged him again. Abby sank into the nearest chair with a sigh of relief.

"They are taking her to recovery just now, so I'd better get back."

"Congratulations papa." I said again as hugged him before he went back. "We'll bring everything in tomorrow."

"Thanks Cat. She'll be wanting to see you both when she's awake." I nod and let him get back to his wife and new-born son. I turn to Abby and find her in tears. I go to her and put my arms around her.

"Come on, let's get home. You need some rest." I help her stand, coffee long forgotten, and we head to the elevators. As we wait, I realise that I had pulled Michael away from the real reason of his visit.

"Sorry, you didn't get to see your sister."

"That's ok. I'll give her a call and explain what held me up. I'm sure she won't mind." We head outside and it is only then that I don't know where Abby has parked her car. She looks so deflated that I don't want her driving anyway.

"Can you stay here with her just now? I'll bring the car around." He nods and takes over holding her up as I walk away quickly to get my car. When I came back, I couldn't believe what I was seeing. Michael was holding Abby in his arms.

As I pulled up beside him, he moved them to the door and opened it and ensured she was in safely.

"Thank you for tonight."

"No problem. I'm glad that your friend is ok. Take care." Before he went to close the door, I called him.

"About dinner, can I take a rain check?" He smiled at my hesitancy.

"Yes. Give me a call when you free." He handed me a card and I held onto it. "Stay safe." He closed the door and I turned back to the road and drove away.

Chapter Thirty-five

Everything now makes sense about that night. A lot of things were clicking into place as the story was being told. I looked to Abby and waited for her so say something.

"I'm sorry. I wanted to tell you, but Michael wouldn't let me. He wasn't lying when he said he was going to visit his sister. It just wasn't in the way you thought, and he didn't correct you. I wanted to go to him that night, but I couldn't as you didn't know about our relationship."

For once, I didn't feel the need to cry which was unusual. I looked at the time and saw how late it was.

"How about we call it a day here and we can pick up again tomorrow.?" Rose said.

"Fine with me, we don't have much more to tell anyway. I would say a day or so should cover it."

"Ok. I've been working on pulling what you have told so far together but I'll send you the full article once it is complete so that you can see it fully before it goes out. It should only take me a couple of days to finalise it." Rose lifted her recorder switching it off as she did. She uncurled herself from the chair and I stood as well.

"Thanks again Rose for what you are doing. I don't think I could have done it with anyone else."

"I'm glad I was in the right place at the right time. That's a big part of finding the right story. Yours is something that I haven't come across before. It takes courage to talk about things and for you talking about this, is something that shows you can get through anything." As she had been talking, she had put on her coat and had walked to the door.

"Bye Abby. See you tomorrow. Same time?" I nod and wave goodbye to her as she leaves. I lock the door behind me and turn back to Abby.

I don't know what to say but knew I had to say something, so I play safe and ask about food.

"What would you like for dinner?" I walk into the kitchen and opened the fridge to see what was there. I was going down so I would need to get a shop in over the next few days. "How about Szechuan chicken?" I shout.

"That's fine with me. Anything will do." I close the door knowing that it was hard for her as well as me, but it was my life we were talking about not hers. Yes, we were intertwined, and she has a big part of my life, but what she did, it take a lot to get over. Tell my history is shedding a new light on a lot of things that happened.

I pull the ingredients out the fridge and my spice cupboard and start preparing. Abby still hasn't come in. I keep going until everything is ready to be cooked then I go back to where she is still sitting.

"Abby." She lifts her head from her phone, and I know that she has been texting Michael. I didn't hear her voice, so she wasn't talking to him.

"He misses you."

"I know. I miss him as well, but I need to get through this on my own. When it's finished, I'll call him to talk and we will go from there." I know she wants us back together again but it's hard to take everything in. I know the reasoning why they didn't, but it still hurts. They kept it from me as if it was a nasty secret.

"He wanted you to love him for himself and not because you thought you had some sort of obligation to him."

"I do love him for himself, but I need to get this sorted out in my mind before I see him again. Is he picking you up tonight?"

"Yes. I've asked him to come around nine if that's ok?" I glance at the time and see that we have enough time to have dinner.

"That's fine. I'll go get dinner on. Do you want something to drink?" She shakes her head and go back to the kitchen. This is the first time where she has not helped me. I miss her help. I get the chicken on to cook along with the rest of the ingredients. Once they have been on a few minutes, I get the rice on cooking so that it will all be ready at the same time. As I was about to plate everything up, she came through and sat down. I put the plates on the table.

"Drink?"

"Just water please." I grab a couple of bottles from the fridge and we eat in silence. It was uncomfortable and it was getting to me. Once we were finished, her phone buzzed, and she glanced at it.

"Is that Michael?" I asked. She nods and stands from the table putting her dishes in the sink to clean up. My heart is racing at the thought that he is so close to me. I leave my dishes where they are and follow her back to living room where she put her coat on and picked up her bag. She opened the door and started walking towards Michael who was waiting at the end of the pathway.

From what I could see of him, he looked tired, and I wondered if he was eating enough. Abby as about halfway down the path when I called to her and she stopped. I took a deep breath and walked towards her. I stopped in front of her.

"Tell Michael Franco's at eight on twenty fifth and not to be late." I saw a smile cross her face and she hugged me before turning away and getting into the car. This was the closest I had been to him since this all started, and it was taking all I had not to run to him. I could feel his stare burn right through me and I had to turn away and force myself to walk back inside and close the door.

I went into the kitchen to clean up then stopped and pulled a bottle of wine from the fridge and a glass and headed back to the living room to sit down. My phone was flashing as I sat down. I lifted it and saw that Michael had texted. A simple message of Thank You.

I opened the wine and poured a glass and drank half of it down before stopping. I lifted the tv remote and flicked through the channels until I found something that would keep my mind busy.

I must have fallen asleep as I awoke stiff, sore and cold. I stretched, working all the kinks out of my body and headed upstairs to bed. I didn't even change as I was so cold, just got into bed the way I was, falling asleep again quickly.

When I woke the next morning, it was early, and I noticed that I hadn't moved at all through night as I was in the same position as I was when I fell into bed. I got up and showered. I had time before they would be back and I knew that I needed to get clear up last night's dishes then some shopping in so once I was dressed, I went into the kitchen putting the coffee on before I did anything and started writing a list for what I needed. Once done, I cleaned the dished from the night before leaving them to drip dry as I would put them away when I came back.

I drank my coffee as I checked my list and as I walked into the living room, I saw the empty wine bottle. That was something to be added to the list but unfortunately, it was too early to buy it yet. I would need to go back out later to get it. I still had a couple of bottles that should do me until I was able to get more.

I grabbed my bag and keys as I headed out to the supermarket to get food. I was feeling a lot better than the last time I did this, but it couldn't hard. I parked up and pulled a trolley out and headed inside. Just doing these routine jobs made me feel better. It gave me something to concentrate on than what I was doing out with this.

I needed to speak with the office to see what needed to be done and when they wanted me back. By the time I was finished, I was feeling better than I had been when I had gotten up. Once I had all the shopping in the car, I headed home and for some reason, I took a different route than normal. I don't know why I did.

I found myself at Grove Park. I parked up but stayed in the car. This was where we had our first date. Even though it was still winter, we had come here. I smiled as I thought about it. I knew that this would come out today. I knew I was nearing the end of my story and I could only hope that it would still feel as freeing as it does just now.

I don't know how long I sat there but it wasn't until my phone buzzed that I realised I had been there longer than I thought. Abby and Rose were waiting on me. Luckily, I didn't have any frozen stuff that would be defrosted.

I left the park and drove home finding Rose's car parked outside but no sign of them both. Abby must have let themselves in. I parked up and started pulling the bags from the car. When I opened the front door, I dropped the bags there then went back to get the last few. When I came back in, the bags were gone, and I found Rose and Abby putting everything by for me.

"Thanks." I said as I put the last couple of bags on the counter. Before I could do anything, I was gently pushed away, and I sat down watching the two of them put my groceries by. A short time later, they were finished, and a coffee mug was put in front of me.

"Ready to continue?" Rose asked me. I nodded and got up and went into the living room. We had gotten into a routine doing this and we all took the seats that we were comfortable with.

Chapter Thirty-six

I was finishing up early a couple of days later after Lydia had her son. I hadn't wanted to intrude on them, but I couldn't keep away now. I had bought a little something the before the baby was born but I was planning on getting something else once they knew if it as a boy or a girl. Now we knew, I was looking into getting something that would suit the little boy perfectly.

I was just about to open my office door when it opened first, and a large blue balloon came at me. I let out a little yelp at the surprise. I leaned around to see who was on the other side of it and saw Michael

"What are you doing here?" I was smiling as I didn't care the reason why.

"I wanted to give a gift to the new parents. I could tell how much they meant to you." My smile grew wider at his thoughtfulness about someone that he had never met before. "Are you going to the hospital today?"

"Yes. I was on my way there just now. I wanted to give them a couple of days alone first."

"Mind if I tag along with you?" He looked sincere about it and I couldn't say anything but nod. I walked past him and headed to the elevator knowing that he was walking with me. I could feel the gazes of those we walked past, and I didn't know if it was them or Michael that was making the butterflies fly about in my stomach.

We stood quietly side by side as the car descended to the basement car park. I headed to my car but stopped just next to it.

"Do you want to come with or follow me?" Why I ask this I don't know.

"I don't think this will fit in your car so it will be best if we take mine." I nod at him and pulled out the gift bag that was there. I stood there suddenly realising that I didn't know which was his car. He pressed a button and I saw the large SUV across from mine flash so that was his car. I crossed behind him as watched as he put the balloon in the back seat and took my bag and put it in the boot. Before I could open the passenger door, he was there opening it for me.

I felt as if I was sixteen again unable to stop the blush rising my face. I kept my head down to try and hide it and to get it under control. He said nothing when he got in the car, only started it up and headed to hospital. By the time we arrived, I had myself partially under control.

I didn't know how easy it would be to get parked, but we were lucky when someone pulled out of a space quite close to the entrance. I got out the car but before I could lift my gift bag from the trunk, it was handed to me along with another larger gift bag that I was curious to see what was in it.

Michael pulled the balloon out and we walked inside. It was fortunate that is was calm otherwise he would have had some job keeping hold of it in the wind. I glanced at the directory board and headed in the direction of the maternity wing.

I knew Abby would be along later so I was hoping that we would be away before she arrived. I don't know why she didn't like him especially as she didn't know him. Not that I knew him, but I wanted to, and I hoped that I go the chance to.

I didn't know where they would be, so I stopped at the desk and asked.

"Excuse me, I'm looking for Lydia Whelan's room." The nurse checked the computer then looked up.

"Only family can visit. Are you family?" She asked the question just waiting to turn us away.

"Yes. I'm her sister and this is her brother-in-law, my husband." I stood strong as I spoke hoping that Michael wouldn't say anything. She looked at us both trying to work out if we were married or not. Thankfully, our hands were full so she couldn't see that we didn't wear rings.

"Room 206." She dropped her head and went back to work ignoring us.

"Thank you." I said and walked away from the desk looking for which direction we needed to go it and fortunately, I found it easily. I kept walking not knowing what to say to Michael. We stopped outside the door and I knocked. Once I heard someone answer, I pushed the door open slowly. Inside I saw a tired looking Lydia on the bed and Lance was sleeping in the chair.

"Hi, is it ok to come in?" Lydia pushed herself up the bed a little

"Yes, please come in. I need someone else to talk to. I walked around the bed putting the bags on the floor and leaned over and gave her a hug."

"Congratulations momma. How are you feeling?"

"Tired and sore. I'm hoping to get home tomorrow."

"Where is he?"

"He should be here soon. The nurses have been keeping an eye on him, but they told me they should be binging him down soon." I saw her look over my shoulder with a surprised look and it was only then that I remember Michael. I turned to him.

"Lydia, this is Michael. We work together. He was with me when Abby called to say you were in labour."

"Michael, it's nice to meet you."

"Congratulations on your new son."

"Is that for Jay?" I looked at her. "That's what we've named him. Jay." I grinned loving he name.

The door opened behind him and he had to step aside, squeezing into a corner with the balloon. At the same time, Lance woke up.

"How are you feeling sweetheart?" He leaned over to kiss her.

"I'm fine but we have visitors." Lance turned and a smile lit up his face when he saw me.

"Cat. Thank for coming." He came around and hugged me then sat in the chair at the other side of the bed and held his wife's hand. We stood watching as the nurse came in with a bedside crib and set it up on the other side of the bed.

"I think someone was missing his mom. He was screaming earlier until we moved him to come down here. I think he knew he was coming to you." Once the nurse left us, I walked around the bed and stood over the crib looking at the tiny baby lying there. His eyes were wide open looking around him.

"May I?" Lydia nodded and I bent down and picked up the little bundle and held him close.

"Hi, I'm your auntie Cat." I stood holding this little person and something inside me seemed to click. I didn't know what it was, but I felt different. I looked up from the Jay and my eyes caught Michael's. The heat in his eyes was something that I had never seen before or expected, especially from him. And if I was honest with myself, I felt the same. I could feel my eyes watering and thought his was as well but put it down to the light.

"Lance, this is Michael, Cat's friend from work." He looked as if he was going to say something but stopped.

"Michael, it's nice to meet you. If you can find a space over there, you can put that balloon there." Michael smiled and crossed to where I was and set up the balloon so that is wasn't in the way. I turned towards as he came closer and my breath caught when he stood behind me. Jay began to fuss then, and it pulled me from the direction my thoughts were going in.

"I think someone is hungry." I handed him over to Lydia and she began to pull down her gown to breast feed. I stood back and looked away and found my gaze on Lance. "How's the new daddy holding up?"

"Tired but good. I'm only glad they are both ok. It was close for a moment and I don't know what I would have done if I had lost either of them."

"You didn't and it worked out. Do you need help sorting things out at home?"

"No, I'm fine."

"Yes, he does. I don't believe he will have everything ready for us coming home. For someone who is normally planned and have everything in place, he has fallen to pieces and getting a little scatter-brained getting things sorted out." I looked between the two of them.

"She's right. I thought we would have more time to get things organised at home, but I haven't gotten the crib finished yet or baby proofing everywhere. There will be other things that I will have missed as well."

"Ok. I'll come and help you get everything sorted out. We want everything in place for this little man coming home. I'll get changed then head over to help. Is there anything you want done first?" Lance opened his mouth, but it was Lydia who spoke.

"Everything. He hasn't left here since we were brought in and I know what the place was like before so I know it will be a mess." She said it with a smile knowing that she wasn't getting on at him. I saw the sheepish look on Lance's face as well.

"Right, I'll get going and will text you when I've gotten everything sorted out." I leaned over and gave Lydia a one-armed hug then kissed Jay on the head before turning to Lance and hugging him. "I'll see you both later." I turn to leave and saw Michael take a few steps towards the door before stopping.

"Michael, can I have a word with you please?" I look between them then let the room. I knew that he was probably going to get questioned about his intentions even though we haven't gone a date yet. I wait outside and a few minutes later he comes out looking like something bad happened.

"Everything ok? They didn't grill you too much about your intentions?" He looked at me so intently, that I felt as if our souls were connecting.

"No, it was fine. You have a lot of people who care about you." He stepped closer and put his arm around me and we walked down the corridor to the elevator and out to the car. "Do you want me to drop you back to get your car?"

"No, it's ok. I'll pick it up over the weekend. If you could drop me home that will be fine."

"What about getting to Lydia's?"

"They live on the property at the back. They have a cottage there." He nodded and was quiet for the rest of the journey. As we pulled up at home, I didn't want him to leave. "Do you want to help me?" I waited anxiously for him to respond.

"I can't, I have some things to take care of."

"Oh, ok. Thanks for the lift." I couldn't keep the disappointment from my voice. I undid my seatbelt and went to open the door but was stopped by his hand on my arm.

"I want to, but I really do have some things to take care of. What are you doing Sunday?"

"Nothing, why?" He smiled as he answered.

"Because I want to take you out. The last day of the winter fest is Sunday and I was hoping that you would go with me?" My heart was racing, and the butterflies were now doing an acrobatic display inside me.

"I'd love to go with you." I couldn't keep the smile form my face as I looked at him. He seemed uneasy as to what my answer would have been, but when I said yes, I saw relief pass over him.

"Great. I'll pick you about two. Make sure you dress warmly as it's forecasted for possible snow."

"I will." I got out the car and closed the door. I knew he was watching me as I walked to the door. He seemed to be deciding something then he got out the car and came towards me. I turned when I heard his footsteps as his lips met mine and my arms had found their way around his neck.

He was gentle but forceful and I couldn't get enough. I opened to him and heard him groan as I tried to get closer to him. He seemed to come to his senses and pushed me gently away from him, but he never let me go. He had a smile on his face.

"I'll see you Sunday." He bent down and kissed me again then let me go and got back into his car. He waved as he drove passed and I moved slowly inside thankful that Abby wasn't there as I needed to collect myself before seeing her.

Chapter Thirty-seven

It took both me and Lance until the Saturday afternoon to get everything ready for Lydia and Jay to come home. I had never known Lance to be so unorganised but knowing the reason for it, it was understandable.

He didn't mention Michael at all which I found strange but didn't want to chance anything. I knew for some unknown reason Abby didn't like him and I wondered if her feelings had spilled over to Lance. I didn't think he would have been like that but then again, his son was just born under trying circumstances so I would take what I could get.

Lydia and Jay should be able to come on Monday, so everything was set up and ready for them. Abby hadn't been around which was unusual as I had thought she would have wanted to help, but I figured she must have something going on at work to keep here away. I wasn't aware of anything major but that doesn't mean there wasn't something big in the works.

I was eager and nervous about my date with Michael. I had been meaning to go the winter fest before now but just never got around to it. The last time I had been was with Abby, Lance and Lydia last year. We had fun wandering around the vendors that had been set up and I finally convinced Abby to go skating with me.

I smiled at the memories knowing that things were going to be different going forward. I really liked Michael and if we were going to spending time with each other, I needed to find out why Abby didn't like him. I was pulling my warmest clothes out when Abby came in. She hesitated a little then sat on the end of the bed. I knew there was something that she wanted to say, and I was going to let her say it.

"Are you going out?"

"Yes, Michael is taking me to the winter fest."

"Oh." She looked down at her lap and then back up at me. I began undressing and put on my thick socks then my jeans. I pulled on my top then a thick jumper and by the time I was ready to put my boots on, she still hadn't spoken.

"When is he picking you up?" I glanced at the time.

"In about half hour." I sat down and pulled on my boots knowing that they would keep me warm as walked about the park. I turned and began brushing my hair then tied it back so that it would be out of the way. I lifted my small backpack along with my hat, scarves and gloves and went to go downstairs when she finally spoke.

"I'm sorry. I didn't know what to do when you came home with Michael at Christmas. You looked happy and good together that triggered something motherly in me and I wanted to know what he was up to. You hadn't mentioned him since your party, so I thought you had forgotten about him. I thought it was just a teenage crush." I moved back and sat next to her as she spoke.

"When he left, I could see how it affected you but thought you would have grown out of it. When I saw you together again, I knew that you hadn't. You looked good together, but I don't want you to get hurt. You don't really know much about him."

"That's what dating is for. You find out things about each and know if you are compatible. You must know something about him. He used to be your assistant."

"He kept to himself and did his work. We didn't really talk much unless it was business related." There was something about the way she was talking that she was hiding something from me. I didn't know if I wanted to know what it was in case, they had been together.

"Were you two together?" The look on Abby's face was something akin to me asking if she slept with her brother.

"No, oh god no, never. We were colleagues that's all. He was quiet and couldn't get much from him."

"Ok. He may have changed since you knew him. He must have been young when he worked for you, so he is now older and wiser. You need to give him a chance. I really like him Aunt Abby."

She looks at me and knows when I call her Aunt Abby, that it something special. I could see tears in her eyes as she sat there. She said nothing but pulled me in for a hug and didn't want to let go.

"I promise I will give him a chance but if he hurts you, then he will have to answer to me."

"Thank you, that's all I'm looking for. I'm sure you will like him when you get to know him." We both stood and headed downstairs. We were halfway down when I remembered I had left the rest of my things in my room. I went to turn back when the doorbell rang. I looked at Abby.

"He's prompt that for sure. Go, get your things and I will entertain him until you come back. I headed back up the stairs but stopped at the top of them and waiting until she had opened the door.

"Michael, it's good to meet you again. Come in please, Cat is just getting her things. She'll be down in a minute."

"Miss McIntosh, it's nice to meet you again." I didn't wait around to see what else they said as I wanted to get my things and get out of there. I didn't want to leave them alone for too long. I came running down the stairs and they were still standing in the foyer.

"Everything ok here?" I ask looking between the two of them.

"Yes, everything is fine here. We were just getting acquainted. Are you ready to go?" I nod and wrapped my scarf around my neck before hugging Abby goodbye. I knew I was rushing away but I didn't want to stay for too long.

A few minutes later we were in Michael's SUV and heading out. It was warm inside, and I didn't want to leave it to go out into the cold. We pulled up at the parking area and were directed to park at the back. Once parked, we got out, wrapped up warm and headed to the entrance to the festival. As we were walking, there were a lot of families heading in as well. The ground was a little uneven and I lost my balance a little, but Michael caught me and took me arm holding onto me as walked around.

The weather was perfect. There had been some snow earlier in the day, but it had stopped, and it gave everything a pretty look to it. There were a variety of vendors from those selling hot drinks and food to those like what you would get at a fairground. Michael tried his hand a one of them and won. He picked the largest prize there and gave it to me.

We spent the afternoon walking around and having fun, it was difficult to move in places carrying a large stuffed animal, but we managed it. There was a booth that was taking pictures of people who could either get dressed up or as they were.

"Come on, let's get a picture." He pulled me towards the stand, and I couldn't help but laugh.

"Yes sir, what would you like?" I was looking at the pictures that surrounded the booth to see what they can offer.

"What would you like sweetheart?" He had his arm around me, and I felt happy.

"That one." I pointed to one and looked at him. He nodded and turned to the vendor.

"The lady wants that one." I watched as the man looked at it then back at us.

"Ok, if you come this way, we can get set up." We followed him behind the stall and a little way away to a hut that sat a little way behind the stall, and it was exactly what I wanted. It was warm and cosy inside and set out beautifully.

The man moved around the room setting things up and I waited for him to say he was ready. A few minutes later he was.

"Ok. If you want to put Mr Furry over here and you can both stand in front of the fire, please." Michael put My Furry behind the camera and took off his jacket and put it along with mine over the chair in the room. He pulled me to him in front of the fire and turned me to him. I felt myself becoming lost in his eyes until I heard someone cough and I remembered where we were.

I turned to the photographer and took his directions as he took some photos. It didn't last long but it was something that I would never forget. As we were walking back to the stall to sort out payment, I was feeling happy, relaxed and content for the first time in my life. Michael had his arm around me, and I was safe.

"If you give me about half an hour, I should have them ready by then." We nodded and left him to it. It was getting dark and colder, but I didn't want to leave. I must have shivered as Michael pulled me closer to him and I felt his heat. I wanted to snuggle in against him.

"How about something warm to drink?" I nod and we head to one of the stalls that had a seating area. We got a couple of hot drinks then found a table that was close to one of the outdoor heaters. We sat and watched as everyone went by.

"I've had a good time today." I said.

"Me too. Thanks for coming with me." I snuggled in closer to him just so that I could be close to him. He put his arm around me and held me tight. It was perfect. I didn't want to leave or for the day to end. We sat there for some time and I must have been dozing as I was jerked awake.

"Hey, watch where you're going." I heard Michael shout. I looked up at him and saw the anger on his face which disappeared when he looked down at me. "Hey sleepy head."

"Sorry, I didn't mean to doze off."

"Don't worry about it. I don't know how you could sleep in this cold, but you must have needed it." I moved away from him and felt the loss of his heat. "Come on, we need to go get our pictures before he packs up." I stand and before I lift Mr Furry, Michael grabs him. He takes my hand and we head back to the stall. We caught him just as he was packing up. I stood a little away and let Michael pay and pick up the pictures.

"Come on. The fireworks will be starting soon." I nod and was about to head back the way we came but Michael pulled me to the exit.

"The fireworks are that way."

"I've got a better place to watch them from." We half ran to the car and then we were driving around the back of the park to an outlook point that was closed in the winter as it was too dangerous in bad weather. Michael parked up and we could see the whole park from where we were.

I was glad to be inside as I was feeling it quite cold after dozing off. We didn't have long to wait until the fireworks began and I must say, I haven't seen anything like it. The view was perfect to see them and being in the warmth was even better.

I didn't want the day to end but I knew that it must. Once the fireworks were finished, we drove back home and as we were sitting outside, I knew that this was what I wanted for my future. I loved living with Abby, but I needed my own space. I had been saving up for some time for my own house and I am about to take the plunge. I had seen a house that was perfect for me and I had a viewing arranged for later in the week.

"Are you doing anything Wednesday?" I asked.

"No, why?" I was nervous about asking him.

"I have a house viewing and would like you to come with me." He looked surprised t my request.

"Wouldn't your Aunt be better to go with you?"

"She will find fault in everything there. She doesn't know that I ready for moving out, but I need my own space." He was quiet for so long that I thought he would say no.

"What time is it at?"

"Three thirty." He nodded

"Ok. I'll go and we can grab some dinner afterwards."

"Thanks, that would be great." I didn't know what else to say. I went to leave the car but stopped when he said my name. I turned to him and he reached across and pulled me to him for a kiss. He pulled back and I wanted to pull him back to me.

"I'll see you Wednesday." I couldn't speak so I just nodded and left the car. I was in a daze as I watched him drive away. I knew that he was my future, and I was going to grab him with both hands.

Chapter Thirty-eight

By the time Wednesday came around, I was jumping at each little thing and the butterflies in my stomach were doing aerial acrobatics all day long. I wasn't just nervous about getting my own place, but that Michael was coming with me.

I was just finishing up a few things when my phone rang, and I answered it automatically. It was Abby.

"Hi, I wondered if you wanted to grab an early dinner?"

"Sorry, I can't. I'm trying to prepare for the Reddick proposal tomorrow."

"Oh okay. How's it coming along?"

"Fine. I think we can do a lot for them if they can ever decide on things. I'm sure I'll convince them."

"This is your first bring on isn't it?"

"Yes. They had been recommended by Slater as they have been impressed with what we did for them." She went quiet on the other end of the phone and I felt bad for lying to her. Yes, I was finishing up a few last-minute things for the proposal, but I was as prepared as I could be.

"I'm proud of you Cat. Your parents would be proud of you as well." I didn't know how to respond to that. Before I could speak, she continued. "I'll let you go. We can celebrate your first solo account this weekend."

"Okay, see you later." She hung up and I found myself staring at the phone. I feel bad for not telling her what I was going to do but I was a grown woman who could what she liked. It was time I stood on my own. I had just put the phone down when it rang again. I answered hesitantly.

"Cat, are you ready?"

"Ahhh, give me ten minutes. I'm just finishing up a few things. I'll meet you in the car park."

"Ok, see you soon." He hung up and again, I found myself staring at the phone like some lunatic. I knew that I wasn't going to be able to finish what I wanted to get done so I packed everything up and switched off the laptop and headed out.

I put the documents I needed in my bag along with the laptop as I may try to finish them later tonight. As I headed down to the car park, I suddenly though that I didn't know if we were travelling together or going separately. As I stepped out the elevator, I saw the decision made for me. Michael was standing next to his car waiting on me.

"I'll follow you as you know where we are going." I was disappointed as I wanted to spend more time with him in the car.

"If you don't mind, I'd rather come with you." He seemed surprised at my suggestion but the smile he gave me made my insides quiver and a heat covered my body. He leaned over and opened the door for me, and I put my bag in the back seat and got in.

"Where are we headed to?" He asked as he drove towards the exit.

"South Shiels." He gave no reaction to the area and we make the thirty-minute journey to where I knew I would be starting my life on my own. When we were closer, I checked the address again to see how far away we were.

"It should be up on the right-hand side." I looked around the neighbourhood and I liked it. It was quiet and quaint and just what I wanted. The houses were different styles, and the size was just what I needed.

"There it is." Michael pulled in and I looked at the house. It was exactly what I wanted. Not too big and homely enough. We get out and I have a strong urge to take Michael's hand as we walk up the path, but I resist. Before we could knock, the door opened, and the realtor was there.

"Miss Mont-Clair, how nice to meet you. I'm Joanne Ronalds." I shook her hand and saw her glance at Michael. I looked at him, but he just smiled. Joanne started giving us information about the house and walked through the living area. I dragged my gaze from Michael and tried to pay attention to what she was saying but my mind was more on what I was seeing.

We walked through the house and by the time we were back at the front door, I'd made my mine up. Michael was quiet as we did the walk through only speaking when he asked a direct question.

"I'll take it." The realtor smiled even more and began talking about the paperwork, but I didn't really take it in. I signed a couple of forms so that it could be taken off the market. As I was buying cash, she didn't think there would be any issues and that I should get a quick entry date. She said she would head back to the office and get the rest of the paperwork sorted out and she would be in contact when I needed to sign the final paperwork and get the entry date.

"Congratulations. I hope you and your husband will be incredibly happy here. It is perfect for starting a family. Good schools nearby and a quiet area." I felt myself going red and I ducked my head so she wouldn't notice. Michael came up behind me and put his arms around m.

"I'm sure we will. Thank you again Miss Ronalds." We left the house and I stood watching her drive away.

"That's the second time someone thought I was your husband." I knew my face would be red, but I looked at him anyway.

"I notice that you didn't correct them both times so it's not all on me."

"I liked the sound of it." We stood close and I felt the heat from his gaze go through my body. I didn't know what to say. He took a step back and took my hand. "Come on, let's get dinner. Is there anywhere you'd like to go?" I was still trying to pull myself together over his response.

"Do you know Franco's?" He seemed to freeze for a second or so before answering.

"Yes, I've been a few times."

"We shouldn't have an issue getting a table at this time." We got back into the car and we drove to the restaurant. Michael seemed a little off and I wondered if he was bothered about being called my husband even though he said he wasn't.

Just as we were nearing the restaurant, the heavens opened, and what I thought was heavy rain at first turned out to be hail.

"I'll drop you at the door, so you won't get too wet."

"What about you?"

"I've got an umbrella and it may not last long."

"Ok. I'll get us a table." He slowed to a stop outside and waited until I had picked my bag up again. He still seemed off and I was hoping that he wasn't regretting coming with me now. I opened the door and quickly got out and ran the few steps to the vestibule. I turned to see him drive away. I shook the rain off me and stepped inside.

Every time I came in here, I got a warm and cosy feeling. From the first time Abby brought me here when I was a little girl, I've always loved coming. There wasn't anyone around, so I moved further inside looking for some of the staff. They hadn't long opened so I knew they would be finalising everything before the evening crowd.

"Cat, it's nice to see you again." I turned and saw Franco coming towards me. He gave me his usual greeting of a big hug and kissing both cheeks. I gave him a smile. "Are you alone?"

"No. I'm with someone. He's just parking the car." He gave me a look that said who is this mysterious man that wanted to get to know me.

"Ok. I'll set you up at your usual table. How's Miss Abby?"

"She's doing fine. Working just as much as usual." We began to walk through the tables to the one that was my usual place anytime I came here. One of the waiters came up to us and handed a phone to Franco.

"Excuse me." He walked away as he spoke to whomever was on the other end. I sat down and waited on Michael. He shouldn't be long, and I hoped that he didn't get too wet getting inside. I was nervous as this would be the first time, we'd had a meal together.

The waiter came back and put some water on the table then left me. I took a drink and was beginning to worry that he had changed his mind but then I saw him at the entrance. I could see him searching for me before he came over.

"Sorry I took so long. I had to park further away, and I waited for the hail to ease off a little before getting out. It's been a while since I was here. Do you come here often?"

"Not as much as I would like. I've been coming here since I've been small, and Franco is like my grandfather. It feels like home here. You should be prepared for a few questions from him as I haven't brought anyone here before."

I stopped talking and lifted the menu. I felt like I was embarrassing myself somehow, but it didn't last hiding behind the menu as Michael pulled it down. He seemed to be back to his normal self, but I still couldn't look at him. He reached across and lifted my chin up so that I had no option but to look at him and the serious look he was sporting.

"I like listening to you talk. I want to know everything about you." I smiled at him and his serious look disappeared. "Now, what can you recommend here?" He let my chin go and lifted the menu and looked it over. Before I could say anything, the waiter came over.

"Are you ready to order?" I kept my gaze on Michael.

"Would you like a starter?"

"Always. I prefer a starter to a dessert." He smiled at me and my insides melted a little.

"Ok. I'll have the bruschetta Pomodoro and penne pollo e pancetta." I put the menu down and waited for him to order.

"I'll have the torte di granchio then spaghetti con filetto."

"What would you like to drink?" He waited for me to answer but I motioned for him to choose.

"We'll have a bottle of the house red and some water." He closed the menu and handed it to the waiter, and I handed mine over as well. Once he had left us alone, I found myself staring at him.

Chapter Thirty-nine

"What did you think of the house?" I asked him.

"It's beautiful and it suits you. You looked at home there and I'm pleased that you allowed me to come with you." I felt as if I couldn't stop smiling. I was happy that he came with me and that he would know where I would be living.

"I'm looking forward to moving in, but I just need to let my aunt know that I will be moving out. I don't know how she will take it but I'm sure she will be ok but I'm still nervous."

"Why would she not like you wanting to have your own space.?"

"It's not that, she's been there for me my whole life and I feel like I am letting her down. No matter what I did, she was always there for me." He gave me a puzzled look and I knew that I was going to have to elaborate on what I'd said. He wasn't going to take it as face value. He wouldn't even ask me what happened, but I wanted to tell him.

"Where to start." The waiter came back over with the water and poured a glass of wine for each of us. He left us and I knew that we were going to have a conversation that I hadn't expected so early in our relationship if that is what we had.

"If you don't want to talk about it, it's fine."

"It's not something that I talk about so it's hard for me." He nodded in understanding and finished his starter. I pushed my plate away from me and took a drink. "I don't want her to feel as if I'm abandoning her. I'm at a place in my life where I want my own space to be on my own. I'll be telling her when I get home tonight. Hopefully, it will go well." I smiled and glanced away.

I tried to get my mind out of the past as I had a new chapter of my life to begin and I wanted the man across from me to be a part of it. I thought back how he looked in my new home and I smiled at the thought. He looked good there even if he did fill the space more than me.

"What's that smile for?"

"Uhh, I was just thinking about what I need to get for my new place. My very own home." My smile got bigger as I spoke knowing that I had something that was all mine. Michael began to smile as well.

"Where are you going to start?"

"I have no idea. I think that will be this weekend's job to work out what I need to get. Once I have the move-in date, I can get yhe bigger things on order or maybe I'll just order them now. It can take up to a few months for sofas and such to be delivered."

"If you need any help, I'm here. Especially for any heavy lifting." He said it in such a way that I knew he was joking.

"Oh, I'll need your help, that's for sure. Having a big strong man to help is just what every female needs." I batted my eye lashes at him, and we began to laugh as Franco came up to us. He didn't look happy.

"Everything ok Franco?"

"Yes, yes, just received some news that I'm not happy about."

"Oh, that's not good. Is there anything I can do?"

"No, you are ok. It's something I need to deal with on my own. Now what are we having today?" Franco looked away from me to Michael.

"We had bruschetta Pomodoro and the torte di granchio."

"Very nice. Let me guess, penne pollo e pancetta for you Cat."

"You know me too well."

"Yes, I do. Now if you excuse me, I have some things to tend to." He said goodbye and left us alone. I turned back to Michael who looked for an instant angry about something then it was gone.

"What about you, do you have any family other than your sister?"

"No, it's only me and her. She practically raised me as my mother's health wasn't the best and was ill a lot. My dad wasn't in the picture, so it was just us. I tried to help as much as I could, but I was only a kid."

"You two must be close?"

"Not as close as we have been. She doesn't agree with a decision I made, and we've not really been speaking lately."

"When was the last time you spoke with her?"

"A few weeks ago." I could tell that he missed her and if they had been close when they were younger, it must be hurting both to not be in contact now. I didn't really know what it was like not to talk to someone you are close to but I had an inkling as to what I had done to Abby over the years yet she still stood by me.

"What do you like to do when you are not working?" I had to get him off that topic.

"What's that? I work all the time and don't have much free time. When I do have free time, I like to chill at home listening to music. I try to run every day, but out with that not much. I used to spend time with A..Annie."

"Is she older than you? I know you said she raised you, but I didn't want to assume she was older."

"She's eight years older than me."

"Does she have a family? Do you have nieces or nephews?"

"No, she spent her time building her business, so she never had time for a family."

"What type of business does she have?" I watched as he hesitated to answer. I wasn't sure the reasoning why, but the waiter appeared with our main courses. Once we were set, I waited for him to answer but he changed the subject.

"What about you, what do you like to do?" I allowed him to change the subject. He must be hurting to want to stop talking about her.

"I like spending time with my aunt. I owe her everything. I don't want to disappoint her as I've done that enough over the years and I can't do that again. That's why I'm nervous about telling her I'm moving out."

It was getting a little morbid and I don't think I can move him away from it this time.

"What happened?" I ate a little of my dinner before answering.

"My parents died when I was three years old. Abby was my babysitter before I was put into the system. I was put into foster care for a few years before being adopted. I spent the next ten years with them." I thought back to my time with the Smythe's and the first time I had seen him.

"Cat, what are you thinking?"

"When I first saw you at my party with Aunt Abby. You were her assistant. Why didn't you tell me?"

"Yes, I remember it. I hadn't thought of that night until the Christmas party. I don't know how I could have forgotten you. You are pretty unforgettable."

"Well, I was only a child at the time and I have grown up and changed since then so it would be difficult not to recognise me." My face was red again and ate something to try and calm myself down but there was no way Michael could mistake what I had said. "Why didn't she tell me that she knew you?"

"We didn't part under the best of circumstances, so she just didn't want to bring up anything bad between us. Well I hope that's what it was. What do you remember?"

"I am so embarrassed about my behaviour then. I didn't know how to act around you. You were my first crush."

"Your first, who was your second?" He stopped eating waiting for me to answer. His tone was something I couldn't quite place but if I had to say something, I would have said jealousy.

"My only." I said quietly.

"What was that?"

"You were my only crush. Anyone after that didn't measure up to you." I mad myself meet his gaze.

"Really, well I need to make sure that you keep feeling that way." I laughed a little as he continued to eat his dinner. I couldn't tell him everything. For me, he was the one I held everyone up to. The one boyfriend I had didn't meet his standards and I had to tell myself to stop it as I was never going to see him again and to get on with my life. I soon forgot about boys soon after that for a long time and that is why I had forgotten him.

We finished the rest of our meals in silence and then began to talk about other things that were happier. Before we knew it, it was late. I tried to pay for the meal, but he wouldn't hear of it, so I let him, and we started heading to where he had parked.

"You weren't kidding when you said you had parked a distance away." The night was fresh but chilly and I wished I had brought a heavier coat as I tried to get further into my own. Michael noticed and he pulled me to him and put his arm around me and we walked in sync. I felt the heat from his body, and I didn't want to leave when we got to the car. Before he drove off he spoke.

"Do you want to get you car or do you want to go home?"

"Home please. I'll pick it up tomorrow."

"How will you get in tomorrow?"

"I'll get a lift with Abby if she's going in. If not, I'll slum it and get public transport." I smiled as I spoke.

"Don't be silly. I'll pick you up. It's only fair. What time suits you?"

"It must be out of your way. I'll be ok."

"What time?"

"Seven okay?"

"Seven is fine with me. If you need to go earlier, just text me." He reached out and I just stared at his hand. "Your phone." I scrambled through my bag looking for it. I handed it to him, and he flicked through it and added his number. He handed it back to me when his phone rang.

"That's me got your number so I'll know it's you." I took my phone back and held it tight. He started the engine and pulled away. The drive was short to Abby's, but it was a comfortable silence which was good. He pulled up outside and parked. He turned to me.

"Well, I'd better go." I put my hand on the door handle but stopped when Michael leaned over and kissed me. It wasn't a long kiss but wow, it hit me right in the heart. He pulled back and smiled at me. I fumbled with the door handle and went to get out.

"Don't forget your work bag." I looked at him and knew that he knew exactly what he had done to me.

"Oh thanks. I opened the back door and grabbed the bag from the seat before leaning back in. "Well, I guess I'll see you in the morning."

"See you tomorrow. Sleep well." I closed the door and walked up to the front door. I watched as he drove away before going inside.

Chapter Forty

"Cat is that you?"

"Yes." I headed in the direction of her voice which was the sitting room.

"Did you get everything done?" I took a deep breath as I knew it would be best to tell her now.

"Not completely." I put my bags down and took my coat off and sat beside her. I could tell she was waiting for me to continue. "I went to view a house this afternoon."

"Oh, I didn't know you were thinking of moving out."

"I feel it's time to be on my own."

"Ok. How was it? Do you want help looking for a place?" I hesitated as I knew she was hurt and would be even more so when I tell her I've already got somewhere.

"No. I've already found somewhere. The one I went to see today I've bought it."

"Oh, ok. I would have come with you if I'd known."

"I wasn't alone." She froze as if she knew what was coming. "Michael came with me then we went for dinner. He's picking me up in the morning as I left my car at the office." Abby stood and began pacing. It looked like she was angry, and this was something I hadn't expected. Disappointment yes but not anger.

"Why didn't you tell me that Michael used to be your assistant? I remember him at my sixteenth birthday party, but you never told me that we had met before."

"We didn't part under the best of circumstances and I didn't think you would remember him. You were only a child." She kept pacing before stopping and looking at me seriously. It seemed as if she had come to a decision about something.

"Do you know much about him?"

"I know enough." She came over and sat next to me.

"Tell me about him." She seemed anxious but eager to hear what I had to say.

"Ok but let me get changed first. I have a feeling I'll need to be comfy to keep going." I lifted my bags and coat and headed up to my room. I changed into my pj's then headed back down. Abby was waiting along with a bottle of wine. She handed me a glass which I took giving her a questioning look.

"Well you're not driving in the morning so why not." I took a sip. "Now, tell me about him."

"He has a sister whom he had a falling out with. She raised him as his mother's health was bad. They were close until recently. I can tell that he is hurting over it. He didn't say what happened only that she didn't agree with a decision he made. I told him to try and make it up with her. She is his only family and I know what it's like not to have any."

"What do you like about him?"

"What don't I like. He's gorgeous, smart, fun to be with, easy to talk to. He listens when I talk. He takes me for who I am not my history."

"What did he think of the house?"

"He loved it and thought that it suited me. It just came on the market and I wanted to get in quick. I ha been looking off and on but not seriously until now. I have saved enough that I can put down a large deposit so the mortgage will be smaller. It's just what I wanted. He didn't even flinch when the realtor thought we were married."

"He didn't that's good. Most guys would run at the mention of marriage. He's going up in my mind now."

"Well, it's not the first time." Abby raised an eyebrow wanting to know more. "When we went to see the hospital to see Lydia, the nurse wouldn't let us in only family were allowed. I told her I was her sister and he was my husband." Her eyes widened as I spoke. "I didn't mean to it just came out. He didn't correct me either."

I took a drink and held the glass. I didn't know how she felt but when I looked at her, she seemed resigned to something and I didn't know if I liked it or not.

"Ok, I'll admit that I didn't want him hanging around you, but I can see that you two are determined to spend time together. I just need to get used to it." I wasn't sure how to take her. She wasn't usually like this, but I would take what I could.

"I really like him. Like really, really like him. We haven't spent a lot of time together but what we have has been great. I want to get to know him more. I want to know everything about him. I want to meet his sister if they ever make up."

"Cat, you are still young, you have your whole life ahead of you. Do you really want to get tied down to one man?" I listened to what she said. It seemed sad that she never had someone, and I wish that could have been different for her.

"Why didn't you ever settle down? Wasn't there someone who set your heart racing at just the thought of him?" I watched her face and saw the sadness there. There had been someone, but she had never said. "What happened?"

"Nothing, now what are you two doing Saturday night?" I allowed her to change the subject.

"I don't know. Why?"

"Well, I want to invite Michael over for dinner. If he is the one for you, then I need to get to know him as well." I smiled knowing that she was trying. We spend the rest of the night talking about nothing and finishing the bottle of wine along with another one. When my alarm went off early the next morning, I could have thrown it against the wall.

I dragged myself out of bed and into the shower I felt a little better after that. After getting dressed I went down to the kitchen to get some coffee. I couldn't stomach anything solid this morning. Fortunately, the machine was ready and waiting.

I switched it on and grabbed a to go mug to fill as Michael would be here soon enough. I had things I needed to finish this morning before the meeting, and I needed to get all my wits about me. My phone chirped and I looked at it. Michael was outside waiting. I smiled as I put the lid on the coffee mug and headed outside. Abby was still in bed so I sent her a text and would see her that night.

I stepped out into the cold morning and shivered. I walked quicky to the car and got in. I stretched around and put my bag in the back before fastening my seatbelt.

"Good morning. How are you?" I grunted at him and took a drink of coffee. I felt it in my bones as it went down. Michael laughed but drove away. We were about halfway to the office when I felt a little more like myself.

"Sorry I'm not with it this morning."

"How did it go with Abby last night?"

"It went better than I expected. She was upset about not telling her, but she was ok with it. She even asked about you. I think she is really trying to like you. So much so that she wants to ask you over for dinner on Saturday if you're free." He remained silent and I didn't know if that was a good thing or bad.

"Are you sure you didn't talk her into it?"

"I'm sure. It wasn't even the wine talking either as we hadn't had much at that point."

"Ahh, that's why you're quiet this morning. Too much wine last night." He laughed and I scowled at him briefly before laughing myself.

"Yes, we ended up talking like we hadn't done in a long time. It was good fun." I took another drink of my coffee and realised that I had nearly finished it.

"Ok. I'll be there Saturday night. Just let me know what time."

"What do you mean what time? I thought we were spending Saturday looking for furniture for me new place." He pulled into the carpark and parked up next to mine. He switched the engine off and turned to me.

"Do you still want me to help you? I would have thought that your Aunt would want to help you out."

"Yes. I'm going to need all the help I can get. I know the big things that are needed but it's the little things like lamps, tables, rugs, pictures that sort of thing. I don't know what to get. I need someone to help me out with that."

"What about Abby? Won't she want to help you out?"

"She will be. In fact, I' m going to ask her to come with us and see if we can get a lot it done. She wants to get to know you and this is a good time." He was quiet and got out of the car leaving me sitting there. I got out behind him and hoped that I hadn't pissed him off about it. I put my bag over my shoulder and headed to the elevator.

"Cat, I'm sorry. Yes, I will come with you and Abby to pick out furniture for your new place." We both stepped into the elevator and as it ascended to my floor, I fidgeted with my coffee mug.

"Thank you. I'll let you know what time later once I've spoken with Abby if she ever gets out of bed today." I stepped out on my floor and turned to him. "See you later." The doors closed as he began to answer.

I headed to my office to get started on my day. I refilled my coffee and got started. My meeting wasn't until eleven, so I had time to finish off what I hadn't done the day before.

Chapter Forty-one

I looked at Abby as she sat on the sofa across from me. I knew Rose was listening, but we had borne so much over the last few days that these last pieces shouldn't be the hardest.

"I know understand the reasoning Michael was so evasive with me. I can't believe I was so stupid to not realise something was going on. It's all so clear now but the hurt is raw."

"Cat, I never wanted to keep this from you. I tried to get him to tell you the truth, but he wouldn't. The longer it went on the harder it became to tell the truth. Why do you think we didn't speak for a while?" I thought back on what I had said.

"Franco knew as well, didn't he?"

"I don't know, maybe he did only he can tell you that. I knew that trying to keep you two apart wasn't going to happen so I thought if we were together, we could ensure that you were ok."

"Oh god, I feel like a fool telling him about my past when he already knew it."

"He didn't." I gave her a puzzled look. "He didn't know everything. I kept some things from him, but this is going to put it out there for him. He is going to be hurt about what you had to go through. He's a man's man, he has a need to protect those that he loves." I felt tears in my eyes as she spoke. She was right. Michael had always been trying to protect me even if I didn't need it.

"How about a break?" Rose asked. I nodded and went to go and sort some refreshments out, but Rose stopped me. "You stay here. I think I know where everything is now." She walked out into the kitchen and I was left with Abby.

"I am sorry Cat. I never wanted it to get this far but you know Michael, he's as stubborn as a bull at times."

"That he is. There is no changing his mind once it has been made up." We sat in silence and I got the urge to hug her. I moved slowly and sat next to her. She looked at me as if I were a rattlesnake about to strike. "Can I get a hug?" I asked quietly. Her expression changed to one of relief and she held out her arms and I fell into them.

As soon as I felt her arms around me, something burst inside me and I let out the tears that I had been holding back. I didn't think I had any left in me, but I was wrong. I don't know how long we sat like that but when I pulled back, I could see that Abby had been crying as well. I felt as if a weight had been lifted from my shoulders. It was then that I knew everything was going to be alright.

Rose came back in with a try of mugs and nibbles. She put in down and began serving. I felt bad at her doing it, but I didn't have the strength to move. The smile she gave me was an understanding one. She sat down before speaking.

"You have certainly had a rollercoaster life. It something that you would never have thought real."

"I know. At times I try not to think about what has come to past but sometimes I just can't help it."

"And you Abby, you have had a lot on your shoulders for so long that I am surprised you are still standing."

"When you must do things for those you love, nothing will stop you. You take on any burden that you must to ensure that your loved ones are safe and loved."

Abby put her arm back around me and pulled me into her. I let her as I felt I needed to let go for once.

"Thank you Rose for doing this for me. I don't think I would ever have spoken about my life like this to anyone else. It's true what they say, if it's meant to be it will be." I gave a wry smile. "Ok, my life was definitely not easy but somewhere they must have wanted me to go through it. I would not have volunteered for it if I had the choice."

"I don't think anyone would have volunteered for your life. You have come through a lot and are standing stronger for it. Even now, having to talk about it is showing a strength of character that not many have. You are proof that no matter how bad life can get, there is always a way through it if you have people behind you." Rose stopped talking and looked a little embarrassed about what she had said.

"Ok, now we must be nearing the end of your story. How about we push on and finish it today?" I glanced at Abby who nodded.

"That's fine with me. Right, I stopped at buying my house, didn't I?" They nodded. I took a breath and began again to finish off to date.

The next few weeks were a whirlwind. I was given a move in date in about six weeks, so I had to scramble to get everything I needed for moving in. I wasn't bothered about a lot of the finishing touches, but I needed to get the main things which by some miracle I was able to.

Lance came to help with Lydia and Jay. It was chaos on move in day, but I couldn't stop smiling. By the time I was all moved in, it was late, and I was shattered. Everyone went home bar Michael who stayed behind. I think Abby was giving us some space and I appreciated her for it. She had been trying with Michael and it was working. They were never going to be best friends, but they could be in each other's company without arguing.

"Well, I think that's everything. Thank you for staying with me. I don't think I would have gotten half of this done if I had been on my own."

"We all helped you. It wasn't just me." I walked around my new living room and looked at all the boxes that were still to be unpacked. I felt Michael behind me, and my heart quickened its pace. His hands landed on my shoulders and turned me around. I looked up at him and saw heat in his eyes. I opened my mouth to say something, but nothing came out.

His lips landed on mine were gentle at first then became harder. I found my hands going around him and pulling him into me. His dropped from my shoulders and moved down to my waist pulling me to him as well.

My body felt on fire and he was the only one who could put it out. He pulled away slowly but kept his gaze on mine. I felt out of breath and a little unsteady on my feet. My mouth opened and closed but nothing came out.

"How about dinner?" He pulled further away from me and I stumbled as he let go before catching me.

"Dinner?"

"Yes, it's been a long day so how about I go and get some food and we can eat." I found myself nodding and then he was leaving. I couldn't stop staring at him. He stopped at the door and came back and kissed me again before leaving. I found myself dropping into the nearest chair thinking about that kiss.

I wasn't a virgin, but I hadn't had a lot of experience with men and I had a feeling I was going to regret that with Michael. He kissed as if he had had plenty of experience and I hated all those other women that he had been with.

I shook myself out of the stupor I was in and made myself sort plates and glasses out in the kitchen. He was back soon enough, and we ate in the kitchen from the cartons, forgoing the plates that I had set out. That was the first night that he stayed and over the next couple of years, some weeks he was there more than at his place.

We seemed to settle into an easy relationship, and it was heaven. I got a promotion at work to head of new contracts and I worked my ass off to get where I was. There were some in the office that felt I didn't have the experience to do the job, but they were soon eating their words. Somehow, I kept my relationship with Abby quiet. Life couldn't be any better for me. Until that night.

It was our second anniversary and Michael picked me up around seven that evening. He hadn't told me where we were going but I had a feeling I knew but kept quiet. I was right a short time later. He pulled into the parking lot for Franco's.

"I take it it's not a surprise to be here?" I smiled at him.

"Not really but this is where we had our first meal together and it is my favourite restaurant." I got out the car and waited until he came around. He was dressed in a fantastic blue suit that showed off his physique. It got me hot just looking at him. I was wearing his favourite dress, a royal blue halter neck that had a split up the side. He put his arm around my waist, and we walked into the restaurant.

"Do you have a booking sir?" the maître d' asked.

"McIntosh." He must be new as I didn't recognise him. He checked his list then lifted a couple of menus.

"Please follow me." We followed him through the restaurant to what I knew was our table. Franco must have seen our names and put it aside for us. He seated us and gave us the menus.

"Your waiter will be here shortly." Over the years, the restaurant had moved upwards. It was difficult to get a booking here, but we always seemed to get one no matter how late we left it. I glanced at Michael and he seemed nervous. It took me back to our first visit here.

"Are you ok Michael? You seem a bit nervous? Is something wrong?"

"No, I'm fine. Just thinking about work and if we are going to get the Schaeffer deal done in time.

"I'm sure we will. Everything has been done it's just a formality now to get them to sign the paperwork." He nodded and looked over the menu. I glanced over the menu as well to see if there was anything that took my fancy, but I had a feeling I would be choosing my usual favourite.

A waiter came and took our order and as we waited, I felt on edge. I couldn't explain it but there was something not quite right about tonight. It wasn't that Michael was still looking nervous, but I knew no matter how hard I pushed, if he didn't want to tell me, he wouldn't.

The wine was delivered to the table and poured. I raised a glass and waited for Michael to do the same.

"To us. The last two years have been the best of my life and I don't know what I would have done without you." He smiled but it seemed a stilted smile. I took a drink and put the glass back down. Michael didn't drink anything but put the glass down and pushed his chair back. Before he could stand, the night manager came over.

"Federico, how are you this evening?"

"I am fine Miss Cat. How are you? Looking as beautiful as ever I see." I blushed. He was one of the newer employees, but he fitted in right away. He turned to Michael. "How is your sister Abby, is she feeling better after being ill?" I saw Michael's face pale slightly as what was said sunk in.

"What do you mean sister?" Federico looked back to me.

"His sister, Abby you know her. She has been ill with the flu and I wanted to make sure she didn't need anything."

"Please leave us." Michael said in a voice that I had never heard from him. Federico looked between the two of us. "Now."

I was trying to comprehend what he had said. Michael knew Abby but she wasn't his sister. His sister had moved away a couple of years ago just after we started seeing each other. They had made up, but they never saw each other anymore.

"Michael, what does he mean?" I watched as he tried to form the words. Federico had seen sense and left us. "Michael?"

"I never meant to keep it from you for so long. The longer it went the harder it became to tell you." I felt as if my heart was breaking and my heart was racing. I could see Franco coming towards us.

"Cat, please let me explain."

"Explain what exactly. You and my aunt are brother and sister and you kept it from me for the last how many years?" I stood and I could feel the anger in my body.

"Michael, Miss Cat, how are we this evening?"

"Did you know?" I turned to Franco and knew by his expression that he knew as well. Everyone had been lying to me. I lifted my purse and started walking through the restaurant. I knew that Michael was following along with Franco and I could feel the stares of everyone in the place.

"No Michael. You lied to me for years. You and Abby. After everything you couldn't tell me that she was your sister."

"Abby tried to get me to tell you at the beginning, but I wanted you to know me for myself and not as someone out of your memories."

"Well, you'll never know now. After all that you knew about me you lied. You knew that I valued family. That was why I tried so hard for you to make up with your sister."

"I know, I'm sorry. If I could take it back I would. Please give me a chance to explain." I started walking again out the door. I had been able to hold back the tears but as soon as I hit the cold air, they started to fall. I could hear Michael calling for me along with Franco.

How could they do that to me? Abby knew how I grew up; she knew what my feelings were on family and to lie about her family to me was unforgiveable. I didn't look where I was going and at the crossroads, I was so in my head that I didn't look properly before crossing the road to get a taxi from the rank a block away.

I froze when I heard the car and as I turned in its direction, I saw Michael screaming from the pavement at me. That was the last I saw before I felt my body rolling and everything went black.

Chapter Forty-one

I took a breath and looked at Abby and Rose. It was done. My story was complete, and it felt good to have it out there. I knew that it wasn't finished but for the moment it was.

"That's it." I said. Rose leaned forward and switched off her recorder. I could see tears in her eyes, but they didn't fall.

"Thank you, Cat. You have been brave telling your story and I thank you for allowing me to write it. I will do my best to put out the best I can to show people that they can overcome whatever is put in their way. Your story is something and it will be my honour to allow the world to read it." She stood and I found I couldn't stand. It felt as if all the strength had left my body. "I will send you the finished article before it goes to press. I want you to be happy with it before it is out there for everyone to read. I should be finished in a couple of days." I felt myself nodding at her, but I couldn't move.

Abby showed her out even though she had spent the last week here it was only courteous to do so. I had a feeling that we would be seeing her again. She was a good person, and I had a feeling we would become friends. When Abby came back in, I still hadn't moved. It felt a if my body was frozen in some way, but I knew that it was more drained than anything.

"You want anything?" I shook my head and waited for her to sit back down. She looked as bad as I felt, and it wasn't just me that had dragged up the past. She had as well, and I learned some things that I never knew, and it made me look at her in a different way. She had been placed in some impossible situations, but she had done the best she could even if she knew that it would hurt some later.

"Please sit." I waited as she sat down, and I turned myself to face her. She looked as if she had aged ten years in the last few days and I couldn't blame her. We sat quietly, each of us in our own thoughts.

"He was going to propose." My head turned quickly to her. "He told me a week before that he was planning on proposing. I told him that he had to tell you the truth before he did. He couldn't marry you with the lie between you both. I don't know whether he was planning on telling you that night or not, but I had had enough and told him that if he didn't do it, I was."

I looked at trying to work out if she was telling me the truth. Michael and I had spoken a little about marriage but nothing concrete. My heart was beating like a bass drum and I was sure that it would burst out of my chest. To know that he had been given that ultimatum by Abby was something that proved she was still watching out for me.

"I had given him a week to do so or else I was going to do it but I had been hit by that flu bug so he had a little extra time to do but I knew that he hadn't. I was going to tell you that weekend as I had a feeling, he wasn't going to do it himself."

I remember Abby wanting to come over that weekend and she had hadn't sounded herself. It was all falling into place now. She was going to do what he hadn't done up until that point. I started to wonder if he had planned it that way by getting the manager to do his job for him. Was he that much of a coward?

"I love him."

"I know. The lies had gone on far too long and any fool could see how you two felt about each other. It had to end. Just not the way it had would have been better." We lapsed back into silence and I felt my eyes getting heavy. They began to droop, and I felt Abby stand and through a cover over me jus before my brain checked out.

When I woke, it was dark and cold, and I uncurled my stiff legs and stood stretching. My whole body ached, and it wasn't just because of the way I had been sleeping. I went into the kitchen putting lights on as I went when I saw the time, I noticed that I had slept the afternoon away. I put the coffee machine on, and it was then I noticed the note on the kitchen counter.

Cat, I am sorry for lying to you and if I could take it back, I would. Family is everything and I was in the middle of the two people of my family. Each of them had reasons for what they wanted to do, and I wanted to protect to you. I know that was wrong, but I didn't stop myself. I would do anything to make this right if you can forgive me. Listening to you talk made me realise that I was adding to the sadness already in your in life. I couldn't be prouder of you than I am at this time and I only hope that you will be able to spend time with me again even if you cannot forgive me. You know where I am if you need to talk, no matter what time it is. I will always be there for. Abby

I felt something drip onto my hand and realised that I was crying. Even though she had lied to me for most of my life, I knew that she hadn't done it out of malice, and I knew deep in my heart that I had already forgiven her. If I was truthful to myself, I had also forgiven Michael but just hadn't told him yet.

At that moment, all I wanted was to be with my family. I wiped my eyes of tears and turned the coffee machine off again. I glanced down at myself and saw that I was need, to do. I pulled on some footwear at the door and grabbed my keys. I left and drove to place that at that moment, was the only place I wanted to be.

The roads were quiet, so I made good time getting there. Thankfully, my code still worked at the gate, so I drove in when they opened and stopped in my usual space. I got out and went up to the door. I hesitated for a second to know whether I should knock or just go in. I went with the latter.

I didn't call out when I got inside only moved through the house to find who I was looking for. I heard voices then a small cry and knew they would be in the kitchen. I walked in but stopped just before they saw me.

Lance, Lydia, Jay and Abby were sitting around the large kitchen table having some hot chocolate. It was unusual for Jay to be awake currently but looking at him, he wasn't long before he was asleep again. He was the one who saw me before the rest.

"Cat!" he tried to get down from the chair but struggled until Lance helped him the last little bit. He came running over to me with a big smile on his face and his little arms held out for me. I knelt and caught him when he reached me. I hugged him tight until he started to squirm to get away. I stood and lifted him into my arms as he spoke away to me in his baby language and I only made out part of what he was saying. Lance and Lydia stood but Abby remained seated with her head bowed.

"Cat, it's so good to see you. We've missed you. How are you feeling?" Lydia came over and gave me a hug as I held her son. She took him from my arms as he was beginning to droop with tiredness.

"I'm good. Still a little sore but I'm good." I was telling the truth. I was good. The physical injuries were healing, and the mental ones were nowhere near as bad as they had been. I knew they would be healed soon after the physical ones. Lance gave me a hug as well but said nothing. I could tell from his face how he was feeling.

"We'll leave you to two alone. This little chap needs to get to his bed." He looked lovingly at his son and wife and took her hand and led her out the kitchen and back to their home. Abby still hadn't moved from where she sat. She hadn't even looked at me since I walked in.

I walked around the table and pulled out the chair next to her. I took her hand and willed her to face me. She did so slowly, and I saw that she had been crying as her eyes were red and bloodshot. I stood pulling her with me. She came stiffly and I felt the stiffness when I pulled her into a hug. After a few seconds she went limp and held on to me as the tears flowed.

I felt some fall from my eyes but nowhere as near as many as she was crying. What had come out over the last few days had been cathartic for both of us even though we hadn't known it at the time. I kept my arm around her and led her out the kitchen and upstairs to her room. She went with me as if it were me that was holding her up when in fact it had been her holding me up over the years, so it was my turn to do the holding.

I steered her into her room and sat her down on the bed. She looked at me and I saw for the first time, the hurt and pain that she had gone through trying to keep me safe. I started to undress her and when she was down to her underwear, I pulled back the covers and put her into bed. I went to leave her, but she grabbed my hand, and I knew that she didn't want to be alone. I stripped as well and got into the bed with her and she held on just like we had done when I had been a younger and had been scared about something and couldn't sleep only the roles were reversed now.

Soon after that, she fell asleep and I lay there thinking about everything and wondering where I would be if it hadn't been for her. If I hadn't had her looking out for me, would I have ended up like Selena? I didn't know the answer only know what has happened and that I was grateful for it.

I don't know how long I lay there beside her thinking, but I knew that it was the starting of a new chapter in my life. Just as I was about to fall asleep myself, I thought of how much I missed Michael and wanted him with me.

Part Four

Acceptance

Chapter Forty-two

The next day was just as emotional as those that had gone before. I awoke before Abby and went downstairs to have some coffee. I had never known her to sleep for so long, but she was drained over everything. I walked into the kitchen and stopped when I saw Lydia.

"What are you doing here? I thought you had quit to spend time with Jay?"

"I had but, in the circumstances, I feel that I am needed here just as much as Jay needs me. Lance is looking after him this morning so he will be over later." I sat down in my usual stool and watched as she moved about the kitchen sorting out food. I could see her giving me little looks as she moved about.

"Talk to me Lydia." She stopped and put a mug of coffee in front of me then stood watching me.

"I didn't agree with what they were doing. I think they should have told you but there was no talking to Michael. You know what he is like, stubborn." I wrapped my hands around the coffee mug.

"I know. It must have been difficult to keep if quiet for so long. When I think back over the last couple of years and the number of times that it could have slipped but it hadn't, I am amazed that it hadn't come out. It also explains a lot of questions that I had over the little things. How I never met his sister or seen any pictures of her.

"He said that it was because they had fallen out over an argument and hadn't spoken in a while and he didn't know if there was any way to make it up. The Christmas's and birthday's that he missed out on due to the lies." I took a drink when I stopped talking.

"I knew that it was hurting them both. A week before your accident, Abby and he had a massive argument over you. She wanted him to tell you now as she couldn't go on lying to you. She told him that if he didn't tell you, then she would. He stormed out and we didn't see him again until the hospital."

"I know that everyone tried to get him to talk to me but as we all know what he is like, he was too stubborn to listen. I wish he would have told me himself and not finding out the way did, but I am glad that it is all out in the open." I reached across and put my hand over hers. "Abby told me that he was going to propose. That was what they argued about. She told me that he had to tell me before he did otherwise, she would." The look on Lydia's face was one of shock.

"I think that regardless of that, it was destined to come out that night. I could have done without what happened afterwards, but I'm glad that everything is out in the open. We can choose what we do and how we react to things. The first few days, I was angry that they had kept it to me for so long but once I heard the story behind how we got here, I understood why it was done. I don't agree but I understand."

"You are more forgiving than I think I would have been if I had been in the same situation. I don't know if I could forgive someone who lied to me for so long."

"How much do you know about my past?"

"Not a lot. I know your parents died and you went into foster care before being adopted then you came to live with Abby." I smiled at her.

"That's not quite everything. Yes, my parents died when I was three and I was put into foster care and adopted. My adoptive parents were killed in a car crash a few months after my sixteenth birthday." I kept my eyes on Lydia's face and saw the shock and the gasp she let out. "I went into a group home for the last two years as they wouldn't let me go with Abby. I went off the rails a little and got into bother. A friend overdosed in front of me and that was when I came to stay with Abby. The rest as they say is history."

Lydia was quiet as I spoke, but I could tell she was listening and was hurting for the girl I was. I had matured over what happened to me and it has made me the person I am today.

"Abby has been the one constant in my life, and I don't know where I would be without her. The same goes for Michael. Now that I know he has known me my whole life, it makes me see him in a different light. He is a protector, and he has been protecting me without me knowing it. I can protect myself and he should have let me make that decision for myself. He should have told me, but I forgive him." Lydia glanced up behind me and I knew Abby was standing there. I turned in my chair and saw her with her hands over her mouth. I got up and crossed to her and pulled her into me. Her body was shaking, and I tried to give her my strength. Lydia came over as well and we all stood hugging each other.

I heard the door open and close and a young voice calling out.

"Mommy." Lydia turned and caught her son as he came running towards her on unsteady feet.

"What are you doing up this early?"

"Had bad dream." He put his arms around her neck and held on. I glanced to Lance.

"He woke up screaming and wouldn't calm down or go back to sleep until he saw you." He looked at the three of us standing close. "Everything ok here?"

"Everything is fine Lance. We all just needed a hug but now that this little man is here, we can get even more hugs from him." I said as I lifted Jay from his mother's arms. He put his arms around my neck and held on tight. I could tell he was still a little upset so I did the only thing I could think of. I started to tickle.

He began laughing and squirming to get down but I wouldn't let him then I put him down and I knew that he wanted to be chased so I happily obliged as I allowed Abby to pull herself together. I played with Jay as Lydia finished sorting the food out. Abby left to get changed and Lance became my partner in crime chasing Jay.

As we sat down to eat, Jay fell asleep in his father's arms and we just smiled at the sweetness of it. It made me wish for a family of my own. Michael and I hadn't really spoke about kids but now, it was something that I was missing.

Soon enough we were finished, and we went our separate ways. I headed back upstairs to shower and see if there was anything that I could wear. I felt refreshed when I came out of the shower. On the bed, there were clothes, and I knew Abby had brought them in. I dressed and headed out to find her. I knew where she would be, so I headed to her office. I knocked on the door and pushed it open and found her behind her desk staring into space.

"Aunt Abby?" I walked in and stopped in front of the desk. She didn't say anything just stared at me. It was as if something had given way inside her. I wanted to find what it was and repair it for her like she had done for me over the years. "I'm going to see Michael today. It's time we spoke. I know I told him I would see him in a couple of days, but I need to see him now."

She nodded her head but said nothing.

"How about we come to dinner tonight?" That got her moving. She sat up straighter and stared at me as if I were going to disappear. "I can't promise anything but let me speak with Michael first and we will go from there."

"Do it here. Ask him to come here." I started to shake my head. "Please, Lydia and Lance will be at their place and I can stay in here out of the way. It makes sense as you are here already, and he can be here soon. There is no point in going somewhere else. This gives you the privacy and in a kind of neutral place." She had a point. I wasn't ready to go to his place or for him to come to mine. I had thought out meeting him outside but then we wouldn't have complete privacy.

"Ok. I'll ask him to come over in an hour so." Abby nodded her head as she seemed to return to her normal self. I stood and headed back into the hallway. I had to find my phone as I couldn't bring myself to call him so I would text him. I found my phone in the bedrooms and as I sat on the edge of the bed, I sent the text asking him to come back. I got a response immediately and the butterflies in my stomach started doing their acrobatics again.

I had to get myself under control before I saw him again. I found myself going through my memories of him and not those that I had spoken about. It was the private memories and how thoughtful and romantic he was.

I remembered our first Christmas together. I felt bad about him not seeing his sister, so I wanted to make it special, but I wasn't sure what to do. He surprised me with a weekend away in a log cabin in the middle of nowhere. It had snowed on our way there and we ended up staying longer than the weekend as we had been snowed in. We had spent the weekend walking in the snow then cuddling up in front of the roaring fire at night. It had just been the two of us and it had been wonderful. We had made plans to go back again this year as we couldn't get away last year. I was thinking of that place as our cabin.

I had to compose myself as I knew this was going to be just as emotional as what had happened up until now and this was just as, if not more, important that everything else. He was my other half and I needed him.

I wished I had something else to wear but all I had was the sweatpants and shirt. It would have to do. I headed back downs stairs holding onto my phone. I wanted to get back to work but I needed to wait until the doctor signed me off. I had a doctor's appointment tomorrow afternoon so I was hoping to find out that I could go back to work. If not, then I was going to need to find something to keep me busy until then.

When I went into the kitchen, I saw the food that Lydia had been prepared siting out ready to be used so I made myself useful and began cooking. I was hungry but I didn't really want to eat but knew I had to.

I loved cooking and I usually got lost in myself as I cooked, and this time was no different. Before I knew it, I turned around and stopped as Michael was standing in the doorway. He looked as if he had aged and he had lost weight. There were dark circles under his eyes, and he looked as if he hadn't slept in a while.

"Hi."

"Hi." He stayed where he was as if he didn't want to scare me. I came around the worktop and stopped at the table and put my hands on the back of the chair. "You look good." He said. I couldn't stop my eyes from moving over his body and seeing all the differences since we had last seen each other. I knew I was to blame for this, but I had good reasons.

"Do you want something to drink?" I asked. He shook his head. "Please sit." I pulled the chair out I had been leaning on and sat down. He moved slowly and sat in the chair opposite me. He clasped his hands together as if he were stopping himself from reaching out to touch me. I was doing the same as it was taking all I had to stay where I was. We had to talk about things before we could move forward.

"I am so sorry I lied to you. I wish I could say that I would do things differently, but I don't know if I would. You have been a part of my life for so long, that I would do anything to keep you safe."

"I wasn't in any danger. You lied to me. For two years. You had Abby lie to me along with others. You knew what she meant to me and yet you had her lie. She told me that she hadn't wanted to, but you made her." He dropped his head as if he were ashamed then lifted it again and met my gaze.

"I'm sorry. I don't know what else to say. I knew it was wrong, but I wanted you to like me for me and not what your memories told you. From the first moment I met you, I wanted to protect you even though I was only ten. You were mine and I wasn't going to let you go.

"When I saw you at your sixteenth, I couldn't believe how beautiful you had turned out. I knew you would have been beautiful, but you took my breath away when I saw you. Abby knew that and wanted to keep us apart, but I told her that I wouldn't seek you out but if we met again, I wouldn't discourage you. That was when we had our first argument over you.

"She wanted to tell you, but I said no. I had to leave so that I wouldn't grab you and never let you go. I heard all about you after that and it broke my heart knowing that I couldn't be with you. When I found out about the Smythe's, I couldn't believe that it had happened again. When I heard that you were back living with her again, I felt as if I had taken a deep breath for the first time in years. Not knowing where you were, what you were doing, if you were safe, ate away at me."

He kept my gaze all the while he was talking. I could see the hurt in his eyes, but it was nothing compared to what I had been through. Knowing that he wanted to be there for me even though I didn't know him, made me feel loved. I wanted to say something, but I had the feeling that he had to get his out of his system before I said anything.

Chapter Forty-three

"Abby sent me to set up the new office when you came back to live with her. I wanted to be there, but she said you needed time to heal before we met again. I don't know what you went through but I know it hurt. I spent two years setting up the office and getting it up and running. The business was growing, and Abby trusted me to do things right.

"By the time I came back, you had moved on and were getting on with your life. I didn't think it was fair to barge back into your life. I didn't know if you would remember me or not. I was scared to find out, so I kept my distance. I kept up with what you were doing through Abby and I was happy that you were happy."

"Why did you approach me at that party?" I waited for him to answer. He smiled and it lit me up inside.

"How could I not? You were absolutely stunning, and I didn't want anyone else spending time with you." I smiled at him.

"You were jealous."

"Yes, I was. When I saw that idiot trying to kiss you when I you didn't want to, I saw red. You were lucky that I didn't punch him out, but I was more concerned with getting you out of there than hurting him. I could always come back and punch him if need be. I wasn't leaving your side again until you were home safe."

My mind went back to that night and Abby's actions now made sense. She hadn't wanted to keep me in the dark it had all been on him. As I looked at him, he knew what I was thinking.

"I twisted her arm to keep quiet. She knew you remembered me from the party but nothing else. I wanted to you to know me and not clouded by our history together."

"I didn't remember our history together. I was too young."

"I know but I didn't want to take a chance. I didn't want you treat me like a big brother rather than something else. I had planned on telling you, but it got harder as time went on." He went quiet and bowed his head before looking back at me.

"That night, I was going to ask you to come away with me and I was going to tell you."

"Were you? Or were you going to ask me something else?" I knew there was anger in my voice. By his expression he knew what I was talking about.

"Yes, I as going to ask you to marry me, but I knew that I had to tell you first. I didn't know how you were going to take it so I thought if we were alone, we would have time to talk without interruptions. I was going to surprise you as I had just completed the purchase on the cabin we love." I looked at him surprised.

"I had planned on taking you up there, telling you about everything and was going to see how things went before asking you to marry me. I know how much you loved that placed and I wanted to give it to you as an engagement present."

My insides were going in all different directions. The butterflies in my stomach were doing constant somersaults, my heart was racing as if it were running for its life, whereas my brain was trying to understand what he was saying. I knew what he was saying but it was taking longer to sink in my mind.

"When Federico said what he did, I knew that it was over. I didn't have the time I had planned on. You wouldn't listen to me as you left me. I knew you were slipping away from me and I would have done anything to get you back. When I got stopped trying to leave, I was ready to explode. I never knew you were so fast on your feet.

"When I saw that car coming around the corner, everything went into slow motion. I could do nothing to stop it and I didn't want to believe what I was seeing. Those few seconds were the longest of my life then everything seemed to speed up. I heard the screams from the restaurant, and I found myself running to you.

"You were unconscious when I got to you and there was blood flowing from your head. I didn't know what to do. I heard people around me, but I didn't know what they were doing. I was handed a towel which I used to try to stem them blood. I didn't know if you were injured anywhere else, so I just held you and talked to you.

"The paramedics had to pry me away from you but I was with you all the way to the hospital and I tried to stay with you in the emergency room but they wouldn't let me. I stood staring through the doors they had taken you through wishing that I could go back and change things.

"I stayed in the waiting room for hours until they told me that they were moving you. At some point, Abby turned up, but I don't know who called her as it hadn't been me. I was lucky to be able to tell someone my name let alone have a conversation with someone. Abby was able to get some information but not much.

"When you were taken to a room, I went with you and stayed with you. They tried to kick me out, but I refused. Abby brought me clothes and food, but I wasn't interested in eating. I just wanted you to wake up. I didn't even care if you shouted at me, just as long as you were awake. Those two weeks were the longest of my life."

Abby had told me that he had been by my side when I had been in hospital, but I hadn't really believed it until now. I don't know why I hadn't.

"I tried to see you, but you wouldn't let me. I was upset that you wouldn't let me see you, but I was mostly relieved that you were awake and that you were going to be ok. I tried to tell myself that if you never spoke to me again it would be ok, but I knew that I would do anything to be able to talk to you again. To try and explain."

"I know. I found out a few things over the last few days and it has made me look at my life differently. I don't agree with what you did but I am accepting it but only under one condition."

"Name it. I'll do anything "

"You never lie to me like that again."

"Done. I promise that I won't lie to you again about anything. I'll be honest with you and tell you everything. I don't want to go through this again." I smile at him.

"You can't keep that promise as there will always be something that you will lie about." His face fell as I spoke. I knew the way he had taken it and I was just a little please with his reaction. "There will be times when you will lie to me," He went to speak but I gave him a look and he closed his mouth again. "The type of times I am talking about are if you are trying to surprise me with something and don't want me to know but that is all. Anything out with this, then I will not accept."

His face smiled as I said that, and I knew that we would be ok.

"I promise that I will only lie to you to keep a surprise from you and nothing else. I don't want to lose you."

"If you stick to that, you have me forever." I smiled and stood, walking around the table. I could tell that he wanted to reach out and hold me but he as letting me make the first moves. He turned in his seat but remained seated. I slipped in between his legs and pulled his head to my body. His arms went around me and held on tight.

I felt his body begin to shake and I knew that he was crying. I felt the tears in my own eyes as I held him. We stayed like that for some time before I felt him pulling away from me. He looked up at me and stood. He towered over me, but his expression was gentle and loving. I held my breath as his head came down to mine.

The lips that met mine were soft and gentle. I could tell he was holding himself back, so I took the initiative and made the kiss into something more. I could feel his breath hitch, but he was soon with me in the kiss. When we parted, we were both breathing heavily.

"Wow, I didn't expect that." He said. I just smiled at him and pulled him back to me. We kissed more and his arms were around me holding me up. I could feel that he had taken control now and it didn't bother me at all. I eventually pulled away as I needed to tell him about the article.

"Michael, I need to tell you something."

"What is it? Is it about the article?" I nodded. "What about it?"

"Well, there has been a lot aired and a lot of it I knew nothing about. I don't have many memories of my early years and this has shed some light on them. "

"I can imagine it has."

"There are some things that were hard for me get out and I don't want you to think any less of me when you read them."

"I don't think there is anything that you could say or do that would make me think less of you. I was there if you remember."

"Not through all of it." He gave me a puzzled look and knew that he was trying to think what I could be meaning. "There will be some things that will get your protective streak up and I want you to promise that you won't try to wrap me up in cottonwool."

"I can't promise that. It's in my nature to protect so all I can promise, is that I will try and not smother you when I find out whatever it is that you have to say. Ok?" I nodded and through it was the best I could get. I pulled out of his embrace missing the heat instantly.

"Do you want something to eat?" Before he could say anything, his stomach let out a growl. We both laughed. I went back to where I was before he came in and finished up what I had been doing. I made him bacon and eggs with toast and as I was plating the food, Abby came in.

"You want some?" I asked. She looked between the two of us and nodded. I saw Michael reach out and take her hand giving it a squeeze. I fixed another plate of food and we sat down and ate in silence. It was a little awkward, but I was happy to be there with the two people that I loved most in the world.

Chapter Forty-four

I received the finished article from Rose a couple of days later and when I had finished reading it, I couldn't believe that I was reading about my own life. It was going to be published in two parts as it was too long for a one off. It would be published next week, and I was suddenly nervous about it going public.

I gave it to Michael and Abby to read and I could tell that they were moved by what they read. After Michael read it, he kept his promise, but it was hard. I knew wanted to keep me wrapped up, but he knew that it made me who I was.

The day the first part was published, was the day that I had originally planned to meet with Michael at Franco's. It was an emotional day for me when I saw my life in print. It seemed a little surreal to me, but I just kept on going.

I was nervous about going back to Franco's after what happened the last time, I was there but I needn't have worried. When we walked in, I was glad that Michael had his arm around me. I heard a shout from the back of the restaurant, and saw other patrons turning to the sound then followed Franco as he came towards us. I really didn't see who else was there as I was concentrating on not freaking out being back here for the first since it all happened.

"Cat, it is so good to see you again. I am so sorry about what happened." He pulled me from Michael and gave me a big hug. "I never wanted any of that to happen."

"I know Franco. I don't blame you. You were doing what you thought was best." I turned to look at Michael who looked apologetic.

"I'm sorry for putting you in that position Franco. I should never had done it. I would like to apologise to Federico if he is here." I looked around for him but didn't see him.

"Yes, he's here but in the back. He didn't want to make things worse between you, so he wanted to keep out of your way."

"There is no need for that. Tell him to come see us." He nodded as he answered.

"I will. I read the article, it's good." I smiled at him and reached back for Michael's hand. "Now, let's get you seated at your usual table." As we walked through the building, I could feel everyone looking at us. I saw some of them whispering and I knew they knew who I was. They had wanted a picture even though I didn't, but I lost that argument.

By the time we sat down, my nerves were getting more settled. Franco took our drinks order and left us. For some reason, I didn't know what to say now. We had talked a lot over the last few days but now, I felt nervous. I didn't know whether it was being back here or the fact that the article had come out.

Federico appeared at our table with the drinks and he kept his gaze anywhere but mine. When he wouldn't look at me, I stood and stopped him from leaving. He looked at me and I saw the hurt and shame in his face. I said nothing only gave him a hug and I didn't let go until he returned it.

When we parted, I smiled at him to let him know that everything was ok. He smiled back at me then left us. When I sat back down again, I noticed that we seemed to be more secluded than we would be normally.

"When did they change this around? It was never this private here?" I took a drink as Michael watched me.

"I asked them to make it a little more private for us. After the last time, I wanted to have some privacy." He stood as he finished talking and came round the table to my feet and got down on one knee. My breath caught and I had to move slowly to put the win glass back on the table so that I wouldn't drop it.

"Michael, what are you doing?"

"What I should have done a long time ago. Cat, you bring light into my life that I hadn't realised was missing. What I did to you should never have happened and I am sorry. These last few weeks have made me realise that I can't live without you. I want to spend the rest of my life with you if you will have me. Catriona Mont-Clair, will you marry me?" I looked down and say him holding a small square box with the most beautiful ring that I had ever seen. I didn't know what to say and knew that my mouth was opening and closing but making no sounds. I knew he was waiting for an answer and I had to give myself a shake before I could speak.

"Yes, Michael. I will marry you." The smile that crossed his face was something I had never seen before. He lifted the ring from the box and slipped it onto my finger. He stood and pulled me to my feet and kissed me.

Behind me, I heard cheers and whistles and I turned to see who was there not hiding the blush on my face. I knew that along with my face being red, my mouth was wide open as I took in everyone that was standing watching us. Abby, Lance, Lydia and Jay, Susan and Tracey, Julie and John. They were all there. I knew there were more people standing around, but I couldn't focus on those behind only those in front. I was smiling as I felt tears fall. Abby came over first and hugged me tightly.

"Congratulations. I'm so happy for you both. Now we will officially be a family." Jay came running over and grabbed my legs and I lifted him up.

"Contulating." I knew what he was trying to say to I just smiled and gave him a kiss on the cheek. He squirmed to get down and his parents came over. There were tears all around, but they were happy tears, and I knew then that I had found my family that would never leave me.

Epilogue

How times have changed. A year ago, the story of a woman who had been through several traumatic events in her life was published in this paper. The response to that article was something that could never have been expected.

The number of people who stood by her was amazing and it has done so much for those who are suffering just now. It showed that having a support system behind you allows you to move on from traumatic events. It has brought to the fore the number of resources that are lacking in this country to help those that are suffering.

The official channels can only work so much but having those other resources behind them help to take the pressure off and ensures that no-one is missed. The Mont-Clair Foundation opened its doors three months ago and since then, they have helped numerous people who have needed in whatever capacity they need.

Catriona Mont-Clair and Abigail McIntosh have worked tirelessly to ensure that there is something for everyone when they need it. You will have seen over the last few weeks, articles in this paper about the new centre opening at the local hospital so that people do not need to go far to the help they need.

This is just the start of their plan to put one of these centres wherever they are need and to offer the services to those in need free of charge. They have done so much in this short space of time that it is my pleasure to announce that as of last night Catriona Mont-Clair is now Catriona McIntosh.

Her story has a happy ending, and I am sure that she will work to ensure that many more people will have their own happy endings as well.

Rose Maguire